SAVING MARS

Book One in the Saving Mars Series

Cidney Swanson

ISBN 978-0-9835621-6-0

For Toby

1

NOT BIG ON PROTOCOL

She was the kind of girl who slept with books on her bed. Not merely collections of books stored on computer wafers, but actual paper-made books from Earth, one of which lay upon its belly, spine protesting. It was this unforgiving surface that woke Jessamyn early, having already imprinted a crease along one side of her face. She sat up rubbing her cheek, rolled over, and kicked off the bed, landing silently so as not to awaken her family.

The getting-out-of-bed-before-the-sun wasn't a preference for Jess; rather, being perennially out of funds forced her into resourceful behaviors where she spent time (which she had) instead of credits (which she lacked.) She wished she were the sort of daughter who purchased thoughtful gifts for the ones she loved, but she couldn't hold on to credits very long. The cause for this littered her bed.

As she crept through the central room of the dwelling, Jess saw her walk-out boots, leaning upside down next to the heat exhaust. The sight made her smile; her older brother had placed them there, of course. Ethan had known his sister would be ice cutting today. He understood, as Jessamyn did, what would make their mother happy on her birthday. As long as you didn't blatantly hoard, Mars Colonial generally turned a blind eye to the mandate against water acquisition for personal consumption. Jessamyn was no water-grubber—she hadn't flown to the northern polar cap for lucky ice since her mother's last birthday, and birthdays only occurred twice annually.

Slipping into the airlock that kept Mars's frigid air from entering their home directly, Jess shivered. The thermometer told her it was well below freezing. Working fast, she shoved her legs through the walk-out suit designed to protect her from the harsh environment outside. A quick seal up the front, feet into warmed boots, helmet secured, and she was ready to go.

No one had questioned her when she put in the requisition for a planet-hopper yesterday. First Lieutenant LaFontaine, whom everyone called Lobster because of his red beard and hair, liked Jess and let her take a vehicle overnight when she asked.

It was just an old settler's superstition about polar ice being lucky, but a gift of ice would give her mother at least a week's reprieve from pain. A sufferer of dry-lung, Jessamyn's mother found relief from breathing humidified air—a practice abandoned a generation ago when the Mars Mandate had been adopted.

Closing the airlock behind her, Jess crossed the permafrozen ground and climbed aboard the tiny craft. Within seconds, she was airborne.

Lobster hadn't asked what Jess wanted a planet-hopper for, and Jess hadn't told. It was both illegal and dangerous to visit the polar caps. Marsian ice only melted when some external heat was applied, such as the heat from a descending planet-hopper. No matter how carefully you flew, hoppers came down hot. And if you came in hot, the ice melted and refroze, holding your craft so that it tended to become a permanent feature of the icescape. A handful of abandoned vehicles littered the northern polar cap.

But Jessamyn was a good pilot. An exceptional pilot, like her mom had been before her accident. When Jess reached the northern pole, she teased the thrusters on and off a handful of times, bouncing the craft up and down until the surface cooled the landing gear to where Jess could sense the ice losing interest in seizing her craft. It was a method she'd invented before she'd turned ten. Her father had tried (unsuccessfully) to have the unusual landing introduced into the pilot curriculum at the Academy. Jess had received a polite vid-mail from the academic dean thanking her for her inventive spirit, but explaining that her method taxed several parts of the landing gear beyond what they were designed to support.

"In other words, Mars Colonial doesn't want citizens running to the poles whenever their refiltration system needs water," Jessamyn's mom had said. Jess's father had scratched his head and agreed with the dean's point that the landing method *was* likely to damage certain models of planet-hoppers. Jessamyn's brother hadn't said anything aloud, but by that afternoon, he'd sent a set of modified ship designs to the Academy which would allow for safer Jess-style landings. These, the Academy implemented in hopcraft design going forward; Ethan's genius had been apparent to them from early on.

Jess hadn't bothered requesting one of the newer modified ships, which required approval by Lobster's commanding officer. Consequently, her borrowed planet-hopper objected to her several land-and-release bounces by groaning and emitting a series of red-flashing blips and beeps. She disregarded these; the hopper was fine. She knew this craft as well as she knew her own brother. Perhaps better, even. Ethan was the less predictable of the two in many ways.

After double-checking the systems that were essential for ignition, Jessamyn began to power down the craft. Standard protocol required leaving a vehicle idling when stopping at a remote locale such as a polar cap. Standard protocol also specified that the correct number of persons in a craft visiting the poles was two and not one. Jess didn't think much of standard protocol. Besides, if she turned the engines off, she could imagine herself as an early settler, living when Mars hadn't held enough air pressure for sound to travel far on the surface.

Jess felt a quiver of happiness run through her as the small craft quieted. She heaved the seal-door open and stepped out onto the planet's frozen crust. There it was: the absolute silence of the red planet. Jess smiled and glanced briefly at the sky—still some stars out—before turning her attention to the land below. Before her lay Mars's true wealth. The discovery of tellurium deposits—rare on Earth—had created a frenzy of excitement once, but since the No Contact Accords had ended all *legal* trade with Earth fifty orbits ago, it had become clear that water, and not tellurium, provided Mars's true hope for a future. As such, water was highly regulated, and even the wealthiest citizens conserved to hurry the dream of a terraformed Mars into reality.

Overhead, the sky was shifting from inky darkness to a warm purple. Jess allowed herself a few minutes to gaze upward. Even the Terran satellites, circling in their deadly orbits, looked beautiful in the pre-dawn sky. She identified her favorite spring constellations before they blinked out—the Apple Tree, the Three Tilapia, and the Horn of Plenty. In the pause before dawn, the stars seemed especially close, as if Jess could reach up and pluck one from the sky for her mother's birthday gift. She smiled, imagining her mother's response. *Oh, Jessamyn. Where am I going to keep this? There's no room!* It was her mother's favorite complaint in spite of the fact that their family had a larger dwelling to accommodate Ethan's alter-abilities.

Low in the sky, Jess identified the warm glow of Earth. *Terra*, the home world of her human forebears, was about to set, dipping below the horizon line. A swelling rush filled her ears, made her fingertips tingle.

Earth.

Terran-Mars relations might be non-existent (dwellers on the red planet went so far as to refuse to be called by the Earth-name *Martian*, insisting upon *Marsian*), but Jessamyn still ached to see vast Terran oceans, to soar through clouds, to catch snow on her tongue. All these things—and many more—her pirate granddad had spoken of. Jess's earliest memories were filled with his tales. She would never have traded her life on Mars for a life on Earth as a filthy *body-swapper*, but she ached to visit, to see the wonders of the blue-green planet with her own eyes. In fact, Jessamyn had enrolled in pilot training for one purpose: so that she could qualify as a Mars Raider, piloting as her grandfather had done, as her mother might have done.

The thought of her mother brought Jess back to the task at hand, and sighing, she pulled her gaze from the heavens. Before her spread a wide expanse of late-spring ice. Today, it was covered in dull, gritty dirt, evidence of a recent storm. Her work was simple enough. It was only a matter of finding a section of cuttable ice, working quickly, and getting away without succumbing to the desire for the riches that a larger and then a larger cut of ice would yield in certain back streets of New Houston. But the acquiring of wealth wasn't a real temptation to Jess. The things she wanted most weren't things at all.

When Jess switched her headlamp on, a stunning transformation rendered the dull surface into a symphony of reds, tans, and dark browns struck through with glistening points of ice. She moved her headlamp from side to side, watching ice crystals wink on and off. She imagined this would be what fireflies (something she'd only read of) looked like. The gutter-and-spark so beguiled her that she forgot for several minutes the task that had brought her to the polar cap. But at last, *twinkling* made her think of *birthday candles* which reminded her of her purpose.

The sun, breaching the horizon, seemed to be telling her to hurry along, now, as well. Squatting, she sliced her heat knife through a layer of frozen dirt. As she shifted the outer layer to one side, her breath caught anew. The ice hidden below the surface glittered, having formed a tiny, crystalline cavern into which her lamplight now flashed. She stared for a moment, awestruck, gazing until her eyes ached from brightness which gleamed like a small mine of diamonds.

Blinking, she bagged her frozen prize and turned back to the planet-hopper. Her mom's birthday had fallen on the same day as the Festival of Singing Ice this annum, and Jess would be hard pressed to finish her academy flight hours if she didn't hurry home *now*. And she couldn't wait to see her mother's lined face soften as she opened the gift. Lillian would scold her daughter for cutting ice, of course, but her eyes would also kindle with a delight that had grown rarer with each passing orbit.

From her mother, Jessamyn had inherited both her red hair and an uncanny ability to fly. Any craft, under any conditions. To some, it looked as if the ships simply acknowledged Jess's inherent right to pilot them. The truth was that Jess understood ships, which perhaps boiled down to the same thing.

"You're not happy this morning," Jess murmured to the planet-hopper as it lifted free of the planet's low gravity. As if in response, the ship shuddered. "We'll get Lobster to have a look at that port thruster as soon as we get you back to base." Her fingers skipped along the control panel, making a series of adjustments to calm the complaining engine. Jess didn't mind the extra demands the hopper made of her this morning; in truth, she preferred flying manually.

She aimed her craft south and to the east, which would take her away from the jet-black sky. She wished she had time to fly west first, then turn to enjoy a second dawn, but what with her mom's birthday and the Ice Festival, it would be a busy day. She waved a goodbye to the night sky, smiling as she picked up speed.

A moment later, an explosion in the port thruster wiped the smile off her face. Orange sparks spun from her craft, bright against the night sky. Even as some part of her mind registered the beauty of the fiery trail on her aft view screen, another part was busy running through scenarios that would not end with her as a splat upon Mars's cold surface.

The ship's emergency systems came to life, and a message flashed across the screen before her: *Contact MCAB immediately!* From inside her helmet, the warnings were reproduced aloud: "Pilot, initiate emergency contact with Mars Colonial Academy Base."

Jess's heart rate jumped as she evaluated the damage to her craft. She'd lost a thrust engine, which was bad, but she hesitated to contact the base. Even though none of her attempts to stabilize the vehicle were working yet, she didn't want some grounded landlubber telling her what to do. She knew that in a few moments, if she failed to call in the incident, the ship's controls would cease responding to her commands and re-route to the Academy Base instead. Ethan had shown her a work-around to keep control of her ship in such a situation, and she quickly keyed in the coding for it. Her gut told her she was seconds away from having the command of the ship shifted to someone on base.

Her gut was not wrong.

"Pilot-in-training Jessamyn Jaarda, this is Academy Base. We've got a report of a thrust engine failure on Planetary Hopcraft Bravo-Tango-One-Three-Four. Please confirm. Over."

Her mouth felt dry inside and she realized she'd left her dwelling without sipping her morning wet ration.

"MCAB, this is BT134. I'm on it," she shouted back.

The ship pitched violently in response to an adjustment she made. "Okay, not that one," she muttered. Her head spun, registering the nauseating effects of the failed fix. Attempting to regain her bearings, she called up a new set of readings on the navigation screen. She didn't like what she saw. The ship didn't like it either, and spewed forth a new series of warnings to eject forthwith.

Jessamyn did *not* need additional warnings clamoring for her attention now. Dancing her fingers along the control screen, she succeeded in disabling the ship's internal audio and visual warnings. Now she only had to deal with a craft careening out of control and a base flunky who probably wanted her to abandon ship.

"BT134, we're attempting to run additional tests to determine the degree of danger associated with your situation," said the base official.

Jess knew what was wrong with her craft: her secondary port engine had blown to smithereens. Without responding to MCAB, Jess addressed the sharp yaw pulling her counter-clockwise. "Easy does it," she murmured, engaging vertical stabilizers to counter the ship's desire to spin like a top.

"Trainee Jaarda? We're having difficulty communicating with your ship's navigational controls."

They wanted to force her off of piloting her ship. *Oh, no you don't!* Jess thought. Aloud, she said, "Yeah, there might've been some damage to navigation."

There was a pause in the MCAB chatter and then came the one order Jess knew she would not obey.

"BT134, we've decided it would be in your best interest to abandon your craft. We have a lock on your coordinates and will send someone to recover you within the hour. Over."

Eject? The thought filled Jess with a hot flush of anger, causing her skin to match her fiery hair. She'd corrected her yaw and roll and she still had one engine on her port side. She would *not* abandon her planet-hopper. They were a valuable class of ship. *Hades*, she had three out of four thrusters. Fueled by anger, she realized what she needed to do. *Forget vertical landing; there's more than one way to bring this baby down.*

"Trainee, you are ordered to eject from your damaged craft *now*. Do you copy?" said the tinny voice.

"I'm having trouble receiving you, MCAB. Please say again." Jess hoped they'd buy that.

"Jess, this is Lobster." A new voice registered in her helmet. "I know you can hear me. Get your skinny little hindquarters off that ship before it blows up."

She shook her head—an answer no one at MCAB could see.

"Jess, that's an order. I suggest you comply."

She could imagine Lobster's face, redder than usual as he tried to talk her out of the sky.

"It's not going to blow. It was just the one engine," she argued. "I can bring her in, Lobster."

A new malfunction warning began flashing on her panel. The *primary* port thruster!

"*Holy Ares*!" she cried.

"Jess, *eject now!*"

"Kind of busy here," she shouted, switching off power to communications.

If the primary port engine gave out, she'd be spinning in circles momentarily.

You are making it home. It was both statement and command, to herself and the ship—they were one creature now, with one shared fate. Jess settled into a cool and quiet place in her head where her mind seemed to meld with her craft. She raced through a power-down like she'd done at the pole. While she knew they couldn't glide all the way back to MCAB, she thought she could bring both of them down safely in the Great Sand Pit.

"You'd better appreciate the efforts I'm making here," she said to her craft. "'Cause we are *both* making it home!" She cut the oxygen supply to her ship's starboard engines and breathed a sigh of relief as the engines flamed out.

Everything went silent and the cabin dimmed, lit only by the rising sun. She felt a moment's panic: had she kept her speed high enough to land using only rudder, stabilizers, and ailerons? It wasn't like they taught this in class. She made an adjustment to the ship's yaw—it responded and she sighed in relief.

This is going to work! She reached out to pat her nav-panel.

For as long as Jess could remember, she'd wanted to try an old-school horizontal landing. MCAB covered the concept in stale texts, all designed to explain how vertical take-off and landing improved efficiency, saved fuel, and cured the common cold. Jessamyn didn't care. Today, a protracted horizontal landing would keep one more hopper operational. She was honest enough to admit she couldn't wait to try it.

With her primary nav-panel powered down to cut off communication with MCAB, Jess would be relying on her memory of the location of the Great Sand Pit. It would have been a lot harder in the middle of the night, but dawn brought vivid color to life: the deep red of Bradbury Canyon, the pinky-browns of Mount Cha Su Bao. Jess knew right where she was and how to get to where she needed to go. She experimented with the spoilers, and her heart beat faster as she felt the ship respond, gliding up and then down in relation to the planet's surface. Once she could see the Haddad Hills, she began her descent.

The ship responded eagerly and Jess murmured to it, "Bet you've always wanted to try this too, huh?" The vast lake of silica opened before them. Using the spoilers to full effect, Jess felt herself descending and slowing. It was noisy as anything, but so easy—almost too easy. She grinned broadly, imagining how she would *demand* this form of landing to be included in the pilot curriculum just as soon as someone came out to get her. As the sand rose up to meet the ship, a memory or instinct told Jess to keep her nose up as long as possible.

Impact, when it came, felt as unlike the gentle descent as possible. Jessamyn hurled forward toward the front viewing window, her harness cutting into her walk-out suit at the shoulders as it prevented her from striking the polycarb. Immediately after, she was flung to the left. She experienced a split second of weightlessness followed by a slamming sensation that made it feel like her skull was parting company from her brain. A final jolt forced her downward into her seat, and then the world tilted to one side as the ship spun clockwise, digging its way into the deep brown sand. Jess held her breath to see if she'd truly landed. Emergency lighting glowed pale blue, directing her to an exit hatch. She scrambled out, noting a sharp pain in her left shoulder where the harness had apparently been overzealous in protecting her. Quickly, she checked her suit's integrity. It was no use setting foot outside if her walk-out suit had torn. But no, her suit remained fully functional. She blinked in the sun, stepping round and round her craft. It was in one piece. The undercarriage would be scratched to *Hades*, but she could tell the hopper would fly again.

Jess began laughing and hugging herself. Shouting to the sand and sky, she cried out, "*Worst* landing *ever*!" She bounced up and down several times. "And I *loved* it!"

Unfortunately, the landing was easy compared with the news that awaited Jess when the rescue crew arrived thirty-two minutes later.

"Pilot-in-training Jessamyn Jaarda, you are hereby suspended from all flight until further notice."

Jess felt her temper flare at the words of the helmeted officer delivering this appalling news. "I just saved a planetary hopcraft from certain destruction. No way are they grounding me. I'll appeal the decision to the Academy dean."

She peered to make out the face behind the speaker's reflective helmet. She'd been certain Lobster would come to find her or her charred remains, but the voice hadn't sounded like Lobster's. She felt a twinge of disappointment that her fate meant so little to him. And then, as she caught a clear glimpse of the face inside the pressurized suit, she felt sick. There would be no further appeal—she'd been sentenced by the dean of the Academy himself.

2

FOR THE LOVE OF MARS

In the early days of Mars Colonial, surviving to another birthday had been an accomplishment worth recognizing. But Mars's annual orbit around the sun took 686 Earth days, and waiting that long for a birthday felt wrong to early settlers. In the end, they kept to the Terran reckoning of age which resulted in almost two birthdays per annum, or single Mars orbit. Later Marsians stuck with the tradition because no one particularly wanted to give up their "extra" birthday.

Today's celebration of Lillian Jaarda's spring birthday had been subdued by Jessamyn's announcement that she'd been suspended from flight. Jessamyn would not be rushing off from the birthday party to training. She would not be dashing from training to the Festival of Singing Ice. Instead, she found herself with seven long hours before she could even think about preparing for the festival—an event she no longer cared about. Even her books failed to console her. What was there left to care for if she'd been grounded?

"Make yourself useful. The solars need scrubbing," said her mom, turning briefly from her algae pots to her morose daughter.

The solar panels always needed scrubbing. It was a job Ethan liked, as it got him out of the house. And Jess knew better than to argue with her mother after this morning's debacle. There had been an abrupt *thank you* for Jess's water gift and silence on the subject of the suspension from flight. Her mother's lack of response wasn't a good thing or a sign of indifference. Lillian Jaarda had been a promising pilot—the most promising of her generation—and Jess now felt the weight of her mother's disappointment pressing upon her like a malfunctioning airlock.

Ethan joined his sister outside before long and the two worked in companionable silence. Ethan didn't tell Jess that he was sorry about her suspension, although she knew he was. But it wasn't a subject she felt like discussing. It was a gaping hole in the center of the universe and if she stared at it too long, it might suck her in like a black hole.

"I am relieved the planetary dog will be at the festival," said Ethan, breaking a two-hour's silence.

Jess knew that if she waited, her brother would probably add something more to give the remark context. The two continued scrubbing side by side. Their oversized home required more heat and oxygen than most houses and a correspondingly greater number of solar panels.

"I do not have any of its hair," said Ethan.

Jess tried to untangle the path of thought that had led her brother to make these two statements. Ethan collected things. Ethan loved the planetary dog—the only animal on Mars. Ethan would be at the festival tonight because he was receiving another award for something he'd invented. This line of thought led Jess to figure out why her brother was thinking about the dog: Ethan was probably worried about the crowds and trying to find a focal point which would keep him from becoming overwhelmed by the high levels of stimulation.

"Collecting a dog hair would be a good thing for you to focus on tonight, huh, Eth?"

Ethan didn't say anything. He'd stopped scrubbing and was staring blankly at the solars.

"Hey, Eth, come back to me," said Jess. "You're going to be fine tonight. I promise." Well, she *hoped* her brother would be fine. Although the festival occurred in a large and open space—the kind of environment

Ethan liked—something about crowds made Ethan respond as though he were in a tightly enclosed space. Now Jess had something to worry about *besides* how miserable an existence she would lead without flying.

"You could stay home," suggested Jess.

"No."

"Mom's staying home this time."

"No."

"You really want that dog hair, huh?"

Ethan smiled. "Yes."

Jess laughed. Her brother was a genius, but he had some very odd quirks, like his collecting. He'd created a series of layered-level boxes holding objects he found meaningful. Or interesting. Or something. Jess wasn't able to divine the guiding principle behind his collections.

When she'd been small, she'd thought of his containers as miniature houses: Ethan would wall off each collected item so that when you looked at one of the levels from above, it was as if you were peering inside a house where the roof had been removed. Each level stacked atop an earlier level so that the whole thing resembled a multi-storied building.

Her brother's soft voice interrupted her thoughts.

"You will fly again, Jessie."

Jess was undisturbed by the abrupt change of subject—normal for Ethan—but she flushed at his use of her baby-name. Her fair skin colored at the least provocation and burned easily. Friends murmured with jealousy that Jess was sure to get her First Wrinkle before any of the rest of them.

"Who wants to be a Mars Raider, anyway," she said, feigning indifference.

"Jessamyn does," replied her brother.

"Yeah," she agreed quietly. "No fooling you, huh?"

"I know that you want this badly enough to risk capture upon Earth, to risk being re-bodied, to risk starting a new war—"

"All right, already," said Jess, cutting him off. "Yes to all the above. And tons more. *Hades*, Ethan. I need a get-out-of-jail-free-card at this point." She bumped into her brother's shoulder—a form of contact he tolerated—as she referenced a Terran game he loved.

But Ethan shook his head. "You need an advocate—someone who will stand up for you and alter the decision of the dean or the board of directors."

"How about you?"

"No," said Ethan. "My skills in the art of persuasion are negligible. Also, I believe you acted wrongly. You need someone who can persuade others that your wrong action was a right action."

Jess laughed, causing her walk-out suit to rush additional oxygen to her helmet. "You're a freak. You know that, right?"

"So you have told me."

Jess shook her head. "Let's call it a day. My afternoon wet ration says I can beat you at a game of Monopoly."

They bounded back toward the house, bantering.

"Jessamyn cannot beat me," insisted Ethan. "There exists adequate data to demonstrate this."

"Then I guess *Jessamyn* will be pretty thirsty come the festival Tea Offering," she replied, subtly reminding him to refer to her with a pronoun instead of by proper name.

After a short pause, Ethan said, "You will be as dry as Mars."

"Oh, good one," she said. Figures of speech were challenging for her brother, who thought almost exclusively in terms *literal.*

They re-entered the dwelling, shrugging out of their suits. Jess felt her brother's anxiety rising in the enclosed space.

"Monopoly," she said, redirecting his attention. "Go find it." She hoped it would be enough to distract him out of a downward spiral that led, ultimately, to panic and the fetal position.

"Yes," he said, a tiny smile forming.

She breathed a sigh of relief. Her brother's phobias and idiosyncrasies became more pronounced when he had a large event looming before him. She appreciated that for most families, the Festival of Singing Ice in spring and the Festival of Coming Cloud in fall were joyous occasions. A time to meet people you hadn't seen all annum. A chance to hear one of the Secretary General's inspiring speeches. But for Ethan, the festivals were primarily hurdles to get past.

Still, the fact that their mom was planning to stay home this annum meant that at least one member of the family felt confident Ethan could handle the crowds and noise. Jess hoped her mom was right.

~ ~ ~

"Take care of your brother," murmured Jessamyn's mother. "You know what your father's like at these things."

Yes, Jess knew that her dad would be at his absent-minded-professor-*est* at this event where so many vied for his attention.

"Maybe I should go," her mother said, frowning.

"No, Mom," said Jess. "It's your birthday. You stay home and enjoy the humidifier. Ethan will be fine. He's a man on a mission."

Her mother raised one eyebrow.

"He wants a piece of dog hair for his collection," explained Jess as her father joined them.

Her father looked surprised. "All those birthday visits to pet the planetary dog and he doesn't already have one?"

"Guess not. At least, not from *this* planetary dog," said Jess.

She had no idea if this was the same dog or if they'd had to bring a new embryo out of cryo since her childhood. Jess had never *once* touched the planetary dog on her birthday visit. She'd refused year after year and given up the visits as soon as she'd turned ten Terran years old. Ethan's visits had continued until his seventeenth birthday.

"I am ready," said Ethan, emerging from his room. He'd dressed up for the occasion, donning a proper lapelled jacket.

Jess could see the orange collar of his favorite tee shirt circling his neck like one of Saturn's rings. "Pull down on your tee," she said. "It's showing."

Ethan adjusted his shirt. Jess knew no one would laugh aloud at her brother anymore. He was too well-respected. But she didn't like to see him looking so obviously *different*. Still, if donning a worn-out tee was what it took to keep him comfortable for the evening ahead, she was all for it.

They arrived at the Crystal Pavilion early to give Ethan the chance to become gradually surrounded by increasing numbers of people. Jess kept him busy viewing exhibits from school-age children, studying works of art, and of course, looking for planetary dog hairs. New Houston's Ice Fest brought citizens from all over the northern hemisphere together for one very big party. While Marsians inherited much of the independent spirit of their pioneering forebears, they knew that their best chance of survival in the unfriendly climate was to maintain excellent relations with their neighbors. "We need one another," was an oft-repeated Marsian proverb.

Lobster lumbered over to Jess, a sad frown disfiguring his face. "I'm sorry Jess, I did what I could for you, but . . ." He didn't need to say it. *You disobeyed a direct order* rang out clearly in both of their minds.

"I know," she said.

Jess had managed to keep her fears about never flying again from the surface until she said those two words: *I know.* She felt a contraction in her throat and a burning behind her eyes. Like all Marsian children, she knew better than to waste water with tears. She squeezed Lobster's large forearm and moved off, herding Ethan toward the front of the Pavilion so he wouldn't have to push through the crowd to receive his award later. The Secretary General and CEO of Mars Colonial would be addressing the gathered crowd shortly. Most of the members of the board of directors had already taken their seats on the raised dais.

You need an advocate. Jess heard her brother's words in her head. She scanned the faces of the board members. Several were friendly with her father, most owed her brother a huge debt of gratitude for some solution he'd proposed during various crises. But none knew Jess on a first name basis. She doubted any would recognize her. And they'd all agree with Ethan, most likely. She'd clearly and obviously committed a *wrong action*. Worse, she'd do it again, given the chance.

Jess glanced at her brother as the Secretary General marched on stage, followed by a black, white, and tan Australian shepherd. The crowd surged forward, clapping and stomping in support of the planet's most popular leader in two centuries. Jess saw her brother reaching for his eyebrow, stroking it once, twice, three times, before replacing his hand at his side.

Only three times, she thought to herself. *That's good.* She wished she could comfort her brother with a quick squeeze, but she knew that her touch would increase his discomfort. Instead, she leaned close, whispering a reminder.

"Don't forget your third eye," she murmured in reference to a membrane-implant her brother had invented. By blinking in rapid succession, the eye forced the membrane to drop into place. It served only one purpose: the membrane allowed a person to see items hidden under or behind high-tech cloaking material. Ethan didn't react well to surprises, and festival organizers loved springing a surprise reveal of an onstage object or person. The membrane helped. When she was small, Jessamyn had pestered him for one of her own 'til he'd said yes.

Waiting for the crowd to settle for the Secretary General's opening remarks, Jess blinked rapidly, causing the membrane to slide down. Sure enough, onstage—hiding beneath a cloak—rested a beautiful ice sculpture of a teapot. A tribute to the Tea Offering, no doubt. She looked over at her brother, who was studying the hidden sculpture with great interest.

Crisis averted, thought Jess.

The Secretary General began her speech commemorating the accomplishments of the past half-orbit since Cloud Fest. Jess's ears pricked when she heard her mother's name praised for her Household Algae Pot Program, but mostly she missed the Secretary's speech. She was moving from face to face down the row of board members, trying to decide which one might be willing to advocate for her, to get her back in the air.

Even thus preoccupied, however, Jessamyn couldn't help looking back to the Secretary General when it came time for the Presentation of Plenty. The entire room silenced as a screen appeared so that every citizen of Mars Colonial could see with their own eyes the store of ration bars in their copper-shiny wraps. Like everyone in the room with her, Jess found comfort in viewing the food supply that would keep starvation at bay until such a time as Marsians could grow non-toxic crops.

The current Secretary provided ridiculous access to Rations Storage, in case there were any doubting Thomases among the citizenry. Rations Storage sat next to the Crystal Pavilion and all were welcome to tour the facility on any non-distribution days. Mostly, families strolled past the rows-upon-rows of foodstuff only during festivals. Jess had never bothered with the tour. She knew firsthand, from her granddad, the exact date upon which the nutrition bars would run out: one annum after the next raid was scheduled to be completed. Which meant just over three annums from now.

Jess's heart rate picked up at the thought of raiding. To be considered for piloting the next raid, she needed hours. To get hours, she needed her suspension revoked. She *had* to get back in the air.

The Secretary continued speaking as the screen behind her cleared. "Citizens of Mars, over three Terran centuries ago, our foremothers and forefathers arrived upon this planet, having determined that humanity could and would prosper upon Mars as it had upon Earth. They came for many reasons: some for fame, others for wealth, many to satisfy an abiding curiosity. But they stayed for only one reason: for the love of Mars."

Secretary Mei Lo paused as heads nodded and a few "amens" sounded. Then she continued. "But after two centuries had passed and Terrans grew desperate upon Earth, battling the dark fronts of environmental disaster, poverty, and hunger, the governments of Earth declared the Mars Project a failure and refused to send needed supplies, even those Marsians had paid for with tellurium shipments. Colonists remained, tightening their belts. Why did they remain?" Her eyes swept the room as she waited before pronouncing the words. "For the love of Mars."

The room grew silent as the Secretary reached the darkest part of the tale. "Some left to join the Re-body Movement on Earth. Yes, *some* chose to leave. But *your* ancestors remained. Every one of you on Mars today is here because your great-great-great grandfather or grandmother thought Mars was worth fighting for. And when war came—a war not of our making—your ancestors fought. When Terrans set their deadly satellites in high orbit surrounding Mars, we protested. When they demanded we return to Earth, we declared our independence. And when Terran aggressors destroyed our orbital mirrors, forcing temperatures back toward frigid pre-colonization levels, we grieved. But did we give up? Did we give in?"

The answer came back, resounding as it did every annum at the festival: "*No!*"

"No," repeated Mars's Chief Executive Officer. "We did not give up and we did not give in." She raised her hands in anticipation as she asked the question, "*Why?*"

The answer thundered through the building: "*For the love of Mars!*"

The Secretary reached her trademark ending: "Citizens of Mars, my friends and my inspiration—we will prevail. We will create the Mars our ancestors could only dream about. Work hard. Be courageous. Be bold." Here she paused, smiling. "And always, be as generous as a dog." She bowed and sat beside the planetary dog, giving it a quick pat on the head.

Jess felt a shiver run its way from her head to her toes. No generation of Marsians had ever known a braver or more inspiring leader. Jessamyn had arrived tonight indifferent to the Ice Festival's marking of the anniversary of Marsian colonization. But she felt certain no one could have remained indifferent after that speech. She wondered how it affected Ethan. She turned to look at her brother as a group of very tiny schoolchildren bounced onto the stage to sing.

But Ethan was no longer beside her.

"*Hades and Aphrodite*," she muttered under her breath, glancing behind for her brother. A few people frowned at Jessamyn's lack of attention to the singing children. Jess smiled weakly and moved off to one side, slipping down the length of the building, looking for her brother. She jerked her head swiftly to one side, activating another of her brother's inventions—an inner earpiece that allowed the two to communicate.

"Ethan?" she whispered. She suspected she already knew where to find him—against the back, where a patch-worked wall of glass soared over five meters high to the ceiling. The Crystal Pavilion had been named for this glass-work, an ancient effort pieced together by the first generation of Mars-born pioneers. Sure enough, Ethan stood, staring out at the planet's surface, his forehead just touching the glass.

"You okay?" she asked softly.

"I am better now. The window helps. I began to feel trapped. The number of people this annum . . ." Ethan broke off.

Jess heard the strain in his voice and her heart melted for her brother and his vulnerability in this environment. "Let's find your dog hair and get out of here," Jess murmured.

"They were using vac-mechs onstage," said Ethan.

"The invention they're giving you the award for?"

"Yes," said her brother. He'd come up with the device to improve the air quality of heavily occupied interior spaces where people with dry-lung suffered worse than in their small homes. He spoke again. "The vac-mechs will have gathered all the dog hairs."

"Can you . . . I don't know . . . empty it?" asked Jessamyn.

"The mech incinerates whatever it gathers," replied Ethan.

"Ah," said Jess.

A sonorous gong rang out across the pavilion, bringing the roar of the crowd down to a soft whisper. "The Tea Offering," murmured Jess.

"Harpreet is as generous as a dog," said Ethan.

Harpreet Mombasu, retired pirate-raider, spoke softly into a voice-amplifier. "Won't you join me for tea?" Some annums she spoke at length. The crowd stood in quiet anticipation, to be sure she had finished. Apparently however, she had no more to say, for the tea servers had already begun handing out small rations of tea from behind a row of tables set end-to-end along one side of the pavilion. This annum, or maybe the next, would see the end of the small stash of tea Harpreet had brought back from Earth. She could have hoarded it. She might have sold it for an untold fortune on Mars. Instead, she had chosen to brew it once an orbit for the Festival of Singing Ice and to offer cups to every man, woman, and child on the planet for the asking.

"How many cups of tea can one woman drink?" she was often quoted as having said, and the saying had been added to Mars's other pithy proverbs.

"Harpreet!" murmured Jess. "*Harpreet!*"

Ethan looked at her inquisitively.

Jess felt a wild, hopeful fluttering deep in her belly. "Don't you see? Harpreet will go to bat for me!"

"Go to bat?" asked Ethan.

"Figure of speech," explained Jess. "I mean, she'll *advocate* for me, Eth! And then they'll have to listen. She's . . . she's . . . well, she's *Harpreet*!"

Ethan's brows furrowed for a moment and then he nodded. "Yes," he said. "I believe Harpreet might succeed where others would fail." He brought a clutching hand to his belly and forced himself to look out the window again.

He's not doing well, thought Jessamyn.

"I'm taking you home," she said aloud. "I'll make your apologies and then we'll go."

"Yes," said Ethan, pressing his head to the glass.

Jessamyn dashed to the front of the hall and explained to festival personnel that her brother felt too unwell to collect his award. Then she found her father, interrupted his technical explanation of the algae pot program to a group of students, and murmured into his ear that she had to take Ethan home.

Her father frowned. "Should I go with you?"

"No, I'll drop Ethan off at home and come back for you later," she replied.

Before returning to her brother, Jess grabbed an assortment of Festival souvenirs, hoping one or more would keep his attention during the brief journey home. He wasn't fond of traveling in the enclosed space of the family's tiny get-about. But in less than twenty minutes, Jess managed to get herself and her brother suited-up for the ride, into the get-about, out of the get-about, and back inside their home.

By this time, she felt desperate to return to the Ice Fest in hopes of speaking with her grandfather's friend, Harpreet Mombasu. When she arrived once more in downtown New Houston, parking was a nightmare.

Her family's original space had, of course, been taken, and Jess ended up leaving the get-about on the far side of Rations Storage.

Grumbling every step of the considerable distance, Jess pondered how best to approach Harpreet. The old raider was known for thinking unconventionally, but could she be made to agree that Jessamyn had done a *right* thing and not a *wrong* thing by disobeying a direct order? Jess threw her arms up. Who knew?

She bounced along the paved surface swiftly in Mars's low gravity, sparing only a quick glance for something that caught her attention as she passed the storage facility's front windows. The building looked empty at the moment, although she caught sight of several of her brother's vac-mechs, hungrily seeking the leavings and detritus of today's thousands of visitors. All of whom were probably back inside the Crystal Pavilion now, cheering as medals and honors were given in the Awards Ceremony. She would have to see about collecting Ethan's.

There it was again, a flash of something caught only by her peripheral vision. She looked into the windows as she continued alongside the rations facility. And then she saw it. A bright tongue of flame.

One of her brother's vac-mechs had caught fire.

Jess hesitated. The building looked empty—predictable during the awards ceremony. Was no one watching the security feed? She could call for help, but fire would spread quickly in the oxygen rich environment of Rations Storage. Someone needed to put that fire out *now*, before it spread. On instinct, she pressed the button of the next airlock door she came to. Not bothering to remove her walk-out suit, Jess pushed through the secondary door and dashed toward the small mech. The quivering flame looked like it was dying, and Jessamyn felt a moment's relief. But as she stepped forward to make certain the fire was out, a terrible thing happened. Jess heard a loud explosion and reeled as something struck the side of her helmet with enough force to knock her sideways.

3

NOT DYING LIKE THIS

The chunk of exploding vac-mech knocked Jessamyn to the ground and sent her skidding along the smooth floor of Rations Storage. Sliding, she reached out with her right leg, hoping to catch it against one of several shelving units. The maneuver worked, but the shelf teetered precariously as she came to an abrupt halt. And then, to Jess's dismay, the entire unit tipped and came crashing toward her. She rolled to one side, narrowly escaping entrapment as a dozen ration boxes tumbled to the ground.

Jess didn't think they would have crushed her, but she had no time to wonder. Looking back to where the exploding vac-mech had first attracted her attention, she saw bits of it, scattered and still flaming. She vaulted upright and dashed back to stomp out the dozen tiny fires. She started with the largest, blazing alone surrounded by several feet of nothing, but then realized this fire was the least likely to cause problems. A few meters away, three other burning pieces of vac-mech threatened to either melt or ignite objects they touched. Jess hesitated, glancing from one to the next, trying to decide which fire to put out first.

"Aw, *Hades*!" she cursed, flying toward one that had, in fact, caught a nearby box on fire. It made no sense—why would a metal box catch fire? Too late, she realized the answer. Flames exploded from the container as an oily and highly flammable substance oozed out the box's damaged corner seams. The liquid followed gravity's call and flared a path to Jess. She jumped back, noticing a second fire growing in ferocity to reach her own height and beyond.

She reached for her emergency call button, hitting it twice before making a true connection. "Fire!" she shouted. "In Rations Storage! Hurry!" She glanced about desperately, seeking something she could use to douse or smother the flames. A banner hung on a nearby wall announcing fifty annums of Marsian independence.

"Make yourself useful," she growled at the outdated piece of fabric as she yanked it from the wall. Turning, Jessamyn realized that the oil-fire had jumped, replicating itself several times. The entire shelf appeared to hold containers of the flammable liquid. She beat the banner against the hungry flames, but her efforts seemed futile. Worse than futile. The banner itself ignited and Jess had to throw it to avoid catching her garments on fire.

Where were New Houston's emergency techs?

Just then Jessamyn heard the sound of another explosion, from somewhere behind the flames now threatening to engulf her. A second vac-mech? Another explosion sounded. And then another. From behind, Jess sensed a sudden brightening. As she turned, she realized to her horror that the cloth she'd thrown aside had ignited several shelves of ration boxes.

"No, *no, no!*" she screamed, beginning to fear for her own life. Flames surrounded her on all sides. She could feel heat through the suit. And that was very, very wrong. Walk-out suits were designed to protect the wearer from temperature change. *How hot was it in here?*

A small memory came to her from early school days, and she threw herself to the ground, seeking out the least deadly-looking of the many flaming objects surrounding her. *You are not dying like this*, she told herself. *Find a way out!* But there was no way out—no way that didn't involve passing through flame. She thought she could smell smoke: was it her imagination or was her suit giving up? Dragging herself forward on her elbows, Jess crept toward the most diminutive of the fires closing in on her. She felt certain she could smell the awful odor of burning suit as she shimmied through a gap between two growing fires.

Black smoke drifted lazily, and she wondered how long her walk-out suit would protect her; it was intended to ward off cold, not heat. *Crawl*, she commanded herself. Groaning and crashing sounds rang out behind her, and she witnessed a large shelf to one side of her buckle, appearing to deflate as it melted from the high temperatures. *Keep crawling! You will make it to one of those airlocks!* She didn't know if the doors would function or seal her inside. *Just crawl!*

A door shimmered into view two meters away and she jumped up and ran for it, noticing that one of her suited legs appeared to be smoking. She beat at it and registered a sensation of *hot* that quickly died back. As she reached to open the door, another shelf collapsed, toppling and pinning her so that, try as she might, she couldn't reach the airlock button.

This is it, she told herself as a yellowish dust filled the air. *Your own personal "the end."*

But then strong hands lifted the groaning shelf from off of her back. Jess scrambled to stand. The air was a mixture of black smoke, grey ash, and drifting soot.

"She's helmeted," cried the woman who'd pulled her free. "I'll get her outside."

Jess felt herself being lifted and carried out of doors. Shaken and grateful, Jess leaned on the tech.

"Are you injured?" asked the woman as she helped Jessamyn inside an emergency vehicle.

"Don't think so," grunted Jess. Her throat felt like she'd gargled sand.

The woman pointed to two medical techs already removing Jess's helmet. "This is Ngala and that's Frank. They'll take good care of you." With that, the woman dashed back outside.

Minutes later, Jessamyn recognized her father's helmeted form as he entered the parked medical vehicle. The med techs stood aside to allow Jess a quick hug from her dad.

"You're okay?" he asked.

Jess spoke, her voice gravelly. "Never better."

For the next hour, with her father at her side, Jessamyn submitted herself to a series of pokings, proddings, and measurings all of which confirmed what she already suspected: she was fine. Her air system had been contaminated during the last minute inside the building, but she hadn't taken serious smoke into her lungs, and the med techs assured her that her throat would feel fine by morning.

When a Mars Colonial Command representative came by to question her, Jess described the fire from her perspective.

The official shook his head as Jess finished. "You're an exceptionally lucky young woman," he said.

But when Jess asked what kind of damage the building had sustained, the official shook his head. "We have a team evaluating the situation," was all he would say.

Jess's father squeezed her shoulder. "I'm sure they'll tell us all about it tomorrow, when they know more."

At last, the medics declared Jessamyn fit for release. She was offered a new walk-out suit which smelled funny and tugged in all the wrong places. Jess fell asleep on the drive home and could barely keep herself awake enough to slip out of the hateful new suit and crawl, exhausted, into her bed.

In spite of the grave ordeal, she dreamed not of fire, but of flying.

4

BOTH KINDS OF WISDOM

Harpreet Mombasu was the most curious citizen ever to dwell in New Houston. She was curious about the weather, curious about technological advances, curious about school essay competitions and sporting events. But mostly, she was curious about people. She appreciated the opportunities that city life afforded for encountering a wide swath of humanity. She loved conversation and good, strong tea. Since her own generosity prevented her from consuming the Terran beverage more than once per annum, she had become a consumer of chat, a connoisseur of the *tête-à-tête*. She'd come closer to speaking with every citizen of Mars Colonial than anyone before her had or anyone after her would.

Harpreet (she refused to go by her official title of Raider Mombasu) had a reputation for seeing a person's future that led many parents to bring their children to her for advice about career paths. In reality, it wasn't the future she could see, but rather the quintessential *person-ness* of whomever came before her. Nine times out of ten, Harpreet could tell from a single interaction with someone what that individual would find most satisfying in life.

In short, she listened well and truly.

Jessamyn hoped the old pirate would follow her regular schedule the next day, going to the New Houston Fountain. Jess left early, avoiding her father's inevitable, "Don't leave the house without your wet ration. It's the most important water of the day." She wasn't planning to skip it.

Lacking anything that resembled an actual water feature, the New Houston Fountain served one product: wet rations. It was housed in a glass-like structure beside the Crystal Pavilion. As with many of the city's popular destinations, pressurized tunnels connected the Fountain to the larger pavilion.

Arriving, Jess passed through the outer door of the airlock. She shifted her shoulders in a practiced move which allowed her to slide off her irritating new walk-out suit. She would need to inquire after a replacement. Looking through the inner windows, Jess searched for Harpreet's dark skin and bright smile. She glimpsed the raider admiring a very new baby in its mother's arms. At least there wasn't a line of people wanting a word with Harpreet.

Jess placed her helmet on a locker shelf and hung her suit below it. She'd forgotten house-shoes, so that meant slipping back inside her walk-out boots. Tapping the airlock button, she stood, impatient. "Come on, come *on*," she muttered to the sticking door.

It released with a gasping sigh and she squeezed through as soon as the gap would accommodate her, hurrying to the side of her intended savior.

Harpreet seemed to be saying goodbye to the woman and child.

"Harpreet," Jess called.

Harpreet, her dark eyes dancing with delight, stood with outstretched arms. "Jessamyn, child!"

The greeting reminded Jess that there were niceties to be gotten through before she could blurt out her problems.

"Goodness," exclaimed Harpreet, "How you've grown! How long has it been since we've sipped water together?"

Jess felt her face and neck heating up. It had been half a Marsian annum; Jessamyn had celebrated a birthday since visiting the old pirate, dear friend of her departed granddad. She'd meant to stop by. She'd thought about sending a video greeting. But she'd forgotten to do either. She mumbled an apology and asked after Harpreet's health.

"I am well." Harpreet nodded her head in a tiny bow and then narrowed her eyes. "And you, child? Your name is upon everyone's lips this morning."

"Why?" Jess felt suddenly worried. "Are they saying it's my fault?"

"No, child. What a dreadful thing to assume," replied Harpreet. "Everyone speaks of your bravery, daughter."

Jessamyn frowned. She hadn't felt at all brave. "Do they know the extent of the damage yet?" she asked.

Harpreet tilted her head to one side. "The Secretary General will be making an announcement shortly. I think it would be unwise for me to say more."

Jessamyn nodded. She wasn't here to talk about the fire, in any case. "Did you already have your morning wet ration?"

"No, child. I have been sitting here, waiting to see who the Divine might bring my way this morning."

"Oh," said Jess. "Well, I don't want to get in the way of anything, um, divinical."

Harpreet gazed for a long minute into Jess's eyes. Then she reached her soft, brown hands to take one of Jessamyn's. "I see only *you* before me this morning."

"Oh," Jess repeated. She smiled a tiny bit.

"Let us go place our orders, shall we?" asked Harpreet.

Jess wondered how the old woman knew she hadn't already sipped water with her family. Maybe Harpreet really *could* read minds.

The old raider leaned in and whispered, "Your lips are still chapped this morning. You weren't planning to skip the most important water of the day, were you child?"

Jess touched her lips self-consciously as the two crossed a small plaza, joining a line of others waiting for their morning fix. When Jess reached the front of the line, she pressed her thumb atop a glowing square.

"One regular," she said. "Please," she added, thinking of Harpreet's easy politeness.

"We'll have that right out for you," said the young man, indicating the far end of the counter.

Jess collected her drink and looked around for an empty table out of earshot from others. She found one nestled into a corner and waved Harpreet over to the lonely nook. Harpreet had stopped to scan her thumb at a ration-vending box. After retrieving a copper-wrapped bar, the old woman walked briskly to join Jess.

"So, my dear Jessamyn," said Harpreet, angling into a chair across from Jess, "How can I help you today?"

Here goes, thought Jess. She took a deep breath and began. "There's been a terrible mistake." As the suspension and the fire swirled together in her mind, she felt her chest tighten.

"Have a sip first, daughter," said Harpreet. Her voice sounded so sad, as though she, and not Jessamyn, had just lost her future.

"I'm so sorry," Jess murmured as she blinked back tears.

"There is no shame in a tear or two," replied Harpreet. "They are a gift from the Divine meant to remind us to pay attention to our feelings. You have survived a terrifying ordeal."

Jess shook her head. "It's not that. I didn't come to talk about the fire."

Harpreet's dark eyes widened a fraction of a centimeter as she raised her eyebrows. *Go on*, she seemed to say.

"I've been suspended from flight," said Jess. "Even though I did everything right. I saved my ship. I kept retrieval costs to a minimum, bringing it in as close as I could. I did the *best* job I could, Harpreet, and now they won't let me fly." She lowered her voice. "For all I know, they may kick me out of the Academy."

The old woman reached for the copper-colored nutrition bar and began peeling the wrap away from the ration inside. The wrapper caught a bit of sun and flashed orangey-gold light back at the window. She smoothed the wrap, preparing it for the recycling mechs, not meeting Jessamyn's eyes.

"You are not being expelled," said Harpreet at last.

Jess swallowed in relief. She'd been worried that with the Ice Fest and the fire, something had slowed down her receipt of an expulsion notice. But if Harpreet declared her still a student, she was still a student. She watched as the old woman examined the date-stamp on the wrapper. It listed a Terran time Jess never paid any attention to.

"I miss your grandfather, Jessamyn," said Harpreet.

Jess looked up and saw that the old woman had now fixed her gaze upon the Marsian landscape.

"He was one helluva pilot," said Harpreet. "I'll never forget his fearlessness, taking on the passage through the satellites."

Jess squirmed. She didn't want to be impolite, but she wasn't here to discuss her pirate granddad.

Tapping the date-stamp with a bony finger, Harpreet spoke. "I remember the day he and I loaded this particular shipment of rations onto the Red Galleon."

"This *exact* ration shipment?" asked Jess.

Harpeet nodded. "He was in a foul temper that day. It was our second on Earth and he thought that, as pilot, he should be exempt from such a menial task. A quick look at the duties roster showed that he was wrong. He'd signed on without reading the fine print." Harpreet laughed. "Oh, he was angry."

Jess wondered how to politely bring Harpreet back around to the problem at hand.

"But a pilot must always obey orders," continued Harpreet, meeting Jess's eye. "Our commanding officer exercised her right to keep your grandfather working the entire day. He swore at her long and loud, but she didn't back down—"

"And when they returned home, she married him," Jess murmured. It was a story she knew well.

"When they returned, they married," agreed Harpreet. "And it lasted just long enough for your mother to be brought into the world."

Jess nodded. Her grandparents' divorce was notorious. Most Marsians, if they married, stayed married for life.

"He could only see things from one point of view, your grandfather."

Jess remembered the arguments between her granddad and her mom. "His point of view," she said.

"Precisely," said Harpreet. She pushed her mostly uneaten ration bar a few centimeters away. "Do you know, I find I have less appetite as the orbits go by. Would you do me the great courtesy of preventing my ration from being wasted?"

Jess stared at Harpreet. No Marsian would ever *think* of wasting their dry ration. It would have been the worst form of sacrilege, a dishonoring of those raiders who had risked everything to obtain food. That aside, Jess wondered how could anyone *not* want two-thirds of their morning meal? As a seventeen-year-old, Jess still received three dry rations a day and couldn't imagine how adults made do with only two.

"Are you sure?" asked Jess, already eyeing the ration hungrily.

"Yes. You sit here for your meal and think about your grandfather." Harpreet swung her feet around as if in preparation to leave the table.

"But—" Jess paused to compose herself. "You haven't told me anything. Please. You have to tell me what to do."

Harpreet sighed, settling back into her chair. "You are very alike, your grandfather and you."

"My granddad's *dead*," replied Jess. "He can't help me."

"Hmm." Harpreet resumed gazing out at the landscape of red dirt and brown rocks. The sky glowed, warm and golden. "He died a bitter and lonely man. I visited him every day, but he had long since given up challenging himself, looking for ways to grow, to learn, to become attuned to the harmonies of minds unlike his own."

Harpreet turned and faced Jessamyn. "You must not make his mistakes, my child." She paused and waited until Jess's eyes met her own. "If you can see things only from your own limited perspective, what does it matter if you are the best pilot of your generation?"

Jess's heart swelled within her. If she was the best pilot of her generation, then why in *Hades* had they grounded her?

Harpreet continued. "To be a pilot, to be a *raider*, especially, one must learn to see things from more than one perspective. What is it that makes you a good pilot, Jess?"

The question caught Jessamyn off guard.

"Take a moment and think about it," said Harpreet.

Jess closed her eyes. What made her a good pilot? How was she supposed to know that? She came up blank. And then she remembered something her father had said to her mother the first time Jess had been at the helm of a flying ship. "She flies from *here*," her father had said, pointing to his belly. It was true, Jess thought. She felt things with her gut that others didn't seem to notice. She acted with certainty when others doubted. It led her to take risks others wouldn't.

"I fly with my gut," said Jess.

Harpreet nodded. "Yes, child. You fly using this intelligence." Harpreet tapped the space over her navel. "Exactly as your grandfather did."

Jess waited for Harpreet to say more. When she didn't, Jess spluttered out, "And?"

The old woman smiled. "Can you learn to call upon your other intelligences? To see things not only from *here*," she pointed at her belly, "But from *here* as well," she said, pointing to a spot on her forehead, just above her eyes. "A pilot must be a member of a team, Jessamyn. A pilot must learn to say 'no' to the voice which tells her to disobey a direct command."

Jess flushed. So Harpreet had heard *everything*.

"There are times, child, for both kinds of wisdom." Harpreet leaned in and took Jess's pale hand once more in her own dark ones. "But even as it takes teamwork to put out a great fire, so also it takes teamwork to keep a pilot in the air. Daughter, if you wish to be more than a merely *good* pilot—if you wish to be a *great* pilot—you must learn the wisdom of working in harmony with others."

Jess wavered, uncertain whether she felt affronted or encouraged.

"And now, my dear, you must excuse me as I have an engagement with the Secretary General." Harpreet smiled as she rose. "It does not do to keep such a busy person waiting."

Jess found herself seated alone, staring at the barren landscape, with no idea how she was ever going to get herself above its surface again.

She knew she ought to go to classes. But if they were grounding her, and if Harpreet refused to help her get *un*-grounded, well, what was the point of returning to MCAB? Expulsion, which had sounded so terrifying this morning, no longer seemed so awful. The really dreadful thing had already happened: she couldn't fly.

And so, after sitting by herself for an hour in a lonely corner, Jessamyn heard the news that the Secretary General was giving an address in the Pavilion about the Rations Storage fire. A Fountain employee found Jess in her corner.

"We're closing," he said, apologetically. "Everyone wants to hear Mei Lo's announcement."

Nodding, Jess followed the crowds exiting through the tunnel that linked the Fountain with the Crystal Pavilion. The news awaiting them was not good. In fact, it was the worst news Mars Colonial had heard in a century.

5

I'LL DO MY BEST

Inside the pavilion, citizens had gathered; many had remained in town after the Festival of Singing Ice, and these were joined by reporters from as far away as New Tokyo. Jessamyn hugged the back wall of windows, settling between two families with small children, one of whom asked in the over-loud whisper of the very young, "*Is that the hero, Mama? Her?*"

Jess felt her face flaming with color and pushed forward into the crowd. She was no hero. For all she knew, her presence at the fire had made things worse and not better.

The Secretary mounted the dais which had been hastily reconstructed from yesterday. She took a moment to survey the crowd before her. Then, gripping either side of the podium, she spoke.

"My friends, I come before you today in my capacity as Chief Executive Officer of Mars Colonial. I am here to inform you of what we know and what we don't know. It is with deep regret that I confirm the destruction by fire of over ninety percent of our dry ration reserves."

Whispers rushed through the building like tiny breezes. *It wasn't possible.* Someone must have gotten a detail wrong. Surely ninety percent was the amount of food which *survived*, not the amount which had been destroyed. The Secretary allowed time for the implication to sink in: Mars could not wait the scheduled number of orbits before sending raiders to Earth to trade for rations on the black market.

Jessamyn felt as though parts of her body had liquefied and were now sinking down, down, settling low in her abdomen, growing heavier with the passing seconds before the Secretary spoke again.

"For a century and more, we have dared violating the No Contact Accords in twenty annum intervals," continued the Secretary. "The fact that it comes earlier than expected is unfortunate but *does not* mean our defeat as a people. *Every* generation has had to face the risk before us now."

Jess, only seventeen, had never experienced the anxious launch, threading a route past the armed

Terran satellites in high Mars orbit, never known the weeks of radio silence while Marsians waited to see if *this* was the raid where they were discovered—the raid which ended in all-out war between Mars and Earth.

The emotional climate of the pavilion felt to Jess as many-layered as a Terran cake. Underpinning all rested a base-mood of anxiety. A thin paste of frantic hovered over this, followed by alternating layers of disbelief and wonder that such a thing could come to pass. Atop everything however, was spread, like a smooth ganache, the sentiment of sobriety.

The Secretary spoke again. "The fire began last night at approximately 7:50 New Houston time. It has been determined that the cause was the small vacuum mechs deployed to keep the facility free of external contaminants. Yesterday, during the Festival, some four thousand persons toured the facility housing our rations. The mech's designer recommended last annum that we install a cooling system in the devices which would prevent conflagration should the mechs become overtaxed by excessive cleaning.

"Because we did *not* heed that advice, we now stand at the brink of the collapse of Marsian civilization." The Secretary took a slow breath and began to outline a plan to prevent widespread starvation.

"Mars Colonial Command informs me that a window for travel to Earth will open in less than six weeks. I am confident that the brave men and women who have been preparing for the opportunity to serve as Mars Raiders will be more than able to meet the challenges brought on by an accelerated timetable.

"Raider Mombasu—forgive me—*Harpreet* has conferred with me and agreed to reassume the role of negotiations specialist aboard the Red Galleon when it launches for Earth."

The crowd stomped and clapped their approval upon the mention of Harpreet's participation. The plan would surely succeed if Harpreet supported it.

But Jessamyn's heart was already sinking with a terrible realization: her life-long dream of flying as a raider had just been obliterated. With the recent suspension on her record, MCAB would never recommend her for *this* raid. And in twenty orbits, her fair skin would look too reddened and wrinkled—she would have a characteristically *Marsian* appearance. Only those with skin healthy enough to pass for Terran were chosen for the journey to Earth. The risk of someone discovering that Mars was in violation of the No Contact Accord was too great—no one who *looked* Marsian could go to Earth.

Harpreet, old though she was, had been blessed with *melanin*, which offered her body natural protection from Mars's high dosage of ultraviolet light. Harpreet's warm chocolate visage was neither reddened nor wrinkled. She was the ideal raider, regardless of her age.

But even if Jess's record was spotless for the following twenty annums, Jess would never be selected for the next raid.

She missed the close of the Secretary's speech. Dragging herself back through the tunnel, Jess waited for the Fountain to reopen, retrieved her walk-out suit, and went home with her heart cut in pieces like a handful of Mars-rock reduced to gravel.

Jessamyn's family sat for evening rations that night, minus Ethan, who had been called to Mars Colonial headquarters. Jess at first assumed this was because the government wanted to blame him for the fire—the mechs were his invention.

"No," sighed Lillian. "No one's blaming him. Ethan told them how to prevent this and they didn't listen. Now they all look like idiots."

"They're asking his advice on ancient Terran computer systems, if you can believe it," said Jess's father, separating two ration bars into four pieces.

He handed Jess a half-bar.

"What's this?" she asked, pointing to her meal.

"We're on half-rations," her mother replied, lips tight and thin. "Weren't you listening to the Secretary?"

Jessamyn stared mournfully at the reduced portion, not thinking it wise to admit she'd left the Secretary's address early. "Won't people starve?" she asked.

"The old and the sickly are at risk," replied Jess's mom. "The very young as well."

Jessamyn felt her heart miss a beat: did her mother's dry-lung qualify Lillian as *sickly*? "Planetary Ag respects you, Mom. You have to tell them."

Jess's mother stood abruptly and left the room.

Her father sighed, smoothing ration wrappers.

"Your mom's upset. She spent the morning running experiments for Planetary Agriculture, and she's worried about a test that calls into question the nutritional value of the emergency rations from New Tokyo," said her father. "And she's angry that her algae pot program wasn't implemented last annum. As a supplement to ration bars, it would have helped."

"We'd be eating that stuff?" asked Jess, staring at an algae pot. "What about health issues?" Everyone knew people got sick on Mars-raised food.

Jess's father gave her half a smile. "Your mom will always have detractors, but even they agree the algae's not going to kill anyone. All the data looks promising."

A call from Mars Colonial Command interrupted the silence between Jess and her father. He took the call, making a series of nods, grunts, and assents before clicking off.

"Looks like your mom was right. Again." He fixed his eyes on a small piece of copper wrapper, rolling it back and forth between his right thumb and forefinger.

"About what?" asked Jess. "Starvation? Algae pots?"

The wrapper made crinkling noises in the quiet room.

"They want to send Ethan on the upcoming raid."

"*Hades*," murmured Jess. "Ethan?"

Her father sighed heavily.

"He can't go," said Jess. "He wouldn't make it."

"I'd better talk to your mother," said Jess's father. But he remained at the table, crinkling the piece of wrapper between his fingers.

"I won't let them stuff my brother in a deep space vessel," said Jessamyn. "No way! In confined quarters like that, he'd be catatonic by the time he reached Earth."

Jess's father rose. "It's not our decision to make," he said. "Your brother's an adult and he's agreed."

That night, Jessamyn waited in Ethan's room for him to return. The book in her hands couldn't keep her attention, and she gave up and watched the deadly Terran satellites roll past her brother's clear ceiling.

When Jess was very young, Ethan's room had been customized to suit his alter-abilities. She had no memories of the changes that had come over Ethan as a result of his new environment. But she believed him when he said it had improved his life profoundly.

Jess knew only too well what it was like to be with Ethan in any sort of confining room or vehicle. She'd helped him through countless trips. "*Eyebrows*," she'd murmur, reminding him to touch his bushy brows. He said they felt like the fur of the planetary dog. Or sometimes she would whisper, "*Counting*." Numbers soothed Ethan, and repeating them in patterns took him away from present discomforts. When things got really, really bad, Ethan closed his eyes and asked Jessamyn to tell him stories. She could always find one that would transport him from panic's biting edge. Jess knew it wasn't the tales alone. One long journey, when she'd told him particularly lame stories, she'd realized it was the sound of her voice, her presence, which restored him.

Jess heard his loud footfall as he came through the front airlock. Although Ethan was sensitive to sound that originated apart from himself, he rarely remembered to modulate his own voice or keep his boots from clomping.

Jess sighed. Her task tonight—that of talking Ethan out of traveling to Earth—would not be an easy one. Ethan was more stubborn than a stain from Mars's red soil.

"Hey big brother," said Jess.

"Jess," said Ethan. It was his standard way of greeting anyone, a compromise between saying, *Hello, how are you,* which his parents preferred, and saying nothing at all, which he preferred.

"I hear they want you to go to Earth," said Jess.

"I depart in six weeks' time," he replied.

"Ethan, I don't know how to say this to you nicely, so I'm just going to say it . . . not-nice. Your brain will be mush by the time you get to Earth. I don't know what they think they need you to do, but it can be done by someone else, whatever it is. You know I'm right." She paused. "Right?"

Ethan stood gazing at Mars's larger moon, Phobos. "Which statement would you like me to respond to? You made six distinct points."

Jessamyn groaned.

"I was attempting humor," said Ethan. "I assume you would like me to assess your statement that the task given to me can be performed by another."

In actuality, Jessamyn had been hoping to go straight to the "brain as mush" part of her speech. She appealed to his rational sense. "Logically," she began, "If your mental state is compromised, you will be in no position to perform critical tasks."

"I will not allow that to happen," said Ethan.

"Eth—" Jess broke off. She'd fought tooth and nail for others to treat Ethan as alter-abled and not dis-abled by his differences. And now she was going to tell him what he could and could not do? She sighed and flopped on his bed.

"Phobos is bright tonight," said Ethan.

Jess opened her eyes and looked up. "Yup," she said. "The big moon's close to us this week, that's for sure."

"When Earth draws near to Mars, I must be ready to travel on the raiding ship," said Ethan.

"Why does it have to be you?"

"I am not permitted to tell you the nature of my assignment."

"It's got something to do with your hacking-genius, I figure," said Jess. "Tell them to send Yokomatsu. He's got mad hacker-skills. You said so yourself."

"Yokomatsu has not studied ancient Terran—" Ethan broke off. "Yokomatsu is not my equal. Also, Yokomatsu's Marsian appearance might cause Terrans to surmise they were the subjects of an invasion. Mars is not in a position to wage war."

"So make them find someone *else* to take your place," said Jess, still determined to keep her brother safe.

"Goodnight, Jessamyn," said Ethan.

Jess twisted her head and raised an eyebrow at him. His polite use of "goodnight" was almost unprecedented. She knew he hadn't become suddenly interested in politeness and what he called "wasted language." No, if he used the phrase, it was because he wanted her to leave *now*.

"All right, all right. I'm going." She stood, resisting her urge to hug her brother, which he would hate. He had enough to distress him as it was.

"Jessamyn?"

She turned.

"I am sorry it will be me going and not you."

Jess shifted her gaze to Phobos, racing for the horizon. "Goodnight, Eth."

She lay awake for hours, her mind running through problems she couldn't solve. Mass starvation. Her broken dreams. Her brother stuck in a tin can for weeks. At last she reached for one of Ethan's favorite stories, *The Snows of Kilimanjaro*. It was the only piece of fiction she knew him to have read on his own, after she'd told him the story on a trip to New Tokyo. And it was sufficiently depressing to suit her mood. She read until her eyes drifted, and when she slept, she dreamt of blue skies, golden plains, and tall, snow-covered peaks.

The next morning wasn't a school day, and Jessamyn's mom insisted Jess should be allowed to sleep as late as possible.

"Sleep burns fewer calories than being awake," Lillian murmured from where she sat calculating starvation scenarios at her wafer-computer.

But a call from Harpreet put Jessamyn's sleep to an end.

"Jessie?" Her father, entering her room, spoke gently. "Jess, Harpreet Mombasu wants to speak with you. Are you awake enough?"

Jess rolled over. She felt refreshed for a brief moment, but then the weight of her planet's calamity and her own flightless future pressed upon her, heavy as heartbreak.

"I'm awake," she said, her voice dull. She held out her hand for the comm. "Hello?"

"Good morning, daughter," said Harpreet's voice. "I am wondering if you would be so good as to meet me at the Secretary General's office in half an hour?"

"Um, sure, yeah," said Jess, sitting up and running a hand through her night-matted hair.

"Excellent," said Harpreet. "Goodbye."

Jess felt a warm glow spark inside of her. *Hope*, her heart whispered. After donning her cleanest Academy whites, she raced through morning rations.

"What's the meeting about?" asked her mother.

Jess shrugged, feeling the hopeful spark zooming around her insides. "I talked to her yesterday, right before the Secretary's announcement. Maybe she's found a way to get me back in the air."

On the outside, Jessamyn appeared calm as she drove to the New Houston headquarters of Mars Colonial. Inside, a veritable galaxy of small bright sparks had big-banged to life. She knew she should care more about the fate of Mars and less about her fate as a pilot. She knew it, but she couldn't make it so.

Glancing down at the chrono-tattoo on her wrist, Jess saw she would arrive early. Her brother, knowing his sister's propensity for behaviors culminating in late arrivals, had created the glowing tattoo for her eighth birthday. They each had one. Ethan had worked in a sort of compass as well: if it told time in red, the siblings were close to one another. The cooler the color, the farther apart they were. Jess's rebellious streak had been the inspiration for several of Ethan's earliest inventions—answers to their mother's frustrated cries of, "Now where's that child run off to?" An orange glow on the skin of Jessamyn's wrist informed her of two things: she was near her brother *and* she still had three minutes to spare. She allowed herself a tiny smile entering MCC.

"Ah," said Harpreet, as Jessamyn stepped into the stark office. "Here is the young woman I told you about." Harpreet, taking Jess's hand, placed it in the hand of Mei Lo, Secretary General and CEO of Mars Colonial.

Jess hoped she had an impressive handshake. Her mother had said that a firm and brief grasp told people that you were someone who meant business.

"Pleased to meet you, Pilot-in-training Jaarda," said the leader of Mars Colonial.

"Likewise," Jess replied, her heart beating faster. Was she still a pilot-in-training?

"It's going to be a very long day," said Mei Lo, "So I'll get to the point: I need a chauffeur. My full-time pilot and both of my back-ups are busy flying redistribution runs of emergency rations. Even if MC Command would let me, I don't know how to fly anything but a planet-hopper. I have several weeks of travel coming up, and I'd like to interview you for the job."

Chauffeur? Jessamyn hesitated. No self-respecting Academy graduate would apply for the position. *You can always chauff the CEO* was a pass-phrase for what a trainee who failed final exams could do with a pilot rating, second-class.

Jess wanted to fall through a hole in the floor.

Harpreet added, "I've already spoken with the Academy dean. He's agreed to grant you immediate second-class licensing in light of our current emergency."

Jess felt her face redden.

"I spoke with him as well," said the Secretary. "He told me you could pass an exam for a first-class license with your eyes closed."

"Probably," she agreed, shifting her weight uncomfortably. She wanted to cry out that she would give up a week's water to fly ration redistribution runs instead, but the Secretary continued.

"He also told me you've been grounded for disobeying a direct order," she said.

"I saved a planet-hopper, Ma'am," said Jess. "I prevented the loss of a valuable Marsian resource."

"Jessamyn," said the Secretary, her voice softening to a murmur. "Our children are Mars's most precious resource. You risked your life, and I appreciate the courage that took, but I need to ask you: will you obey orders if I accept you as my personal pilot?"

Jess looked at Harpreet, who gave a subtle nod. *Go on, child, this is the only way you are getting back in the air*, she seemed to say with her wide dark eyes.

"I'll do my best," said Jessamyn.

The Secretary's eyes narrowed. Then her mouth turned up on one side. "You didn't give me the answer I wanted to hear. You gave me the truth." She smiled. "I like that. And I don't believe in coincidences; I think you're here for a reason. Pilot-in-training Jessamyn Jaarda, you are hereby granted the title of pilot, second-class."

Mars's diminutive leader struck her hand forward once again and Jess took it, holding it a second longer this time.

The Secretary turned to leave, calling over her shoulder, "My assistant has your uniform. I'll see you in the launch hangar in forty-two minutes."

The forty-one minutes following Harpreet's brief hug and best wishes were a blur. Her father and mother congratulated her during a hurried call. But it was her brother's words that stuck in her head: "*You will have the ear of the most influential person on the planet.*"

Jess had been so struck by what Ethan said that she hadn't even praised his use of figurative language. It was true. She, Jessamyn Jaarda, would have direct access to the Secretary General and CEO of Mars Colonial.

Thinking of her eyebrow-stroking, junk-collecting brother, she knew exactly what she would ask for: to spare Ethan the three week journey through hell. Jess straightened her uniform and tidied her flyaway red hair. She had six weeks to gain the Secretary's trust.

6

THE PLANETARY DOG

The earliest Marsians, sailors of the heavens, swore vigorously and frequently, often adopting the creative phrasing of their fellows without understanding precisely which body part, saint, or god was being invoked. So long as the settlements were composed of military men and women, this arrangement worked quite well. However, with the introduction of a pluralized civilian population—and in particular the introduction of *children*—there came an increase in outbreaks of violence when certain salient phrasings were uttered before those who deemed them offensive.

Marsians, more than their Terran counterparts, understood the importance of getting along with their neighbors. Opportunities for saving the lives of your fellows occurred with greater frequency on the inhospitable red planet. Marsian settlers learned the value of maintaining cordial relations, and, by common consent, it was agreed that the use of curses which gave grave offense to the person who might save your hide in the next dust storm was probably inadvisable. *Only a fool gives offense* was a proverb frequently murmured under the breath, even by those who very much wished they could afford to offend.

Early on, a thoughtful Secretary General came to the conclusion (through experimentation) that no one minded if she swore by the Greek names of the solar planets. Forward-thinking citizens followed her lead, and within a generation, the entire Mars colony railed against *Ares*, swore by *Hermes*, and invoked *Aphrodite* when upset, injured, or deeply moved. To swear otherwise—at least in the hearing of others—was, quite simply, not *Marsian.*

During Jessamyn's first week as the current Secretary's personal pilot (Jess refused to refer to the position as "chauffeur") she had ample opportunity to observe Mei Lo's preferences in cursing. Jess shuttled the busy woman from one settlement to another so that the Secretary could provide personal reassurance that all possible measures were underway to keep Mars from starving.

They discovered one remote outpost where half-rations had been the norm since the last raid. The

Secretary wasted the water of half a dozen tears as the citizens of that locale politely returned the emergency rations they'd received earlier in the week.

"Send 'em somewheres they need 'em," said the enclave's spokesperson, a haggard-looking woman whose ruddy skin spoke of more than forty orbits.

They'd done just that.

Today Jessamyn had flown Mei Lo to a meeting in New Tokyo. On their return flight to New Houston, the Secretary repeated a now-familiar pattern of spending nearly every minute on a comm-call.

So much for having her ear, thought Jess. She couldn't complain about the job itself. Nearly every day brought a new craft to the Secretary General's dedicated launch pad at headquarters, and Jess loved the challenge of mastering each vessel's quirks and traits. Today, however, they flew in the Secretary's personal ship.

"*Ares*, but it's good to have my Cloud Runner back," sighed the Secretary.

The Cloud Runner was a luxury-class personal ship with non-standard landing requirements. None of the settlements they'd flown to last week could have accommodated the strange craft: when docking, the ship was designed to settle onto a series of prongs allowing it to recharge. The Secretary's executive dwelling had the necessary dock, which meant Jessamyn could fly her directly home today.

Jess ran her fingers down the launch schedule. "Looks like I can take you out in the Cloud Runner all this coming week," she said.

"Mmm, that will be nice," said Mei Lo with a pleased sigh. "*Decadent,* but nice."

"You're planetary CEO," replied Jess. "There's nothing decadent—"

An incoming comm-call interrupted Jessamyn.

"This is the Secretary General." Mei Lo launched into a discussion that cut short Jess's hopes of an actual conversation with her new boss.

Jess scowled and aimed the Cloud Runner at the setting sun. A distant dust storm had filled Mars's shallow atmosphere near the horizon, creating a brilliantly burnt-orange sunset. It was stunning. Jess adjusted the speed of the craft so that she could keep the sunset in sight all the way to Mei Lo's home. The beauty relaxed her. She ached to fly and fly, chasing nightfall around the planet.

Once, Jessamyn had overheard her father trying to explain his daughter's response to natural beauty. *Most people have five senses*, he'd said. *Jess has a sixth: the sense of wonder.*

Jessamyn hadn't understood what he meant at the time, and she still wasn't sure she could explain it to anyone else, but his words sounded right to her somehow. On the other hand, she asked herself, how could anyone be other than wonder-struck by the flaming sky spread before them?

She turned back to smile at the Secretary, who had ended her comm-call. But Mei Lo's eyes were closed, her head sagging at an angle that suggested sleep. Returning her gaze forward, Jess sighed. The Secretary had fallen asleep without re-securing her harness. Now Jessamyn had a decision to make: follow standard protocol and wake the exhausted Secretary, telling her to buckle in, or let the poor woman sleep. It wasn't like Jess would have trouble landing the ship. But harnessing was standard on this vehicle for a reason.

The decision was no-contest, actually. If Jess wanted to prove she could fly by the rules, she'd darned well better wake her passenger.

"Madam Secretary," Jess called. "We're nearly there."

Ahead, Jess could make out the yellow lights of the Secretary's home and the blinking blue lights of the landing pad.

Mei Lo yawned and sighed contentedly. "Thank goodness," she said, buckling herself without Jess needing to remind her.

Jessamyn brought the craft in slowly, nearly silent. She spun the ship, aligning the prongs to the receiving outlets. And that was when she saw the blur.

"What the . . .?" Jess took an infrared reading. "No, no, *no*!"

She pulled the craft out of the landing pattern, causing the Secretary to cry out, "*Holy Ares!*" just as Jess shouted, "Hold on tight!"

Jessamyn had, in fact, decided to do something very stupid and most likely career-killing. But she knew she could never face her brother again if she landed on top of the planetary dog.

To her credit, Jessamyn *attempted* to land the craft such that it wouldn't tip sideways. But the uneven Marsian surface was set against her and within seconds of touching down, the ship wobbled, tilted, and collapsed, tumbling down on its side.

In the silence that followed the crash, the Secretary spoke.

"What in the name of *Hades* happened there, Pilot?"

Jess licked dry lips. "I wrecked your Cloud Runner, Madam Secretary."

"Yes, I did notice that," the Secretary remarked dryly.

Another moment's silence. *This is going to be so, so bad*, thought Jessamyn.

"Would you care to tell me why?" asked the CEO of Mars Colonial.

Jess wanted to reply, *Because your idiot dog was about to get ground into dog-burger.* But she held her temper. Anger wasn't going to make this mess any better. "Your dog was bouncing around down there in its . . ."

Jess struggled to remember the word. "Inside its *hamster-ball.* It was trying to bite the landing lights or something. If I'd attempted to take us back up again for another pass, I would have cooked your dog with the heat from the thrusters. I chose to land the craft . . . unconventionally."

"You made a split-second decision to kill my Cloud Runner instead of my dog."

It sounded idiotic to Jess's ears when the Secretary put it like that.

"I'm afraid so, Ma'am." All the fight *whooshed* out of her and suddenly she felt very, very young. She was an idiot. She'd destroyed her *career* just as surely as she'd wrecked the Cloud Runner.

The Secretary shook her head slowly and began sealing up her walk-out suit.

"Suit up, Pilot. You won't be taking this thing anywhere else."

Jess swallowed against the lump in her throat, wondering why the Secretary wasn't shouting and cursing. Perhaps the planetary CEO had moved past mere anger and into quiet rage.

Jess hoped the door allowing them to exit remained functional. She pushed the release locks and breathed a sigh of relief as the door opened outward, allowing them to crawl free. The planetary dog rolled his habitat to the Secretary's side and the three of them walked into the Executive Dwelling.

Once she'd stripped out of her walk-out suit, the Secretary focused her attention on the dog instead of Jess, freeing him from the globe-shaped unit that allowed him access to the outdoors.

"Come over here, you! Someone is trying to lose his nose! Oh, look at you. If that's frostbite—oh, come here, come here. Goo-ood boy. Oh you are such a naughty dog! Goo-ood boy."

Jess stood awkwardly to one side, watching the interaction between the two. When, at last, the Secretary stood and turned to look at her, Jessamyn had calmed enough to be able to speak rationally.

"I acted on impulse. I'm sorry, Ma'am."

The Secretary tilted her head to one side. "Sorry? Are you apologizing to me for saving the life of the planetary dog?"

"It was inexcusable of me, Ma'am."

"Pilot?"

"Yes, Madam Secretary?" *You are so dead*, said a voice in Jess's head.

"Thank you for sparing the life of Mars's most iconic and best-beloved inhabitant. Our planet has never been more in need of good cheer than we are at this moment." Mei Lo smiled. "And frankly, even on a cost basis, activating a new canine embryo is more expensive than replacing my ship. Not that Rover could ever be replaced."

Hearing his name, Rover thumped his tail twice.

Jessamyn stared, at a loss for words. She'd done something right by doing something wrong.

"May I?" The Secretary extended her diminutive arms as if for a hug.

Jess gave half a nod and then felt the arms of her planet's leader encircling her.

Pulling back out of the hug, Jess asked, "So, does this mean I still have a job?"

The Secretary threw her head back and shouted to the ceiling, "*Do you still have a job*?" She bent down to scratch her dog's head. "Does the nice pilot still have a job, huh, Rover?" The Secretary stood again, recovering herself from laughter. "You've got any job you want, kid, saving Rover's life like that! *Ares!* If I had a son, I'd make him marry you right now!" Mei Lo's eyes danced. "My job's a very lonely one at times. You've saved me from . . . from . . ." She blinked several times. "You've made my life *immeasurably* better by not barbecuing my dog. Thank you, Jessamyn."

Embarrassed, Jess didn't know where to look and found her eyes resting on the dog. It sat, head cocked to one side, eyes fixed on the Secretary.

"Would you like to say hi to Rover?" asked Mei Lo.

Jess wondered if the Secretary would be offended if she declined. She'd never wanted to meet the dog before, and she didn't feel particularly interested in meeting it now. Then she thought of her brother.

"Sure . . ." she said. It came out sounding almost like a question.

The Secretary smiled. "Rover, come. Meet Jessamyn."

The dog stood and quickly closed the few feet between himself and Jess.

Jessamyn lowered herself to one knee as she'd seen countless children do when she'd been young enough to be taken for her birthday visit. Remembering the other celebrants making fools of themselves with the planetary dog, she decided it would be best to get it over with quickly.

But something happened when Jess's eyes connected with Rover's. His eyes, light-blue like Ethan's, caught her at once with their intelligence. *Who are you?* the dog seemed to be asking. He tilted his head from side to side, never loosing her from his gaze except to blink.

"The blinking is one of the ways he's acknowledging you as being ahead of him in the pack," said the Secretary.

"Huh," said Jessamyn. She wasn't really paying attention, though. She felt a rush as something swept through her. A something that reminded her of taking her craft toward breaking day or of watching Phobos as the swift moon zipped across the night sky. The dog was . . . *wondrous.* A shiver ran along her spine. "Hi," she said to the gentle-eyed creature before her.

Rover leaned in and licked her.

"He gave up water—to *me*, a total stranger," gasped Jess.

"It's a shock the first time," said Mei Lo. "Think of the proverb, though, and it all makes sense."

"Be as generous as a dog," murmured Jessamyn.

"Exactly," agreed Mei Lo. "Put your hand out where he can get a good sniff. Dogs learn from their noses as much as from their eyes. Maybe more."

Jess extended one hand. Rover leaned in snuffling, blowing, and, incredibly, licking her once again. She giggled this time. Looking at Rover's black, tan, and white coat, Jess grew curious. *What does it feel like*? She plunged one hand into his thick fur. It reminded her for a moment of her granddad's bristle-y mustache. But underneath she found a softer silken layer.

"Incredible," she murmured, pulling her hand back and forth through his fur.

Rover's muzzle darted toward Jess's chin and he licked her again.

"Unreal," she said.

"He reminds me to act with generosity," said the Secretary. "It's hard to have a water-grubbing attitude with Rover giving up moisture ten times a day."

Jess didn't want to stop pulling her hand through the soft furry layers. Incredibly, she realized she was *petting* the creature. No wonder Ethan liked the planetary dog so much. No wonder Mei Lo was so grateful. *Why don't I see these things coming?* Jess asked herself. Of *course* saving the dog had been the right thing to do. Of *course* the Secretary would be grateful and not angry. Harpreet's words of the other day floated through Jessamyn's mind: *You must learn to see things from more than one perspective.* But how was that even possible when she was stuck inside her own mind? Jess sighed in the quiet room.

Then, with a kind of shiver, Jess realized this was the moment she'd been waiting for: she had the Secretary's undivided attention *right now.* Like she might never have it again. It made her a bit dizzy, like coming in too hot on a fast ship.

But Jessamyn found, as she considered this waited-for moment, that she did not wish to take unfair advantage of the Secretary's current state of gratitude.

"Listen, Madam Secretary, there's something you should know. I wasn't thinking about you just now when I saved Rover's life. Or about Mars," she added. "I saved your dog's life because I don't think I could've faced my brother otherwise. He's crazy about your dog."

"*Mars's* dog," corrected the Secretary.

"Yeah, well, Ethan's the reason I did what I did. I don't want you having any false ideas about how I was trying to be all noble for the citizenry of Mars or whatever. 'Cause I wasn't." She noticed her fingers gripping tightly to a handful of fur and forced herself to relax. Rover didn't seem to mind. She spoke again, quietly. "It was all for my brother's sake."

"All right," said Mei Lo, nodding, narrowing her eyes as she examined Jess. "I can still be grateful for the end result, you know, regardless of your motives."

Jess swallowed and continued before she had a chance to get scared and freeze up. "Listen, I know you want Ethan for some secret assignment, but it won't work. Eth won't make it to Earth. You put him in that ship for three weeks, and by the time he comes out the other side, his mind will be destroyed. He's claustrophobic. *Severely* claustrophobic. And that's only *one* of his peculiarities that I can put a name to. He's got other . . . habits and preferences and quirks that don't have names. But I can guarantee none of it will look good aboard the Red Galleon."

"I've noticed he is . . . different," said the Secretary. "But he seems strongly committed."

Jess released Rover and straightened up so that she could look the Secretary in the eye. "Let me ask you something. Can you afford for him to fail at . . . whatever this is?"

The Secretary turned sharply. "Has he told you what I'm asking him to do?"

"No," said Jess. "And you can bet he never will."

Rover shook his coat and wandered off to a pillow that had his name on it.

Frowning, the Secretary crossed her arms and looked at Jess. "Why do you ask whether or not I can afford for him to fail?"

"I know my brother. I understand that whatever you want him to do, he's convinced that only he can do it, and he believes it ought to be attempted. But he's not sure of himself. Asking my brother to climb inside a small, enclosed space with no escaping for three weeks is like . . ." Jess struggled to come up with something the Secretary might be able to understand. She saw Rover. "It's like your dog wanting to be outside. Sure, Rover can survive in his hamster-ball for a short time, but if you left him in the cold for three weeks, what would you find when you went back to collect him?"

"He'd die," said the Secretary.

"Yes," said Jess. "Even though your dog *wants* to go outside, it isn't an environment he can survive in for long."

"You're saying your brother can't survive three weeks in the *environment* of the Red Galleon."

Jess pinched her lips together then spoke. "Maybe if he had a couple of annums to prepare for it, he might make it. As he stands now? No."

The Secretary stood as still as one of the ice carvings from the Festival.

Jess felt the long pause that followed as if it were a physical thing pressing down upon her.

"Would you bet the future of Mars on that certainty?" The Secretary's face blanched as she whispered the question.

"The *future* of Mars?"

The Secretary nodded.

Jess hesitated. She remembered trips with her brother that ended with him rocking back and forth, eyes closed, making a steady humming noise at the same pitch for hours on end. She remembered other times she'd worked hard with him, sitting beside him and feeding him distractions, telling him stories, keeping him protected as best she could from the deleterious effects of an enclosed space.

She looked up and met the Secretary's eyes. "He can make it if he has me with him. But otherwise, no, Madam Secretary. My brother's mind wouldn't be the same by the time he reached Earth. If you need him in his right mind, send me with him."

The Secretary was quiet for several minutes. Jess stared into the black expanse beyond the large windows. *Ethan would like it here*, she thought. She saw the small moon Deimos and wondered if Earth had risen yet. Beside the window, Rover rested his chin on his paws, lying on his pillow. His eyes darted from the Secretary to Jess, back and forth in clear acknowledgement of the tension in the room.

At last, the Secretary, who'd been staring out the window as well, spoke. "You could have lied to me about your motivation for saving Rover's life. But you didn't. Just like the day I hired you: you told me the truth instead of what I wanted to hear. I abhor lying and dissembling, Jess. I've seen plenty of both as CEO of this planet." She turned so as to face Jessamyn directly. "As I'm sure you are aware, raiding parties are formed with five team members."

Jess nodded, recalling the pang of jealousy she'd felt when she'd heard that a young woman only two orbits her senior had been named captain of the mission.

Mei Lo continued. "What I have not yet announced is that we will be sending two teams of raiders this time—two teams with two separate missions."

Jessamyn's heart beat faster, clattering in her chest like storm-tossed pebbles upon a window.

"I need your brother to accomplish a task that I believe only he can complete as a special mission. At present, the board of directors is locked in disagreement about the choice of a pilot for this mission. Obviously we need someone capable of guiding a ship past the Terran satellite lasers in high orbit around Mars." She smiled softly at Jessamyn. "As you already know, I don't believe in coincidence. I have the final authority to decide this assignment, but the awarded duty comes with a caveat."

"I'll do it," whispered Jess.

"You haven't heard me out," replied the Secretary, her face now sober. "I am sending your brother to hack the control codes of the satellite array, placing them under our direction. That is the top-secret task that falls to the second crew. There is a very real chance he may fail and that some or all of you could be captured with no hope of rescue."

Jessamyn thought of her granddad's tales of body-swapping and shuddered.

"The Terrans would certainly re-body you or kill you." The Secretary paused. "This is a far more dangerous assignment than merely retrieving ration bars."

Jess nodded. "Send me."

7

SENSATION OF WEIGHT

Two days later, Jessamyn officially received the assignment as pilot and first officer of the Red Galleon. She wasn't permitted to divulge the true mission, so her parents, along with the rest of Mars, assumed Jess would be on an ordinary raid with the second crew acting as a safety-net and possibly obtaining additional food.

Lillian glowed with excitement, certain if MCC had ordered double shipments, then the Secretary General was making a commitment to develop a domestic food-source within forty orbits.

"This is everything we've worked for," Jess's mother said, hugging her daughter.

"We're deeply proud of you both," Jess's father said to the siblings.

At the words of praise, worry creased Lillian's red-dry face.

"They'll be fine," said Jess's father. "MCC doesn't make mistakes when they choose a crew."

Ethan walked back to his room, returning a moment later.

"Here," he said, handing Jess what appeared to be a piece of clear plastic half the size of his palm.

Jess took the object.

"It is from my collection," he said.

She looked closely at the clear card and discovered a thin hair enclosed between two layers. "What is it?"

"I obtained a strand of Rover's hair. Now that you have met, I would like you to have it. For luck." Ethan smiled.

Jess shook her head. "What about you? Don't you need good luck?"

Ethan shrugged. "I will have Jessamyn."

~ ~ ~

Jess's congratulations from the Secretary General were mixed.

"Having you at the helm of the Galleon gives me great peace," said Mei Lo as Jess flew her home one last time from a meeting in New Tokyo. "But it also means I'm losing the best chauffeur I've ever had."

"I'm sorry, Ma'am," said Jess. "I could ask for another couple of days, to get you settled with someone else."

"*Holy Hermes*, no!" replied the Secretary. "You've got a job to do, Pilot Jaarda. I hereby order you to forget my self-indulgent complaint."

Jess smiled.

"Between you and me, they're going to ride you extra hard the next four weeks because of the suspension on your record. You may feel less enthusiastic about this assignment before long."

Jess glanced over at the Secretary, who chewed on her lower lip as she gazed at Mars spinning past below them.

"I've thought long and hard over the resolution to destroy Earth's hold on our planet by seizing control of the satellite array," Mei Lo said softly. "*Ares*, I hope I've made the right decision."

"I won't fail you," said Jess.

The Secretary nodded and then seemed to lose herself in dark contemplation of the red-brown planitia for the remainder of the journey.

Jess piloted the Secretary's ship into MCC for the last time strictly according to standard protocol, landing with a textbook precision the Academy dean would have been proud of.

~ ~ ~

Jessamyn's pre-launch training proved both difficult and unpleasant. She consoled herself with the fact that it gave her more time with her brother, whose official function was as the crew communications specialist. Besides her brother and Harpreet, Jess had to learn to work with the payload specialist, a quiet mechanic nicknamed Crusty, and the young captain of their crew, Cassondra Kipling, a woman with political aspirations. "Kipper," as she was called at MCC, was only four years older than Jess, but within the first week, Jess became convinced there was no world in which the two might have been friends.

"She's awful," Jess confessed to Lobster, who would serve on the other ship, as they walked together after a full day's training. "She has no sense of humor. I asked what she liked to read for fun and she said stories were for children and that she had better things to do with her time. Honestly, I don't think she likes flying all that much. I wish you were captaining my ship."

"Kipper's all right," replied Lobster. "You'll get to know her on the flight to Earth."

"Won't that be fun," Jess murmured.

"Between you and me," said Lobster, "I asked for you on my team. Took it up with Harpreet Mombasu *and* the Secretary General."

Jess looked hopefully at her red-bearded friend. Everyone knew Harpreet had tremendous influence over the planet's leader.

He shook his head. "It was no good. It seems Harpreet put a lot of thought into the balance of each team. She spouted about the combination of hot and cold, head and heart and stomach and I don't know what else. Most of it went right past me, to be honest, but I left that meeting confident she knew what she was up to."

Jess sighed heavily. "I'll make it work." She gave Lobster a quick hug. "But I would have loved flying with you."

Ethan stood waiting for his sister, already in his walk-out suit, eager to return home. She wondered how he would manage the final week before launch when they were required to live on base. She'd noticed a determination in her brother to meet every new situation as if it were a game he had to win. It made her proud, but even more importantly, it gave her hope for the weeks to come.

"This extra weight makes me feel like I'm tired all the time," Jess said to Ethan as they climbed into the family get-about. Like the other raiders, she'd been outfitted with weighted garments which she would wear for the duration of her time on Mars. On Earth, she would weigh almost triple what she weighed on Mars. To accustom the team, the weights were increased every three days; the process would continue aboard ship, by increasing its artificial gravity

"I find the sensation of weight pleasurable," said Ethan.

Jess laughed, thinking her brother was attempting humor, but it turned out he genuinely liked the feeling of being more solidly anchored to the ground beneath his feet.

Neither sibling, however, enjoyed their daily "tonic." All crew members were required to consume a noxious mixture of fermented cod liver oil and whey protein, a beverage kept in deepest storage for strengthening the bodies of the raiders.

"Tastes like it's been sitting around for the past eighteen annums, all right," muttered Jessamyn as she sat with her family for evening ration. Secretly, she enjoyed watching her body respond to the increased demands and supplements. She'd always been wiry; now she grew muscled.

But far worse than the weights or foul-tasting drinks were the flight trials and simulations, which Jessamyn had fully expected to enjoy.

"I swear it's like they're waiting for me to screw up," Jess remarked after downing the tonic.

"Well, of course they are," said Jess's mother. "Honey, half the board members glower at me every time I show my face at MCC. These are smart men and women who think *you* can't be trusted to obey orders." Lillian shook her head. "You'd better prove they're wrong."

~ ~ ~

Earth and Mars approached the positions from which the raiding ships would launch. By day Jessamyn drilled and simmed and watched vids of previous raiding ships as they traced the dangerous path between the satellites circling Mars. She noted the caution with which previous pilots had "threaded the needle," as they called this path-finding, and she began to see possibilities, ways to demand more of the ship, ways to confuse the satellites. She was terrified and couldn't wait all at the same time, and one or the other made sleep challenging. She took to hauling a sleep-mat into Ethan's room and watching the satellites as they swept overhead until, at last, the steady sound of her brother's breathing lulled her to sleep.

The lasers weren't designed to rain terror upon the planet's surface. The war against Mars had lacked popular support on Earth, and the Terran government had understood that bombarding the surface could only amplify sympathy for Marsians—something the Terran government had no intention of increasing. Instead, they'd placed a series of satellites in high orbit which would systematically strike with high intensity lasers anything trying to leave Mars. The weapons derived power from the sun, so they would never "run out" of ammunition.

As the lasers couldn't focus upon planetary targets—something Terran government officials repeated frequently—Earth's military appeared less greedy for a high civilian body count. Of course, the high body count would be provided courtesy Mars's harsh environment, they whispered, grinning smugly.

"Cut off Mars's ability to reach Earth, and you seal their fate," Terran Brigadier General Bouchard had said. But Bouchard, the same officer who had ordered the destruction of Mars's orbital mirrors, hadn't counted upon Marsian determination, their love of their planet, or their independence.

And he certainly hadn't counted on Secretary General Mei Lo, born long after his death. Her sworn objective was a completely and truly independent Mars. For that, she needed crops that wouldn't poison the population with soil toxins and a way to defend Mars against possible attack. A group of agricultural specialists were seeing to the first goal. By seizing control of the hated satellites, she could accomplish the second. The lasers, once under Marsian control, could be used to destroy undesired incoming ships, missiles, or even the occasional meteorite.

It was no wonder Jessamyn had difficulty sleeping. Much rested upon her ability to pilot her ship free of the lasers and safely onward to Earth.

~ ~ ~

The requisite number of sun risings and settings passed and the final week before launch arrived. Although they'd been allowed to return to their own homes each evening after training thus far, the crews of the two ships would live on base at MCC this last week.

Jessamyn and Ethan were awakened by their father, who placed a kiss upon his daughter's forehead. Jess rolled over, looking automatically to Ethan's clear ceiling. Mars's yellow sky glowed softly. So long as the clear weather held, they would launch in one week's time.

"Good," muttered Jess, rising. She was ready for the next step. She hoped her brother was. Time flowed oddly during that final week, and when the day arrived upon which the crews boarded their sister ships—Red Dawn and Red Galleon—Jess felt as if minutes and not days had slipped past her since leaving home.

The week leading to the launch had felt to her like a combination of graduation exercise, planetary holiday, and funeral. The impression of the latter had been strong enough that, as she sat aboard the Red Galleon, waiting through the final countdown to launch, Jess had composed an impromptu epitaph:

Here lies Jessamyn Harpreet Jaarda, a Damn Fine Star Pilot.

During Mars's first raid after the No Contact Accords, a very brave pilot had destroyed two lasers on one of the satellites before her craft was carved into pieces by four remaining lasers. Having created a narrow window for raiding vessels to escape, Pilot Dorothy Bin Puri was posthumously awarded the title

"Star Pilot," and while Jess planned to survive her flight, she still liked the sound of the honorary title. It had only been awarded once, as future endeavors to take out the lasers had ended badly. A ban against such attempts had been in place for forty annums. If there was one thing more important than water to Mars Colonial's survival, it was her citizens.

Today Jessamyn's ship, the Red Galleon, and Lobster's ship, the Red Dawn, would fly together past the satellite Bin Puri had damaged. Their hope for escape was two-fold. First they would attempt to pass by in range of only the defunct lasers. But a tandem passage through high orbit had never been attempted before, and in preparation for what would undoubtedly be a more difficult getaway, MCC had coated critical portions of the Galleon with cloaking material. The Galleon would stand between the Dawn and the lasers. If all went well, the Galleon wouldn't be noticed and the Dawn, shielded, would be invisible as well. And if all didn't go well, then Jessamyn's piloting skills alone would have to save them.

When she'd asked Harpreet about sims versus real maneuvers through the dangerous high orbit zone, the old woman had laughed. "The two can't be compared. In simulation, they spin us around, mimic g-forces, give us a pretty screen to look at, but when the real thing comes—well, you'll see what I mean."

Jess felt the hum of her ship's anti-gravity as it came alive. She had the urge to hold her breath, watching the instrument panel while seconds ticked past. Jess had badly wanted to be the one who chose the moment of ascent, but MCC insisted upon a computer-initiated launch. Which gave her little to do but watch the clock before her as the digits to the left of the decimal point zeroed out. Once this happened, she lifted her gaze from the screen, eyes wide for the moment MCC passed control of the ship into her hands.

The Galleon thrust free from the surface and began a steady trajectory that would place her between two satellites, skewed toward the one with non-functional lasers. But no one knew the exact size or shape of the blind spot in the damaged satellite's lasers. It was guess work, based on repeated viewings of past flights. Detection by the lasers remained a distinct possibility.

Jessamyn looked behind her for one last glance at her crewmates before they attempted to "thread the needle." Harpreet looked at peace, smiling softly at Jess. Ethan was too engaged by screens to acknowledge his sister. Crusty was in a different part of the ship. Kipper glared at her first officer—Jess had no idea what for. She turned back to her navigation panel.

"Come on, baby, let's do this." Jess murmured to the Red Galleon. They approached the range where detection by the array grew more likely. Jessamyn's jaw clenched tight as she waited for MCC to release control of the ship to her. When the moment came, she sensed it as strongly as a blind person might experience a sudden shift to sight. "Woo-hoo!" she hollered. Working swiftly, she initiated a total dark sequence where all of the ship's systems were powered off.

There was no engine noise. The only light came from a micro-voltage nav-screen. Artificial gravity disappeared and Jess felt her body's attempt to tug free of the seat harness. Going full-dark might help them evade the satellite's sensitive detectors.

"Don't give 'em anything to notice, my beauty," murmured Jessamyn. She felt a surge of love for the ancient craft and couldn't resist patting the ship's wall beside her. *This is the tough stretch*, she told herself, her jaw clenching tight. Four minutes of dark where the ship seemed to float like a mote of dirt on a Mars breeze. It was almost peaceful, if you could put the thought of lasers and destruction out of your mind. Jess found she couldn't, quite.

Two minutes passed. Jess's fingers, sheathed in tight-fitting gloves, itched as they hovered over the controls that would initiate thrust if it were needed for escape. Another minute ticked by. She practiced clenching her abdominal muscles in a g-straining maneuver. She noted the subtle fluid pressure of the g-suit. Another couple of minutes and the ships would be out of range. A blip on her screen told her the Red Dawn remained precisely where she should be in relation to Jessamyn's ship.

And then something very bad happened. The satellite boosted power to the detector array; it must have seen something. Shrill pips from the Galleon's monitors indicated they would be discovered in seconds. They'd slipped past the dead targeting lasers—would the live ones be able to reach them? Jess knew the answer, although she didn't want to.

Immediately, Jessamyn burned her aft engines full blast, hoping to avoid becoming locked by the satellite's targeting system. As everyone aboard was smashed into their seats by the acceleration, Jess felt her g-suit responding to the sudden and intense shift in gravity. She forgot to tighten her abdominals and felt her peripheral vision degrading.

Slamming the engines off, the pressure shifted—*hard*—as Jessamyn rotated the ship ninety degrees. She executed another brief but powerful engine burn to send the ship along the new trajectory. It felt wrong not to be aiming *away* from the deadly lasers, but this sort of bait-and-switch was her best hope for confusing the targeting system on the satellites. Cutting all power and bringing them to black out once more, Jess held her breath. Or tried to—her g-suit's partial-pressure breathing made that impossible.

Are we safe? Jess wondered. The Galleon's monitor continued its shrill warnings that the satellites were searching for them. She glanced quickly to see if the Red Dawn had slipped through or if it had mimicked her maneuvers. She cursed. Lobster had matched her move for move, which meant his flank was now partially exposed to the live lasers. For several seconds, it looked like the confused satellite had decided no one was there after all. And then Jess heard Lobster's voice in her ear.

"They've got a lock on you, Red Galleon. You are hot, I repeat, YOU ARE HOT!"

Cursing again, Jess confirmed what Lobster reported. A laser had begun its deadly work, cutting through the outer surface of her ship, melting a streak across the hull.

"No you don't!" Jess shouted. She initiated another blast full forward while shouting to her brother. "Missiles, Ethan, *now!*"

He'd anticipated the command and released a dozen missiles which mimicked the Galleon's heat signature, aiming them at the satellite. Jess waited to see if the missiles would grab the laser's attention. They did.

She felt buoyant, jubilant as she shouted to her brother, "It worked, Eth!" Then she cut all power to her ship, hollering to Lobster, "Get your ship out of range, Lobster! You've only got a few seconds! You might not get another chance!"

Meanwhile, the satellite laser ruthlessly targeted and destroyed the Galleon's missiles within less than one minute's time. Jess used the distraction to turn the ship away from Mars and the high orbit death traps. She initiated a brief burn to pick up speed and then went dark. There was a tense minute's silence. Was the cloak providing some protection, confusing the laser's targeting protocols? The satellite knew what quadrant to search. Before Lobster called the warning, Jess saw the laser targeting her ship's aft section once again. She felt a boiling fury at the thought of the blackened streaks, the melting metal.

She fired her engines once again, sending the ship hurtling forward, but the laser adjusted course as well and continued heating its way through the metal exterior. Jess heard an auditory warning.

"*Twenty seconds to hull breach*," said the ship's audio.

"I've got you, baby," Jess muttered to the ship, hoping the Galleon could handle what she planned—it was time for something unconventional. She shouted at Lobster to get clear and abruptly cut the aft engines, flipped the ship 180 degrees using the side thrusters, and then fired the thrust rockets well above safety ratings. The ship groaned and Jess shut everything off once again. She felt a blackening rush that told her she was about to pass out. Vaguely she recognized the sound of someone being sick in their helmet.

A second later, her pressure suit and her own efforts brought her back to full consciousness. She noted with intense relief that the Galleon had evaded the laser, which continued to overshoot its target. No ship should have been asked to do what Jess had just demanded of the Galleon. The satellite locking system was baffled, and the cutting laser shut off, seeking its target anew. Jessamyn saw multiple warnings flashing on the panels before her.

"I know," she whispered to her ship. "I know. Hold together for me." She double-checked the calculations she'd made before throwing the ship in the new direction.

"By *Ares*, Lobster, get yourself out of range, *now*!" Jess called. Her limbs felt odd and she suspected she'd see pervasive bruising from the g's the next time she had a chance to look.

The Red Galleon continued on a silent trajectory away from Mars, away from the Terran satellites designed to confine her people to low Mars orbit. She heard several deep sighs over her comm-system.

"Everyone okay?" she asked. "I sure hope so because we are *out of danger*, people! I repeat, we are out of range!"

As if in response, Jessamyn heard the laser detectors wail once again as the targeting system locked onto her ship once more, but at this range, the cutting laser was too weak and unfocused to give the ship anything more than an ugly sunburn. The Galleon continued on her silent course for a few last seconds before Jess fired the engines again and corrected course for Earth.

"Red Dawn, we are en route," called Jessamyn. "You ready to go grab some rations?"

Jess heard a crew member coughing, fighting nausea.

"Lobster, you okay?"

And then, with a certainty that didn't require checking her instrument panel, Jessamyn knew what had just transpired. Her mouth filled with a metal taste which she tried to swallow away. She felt the void created by the Red Dawn's absence. She had no need to search the skies for dismembered pieces spinning away from one another. She knew the truth. They were gone. All dead.

8

WE ARE SMALL CREATURES

No!

Her mind pushed back, hard against the insistent fact: the Red Dawn was no more.

It's a mistake, thought Jessamyn. And weren't mistakes things you went back to fix? You gathered the pieces together, put everything back where it ought to be, and said, "Let's try that again, shall we?"

Death, always intrusive, felt so wrong here—a *wrong*-ness that grated along her spine like a rock traced upon glass. Lobster, red-bearded and laughing, *couldn't* be merely "no more."

Seated alone in the pilot hotseat, Jessamyn couldn't see the others. But she could hear their feelings in the way they breathed. A hitched gasp, an inhalation suddenly held, a sigh too agonizingly long.

The Captain broke the silence.

"Communications specialist, you will please send a transmission to MCC indicating the loss of our sister ship and the loss of . . ."

Jess heard the strain in Kipper's voice as she forced herself to continue.

"The loss of Captain LaFontaine, First Officer Tedjomuljano, Payload Specialist Ben-David, Communications Specialist Neru, and Negotiations Officer Wu."

"Aye, Captain," replied Ethan.

"First Officer Jaarda, will you please confirm our course heading?" asked Kipper.

"I've adjusted course to take us to Earth," replied Jessamyn. There was no question of doing anything else—the Red Galleon would have to accomplish both missions now.

Behind the Galleon, the golden globe of Mars seemed to watch as the lasers continued their work, cruelly reducing the Red Dawn to finer and finer pieces, so much space debris. Jess flicked off the screen showing what was now, irrevocably, a part of the mission's past. A chill that originated in her bones hummed and vibrated inside her, cold as space.

She felt a primordial impulse to close her eyes and scream, but instead forced herself to run checks using her instrument panel. The Galleon appeared to have forgiven Jessamyn's exacting treatment. *Are you grateful you were spared?* wondered Jess. The question pinged back to her: *Are you grateful? Are you?* Her fingers made course adjustments automatically, and it seemed to Jess almost as if she was watching someone else piloting the ship.

Below, her home world retreated, and she allowed herself to gaze at Mars, to watch it as it raced away, or as she did. The planet shifted from a yellow-orange sphere to a smaller orange-y circle and finally a reddish smudge against a backdrop of velvety black. Jess lost all sense of time as she sat, immobile, watching her world shrink away.

"First Officer," said the Captain's voice inside Jessamyn's helmet, "I'd like a word on a private line."

Jess felt a cool emptiness in her stomach. She knew she should feel something more: Kipper was almost certainly going to offer praise for the quick thinking that had allowed the Galleon to escape.

"This line's secure, Captain," Jess replied with a sigh. She wasn't in the mood for congratulations. Or for Kipper.

"What in *Hades* did you think you were doing back there?" asked Kipper, sounding like she had Mars-sand stuck between her backside and her flight suit.

The question caught Jessamyn off balance. *I could win an award for my inability to predict other people's responses to my actions*, she thought. Closing her eyes wearily, she asked, "Could you specify *which* part of my rescue of the Red Galleon and her crew you're referring to?" She heard the sarcasm in her voice and found she didn't regret it.

"We could start with the part where you began shouting orders to LaFontaine, without reference to the fact that your rank is inferior to—*was* inferior to—"

Jessamyn cut Kipper off. "I was trying to save his life. Which I think you can agree was more important than worrying about who outranked whom. Sir."

"It was insubordinate and unprofessional in the extreme, First Officer, and it may have cost the crew of the Red Dawn their lives," said Kipper. "If this ship had a brig, you'd be cooling your heels in it right now."

Jess's throat burned with the words she couldn't say with certainty—that it wasn't her fault. Instead, she lashed out. "Fine. Send me to my room."

"You will address your commanding officer with respect, First Officer Jaarda."

"Send me to my room, *sir*." Jess knew she sounded like a child. In truth, she felt angry and frightened to a degree she hadn't known since childhood.

She heard Kipper's loud, angry exhalation.

"Jaarda, you will confine yourself to quarters for the remainder of the watch. You will write up a full report detailing the possible harmful consequences of the maneuvers to which you subjected the Red Galleon and her crew. You will evaluate the possibility that you endangered our sister ship, and you will compose letters of condolence to the family members of the crew of the Red Dawn."

Jess sighed. "Okay."

"First Officer, you are a member of my crew and you will answer your captain according to standard protocols."

Jess closed her eyes. She could do this. "Aye-aye, sir."

Another loud exhale. "Captain out."

Jess wasn't surprised by how her commanding officer treated her; rumors had reached Jessamyn that Kipper had tendered her resignation when she'd found out Jess would be her first officer. And Jess knew exactly why Kipper had, in the end, remained on the mission: returning home as a victorious raider would help her politically. Jess despised her for using the command of such a mission as a stepping stone.

But Jessamyn had promised Lobster she would try to get along with Kipper. Her throat tightened as she remembered the conversation. She owed her fallen friend this much. Jess entered the quarters she would share with Harpreet for the next three weeks. She found that she craved the relief of examining every choice she'd made upon the bridge, laying bare what had happened and why and how. Far better this than the haunting question: *Could I have done something that would have saved both crews?*

Collapsing on the upper bunk, Jess pulled up the ship's vid log. *How quickly everything happened.* From the ship's first warning of discovery to her final, daring maneuvers, only four minutes of time elapsed.

She replayed the moment where she had put her ship into a hard turnabout—the moment the lasers lost the Red Galleon. She saw how they overshot their target and then ceased firing, seeking the missing ship. It had been pure dreadful luck that placed the Red Dawn square in the line of fire. Jess steeled herself to observe the video and saw how the laser had sheared through the Dawn's wasp-like midsection, cutting the crew off from the bulk of their propulsion rockets. Horrified, she saw Lobster trying what she would have done herself: burning side thrusters in small bursts to turn the crewed half of the vessel back toward Mars and the safety of a lower orbit. But the laser tracked the movement and opened steady fire upon Lobster's helm. Without the big thrust engines, the Dawn hadn't stood a chance.

Jess stopped the vid and leaned back in her bunk. In saving her own ship, she'd exposed Lobster and his crew. The image of the laser burning through the Red Dawn kept repeating itself in her mind's eye, a torment never to be forgotten. She rose desperate to go somewhere, but then she realized where she stood—

aboard a space-faring vessel confined to quarters. There was no planet-hopper to take her deep into the Marsian desert. And so, kneeling in the center of her quarters, Jess grieved in the manner of her people, moaning tearlessly, her arms wrapped tightly around herself.

Harpreet found Jessamyn like this during the hour before evening rations.

"Child," she said, placing her own strong arms around Jess. "Ah, daughter. We blame the wind when it blows dust upon our windows. But the wind blows for a thousand reasons we cannot name, sparing our neighbor's windows one day and our own another."

Jess felt the strong arms surrounding her and curved her head into the embrace.

"Let blame go, daughter. Cast it to the wind to be borne far away."

Jess pulled back, nodding. "I'll try."

"Come and eat, child. Our stomachs are permitted no rest, even though our hearts have broken."

Together, they rose and joined the other three. Kipper seemed to have calmed herself. No longer accusatory, she greeted Jessamyn with a curt nod.

Over the subdued meal, Kipper addressed the other four crew members. "We have received three transmissions from MCC in the hours since the destruction of our sister ship. The first contained the Red Dawn's audio log." Kipper paused. "It appears that once the Galleon was initially struck by laser, Captain LaFontaine determined to draw fire from the Galleon no matter the cost to himself, his ship, or his crew."

Jessamyn's heart wrenched. Of course. It made sense. Why else would he leave his entire flank open to fire?

"In doing so, he was following orders given by the Secretary General. In the event that the safety of one ship became compromised, the Red Galleon's safety was to be held paramount." Kipper's eyes rested on the table. "The men and women of the Red Dawn, under orders, sacrificed themselves to give us a chance."

The Galleon crew sat in silence, digesting the revelation.

Then Kipper spoke again. "In the second transmission, the Secretary General extended solemn congratulations to our crew for having passed into deep space, along with a special commendation of First Officer Jaarda's bold tactics, without which, and I quote, 'evidence suggests the Red Galleon would have been lost as well.'"

Jess tried to feel satisfied with the commendation. But she felt only empty. She would never again swap stories with her red-bearded friend. Never again ask him for a vehicle it would have been wiser for him to withhold. She swallowed hard against the lump swelling her throat.

"In the third transmission, the Secretary informed me that while the final decision is hers, MCC is split as to whether or not to recommend the assignment of both missions to our single crew. She added that it will likely be days if not weeks before they are able to agree upon a recommendation."

Harpreet placed her hands atop the table, bringing her fingertips together as if in prayer. "Yet our time is limited by the length of the journey. So it will fall to us to create a course of action," she said quietly, her gaze upon her hands.

Kipper nodded. "She suggests we determine for ourselves whether the two tasks can be accomplished by five persons using only the Galleon. There are no other space-worthy vessels to send. The Galleon *must* retrieve rations for Mars. The question is whether or not we will also attempt to transfer satellite command from Earth to Mars Colonial."

"*Hades*, yes," said Jessamyn. "We've all seen what those death-rays can do."

The Captain bristled but did not reprimand Jess for the interruption. Instead, she continued. "I would like to ask Negotiations Specialist Mombasu to consider this matter. As the only one of us with prior experience of the conditions on Earth, I will be guided by her when I present my evaluation to the Secretary."

Jessamyn refrained from rolling her eyes at the Captain's stiff formality. Jess had made the point she wanted. She hoped Harpreet would agree with it.

The Captain addressed Harpreet. "Will you please prepare a recommendation for me by 06:00 tomorrow?"

Harpreet bowed her acquiescence.

"Very well," said Kipper. "We will begin our deep-space rotations immediately. Crew dismissed."

The Captain, Harpreet, and Crusty, the on-duty officers, filed out of the rations room. Ethan remained and Jess approached his side.

"You okay?" she asked softly.

"The Galleon's supply of tellurium must prove adequate," he replied.

Jessamyn frowned. "Adequate for . . . ?"

"Harpreet must now convince our Terran contact that the supply of tellurium currently in our hold is as valuable as a double-amount of ration bars."

"Oh. I hadn't thought of that." Jess shrugged. "Harpreet's a shrewd negotiator."

"She will have to be."

"Hmm," agreed Jess. "But you didn't answer my question, Eth."

"The tellurium must be enough, so it will be. Ethan must survive this journey, so he will."

Half a smile crept onto Jessamyn's face. "You amaze me, Eth."

Ethan checked the chrono-compass tattoo on his wrist. The deep red glow matched what Jess knew she would see on her own.

"It is time for me to visit the observation deck," said Ethan, rising.

Jessamyn raised one eyebrow. "It's *time?*" she asked, following her brother on the brief walk.

"I believe that regular visits, in six-hour intervals, will allow me to better manage the three weeks before us."

"Oh. That's really smart, Eth."

The two entered the ob-deck, kept darkened for better viewing of the heavens.

The stars! Jess saw them as sharp prickling points, scattered carelessly by a sower of star-seed. They swam dizzily before her as she tried to take them all in at once, differently colored and sized, in quantity beyond what anyone could number.

"It's beautiful," murmured Jess, after they'd sat in silence for several minutes.

"I find the outlook to have a balancing effect upon my autonomic nervous system," replied Ethan.

Jess laughed quietly. "Yeah, I guess that's what I meant."

"You will pardon me," said Ethan, "But I do not believe that is what you meant. Jessamyn finds *beauty* where others are not able to appreciate it. I do not believe that it is the *beauty* of what I observe that calms me. It is simply that when I view the vastness before us, I do not feel as uncomfortable as when I am confined to . . . other parts of the ship."

The two sat in silence before the canvas of ink-black, spattered with the bright dust of a thousand worlds. Jess felt a tugging grief, a Lobster-shaped space inside her that was now empty.

"I can't believe I'm not going to see him again," Jess said.

"Him?" asked her brother.

"Lobster. All of them. You'll miss Wu, won't you?"

"Wu was a formidable opponent in Monopoly," said Ethan. "I will think of him often, and when I think of him, yes, Jessamyn, I will regret his absence."

Jess felt a flash of hot anger against Earth and the cruel satellites. "Promise me one thing, Eth. Promise you'll take control of that laser array."

"That is what I am meant to do."

"It shouldn't have happened," whispered Jess. "It's wrong. As wrong as . . ." Jessamyn broke off, unable to think of anything that was comparably unwarranted.

Her brother sat beside her, not speaking, not demanding that she complete her thought. She found his presence deeply comforting.

At last, pointing to the heavens, she spoke again. "We're traveling fifty-five million kilometers and the stars don't change. They should be different, don't you think?"

"What other stars would they be?"

"I don't know. It seems like, if we journey so far, shouldn't the stars be different?"

"Fifty-five million kilometers is a very short distance, Jessamyn. We are not leaving our solar system."

"I know. It just feels like . . . I don't know how to explain it, Eth."

"We are small creatures, Jessamyn, and the universe is infinite."

Jess followed the arch of the treated observation window from one side to the other across the field of stars. "Yeah, guess we all got a good dose of our insignificance today."

"We are small, but we are also infinitely great, Jessamyn. Infinitely important."

"You figure?"

"Our companions are gone, but their importance reaches outward and onward. For each of us. For everyone on Mars. Their importance is boundless. Like the universe."

The pair sat in silent contemplation of the heavens. At last Jess spoke again.

"Do you believe that, Eth? That the universe simply goes and goes and goes?"

"Of course it does."

"I know it's *infinite.*" Jess said, repeating her brother's word. "But do you actually *believe* in it? In infinity? In something that has neither beginning nor end?"

"I believe," said Ethan.

"Hmm," sighed Jessamyn.

Between Mars and Earth, while clocks kept time with the stars, the Red Galleon and her crew advanced toward hope.

9

ANOMALOUS READING

Prior to the inception of the Terran Re-body Initiative, Earth faced several grave problems. Overpopulation had led to hunger and war on an unprecedented scale. Local governments attempted to eliminate these problems, but none had anything like the success of those who recompensed desired behaviors using a variant of a re-bodying program. Such plans offered a reward, in the form of placement inside a new younger body, gifted to those citizens engaging in behaviors that combated their nation's worst problems. Put simply, the Terran obsession with youth provided an incentive to work toward peace and plenty. But where to find healthy young bodies in numbers sufficient for those who had earned them? A program in Belarus gained precedence and became the model for the worldwide Terran Re-body Initiative.

Predicated upon the idea that youth was wasted on the young, eighteen-year-olds "swapped" places with fifty-four-year-olds using a method of consciousness transfer. The eighteen-year-old, now said to be in "twobody," spent the next eighteen years in the *aging* fifty-four-year-old body whilst apprenticing for the work that would be his or her life's contribution. At the end of the apprenticeship years, another body transfer was made into "threebody." (Most Terrans agreed that the switching from a seventy-two-year-old body into a thirty-six-year-old body was the single most satisfying transfer.) *Threebodies* thus had a body age that matched their chronological age. And when they completed their eighteen years of useful contribution and good behaviors (their "working years"), they retired, at the age of fifty-four, into svelte, young, eighteen-year-old bodies for the last quarter of their lives.

A beautiful solution, agreed most Terrans, providing severe checks against anti-social behaviors at eighteen year intervals. The one fly in the ointment was that, in order to provide a steady stream of correctly-aged bodies at correct intervals, life spans had to be limited to seventy-two years. No one was allowed to reach a seventy-third birthday, in *any* body. It was a price most Terrans were content to pay. They had peace, they had food, they had a lovely retirement plan for eighteen truly golden years. And besides, prior to the peace brought by the Terran Re-body Initiative, life spans of seventy-two years, though possible on Mars, had become rare on Earth.

Earth's problems prior to the Terran re-bodying solution had been the same issues that created funding cuts for the Mars Project. However, when it was discovered that tellurium allowed for better success rates in consciousness transfer, Terrans demanded more of the precious metal from Mars, coming up with large bills for "advertising" the Mars Project on Earth.

Marsians laughed. They shook their heads at both the advertising bills *and* the bizarre practice of re-bodying. Their refusal to pay for "advertising" on Earth, when combined with Earth's refusal to send food and supplies Mars had pre-paid, led to a breakdown in relations between the two worlds that culminated in war, a cease-fire, and finally, the No Contact Accords.

What this meant for Jessamyn and her fellow crew members was that the two cultures had grown to have completely different attitudes towards aging and life expectancy, among other things. Yet Jess's crew, as the Marsians disabling the satellites, would be called upon to act as Terran twobodies or fourbodies whose chronological age didn't match their body age.

Jessamyn found re-bodying all rather confusing. It was silly, as well, from her point of view. Who didn't want to age? On Mars, growing old was a sign you were clever, resilient, and a survivor. She had tolerated role-playing as a "fourbody" during her MCC training because she couldn't pilot to Earth without agreeing to it. But she had dreaded assuming the fake role upon Earth, and during training, she frequently lamented not being a part of the team whose mission it was to simply retrieve ration bars. However, the loss of the Red Dawn changed everything. Whereas there had been two teams, now there was only one. This meant extra days planet-side on Earth, and she would almost certainly have to pretend to be an aged person in a young body at some point.

18:00 hours meant the end of Jessamyn's twelve hour "day" shift which had begun with morning rations at 06:00. 18:00 also meant evening rations. With neither sunrise nor sunset, the distinction of day or night could hardly remain important. The crew operated on a Terran twenty-four hour clock with some overlap in their waking hours, and it was during these overlaps that morning and evening rations were shared among the crew.

Jessamyn didn't miss the extra minutes from Mars's slightly longer twenty-four hour and thirty-eight minute day. On Mars the extra time was allotted to mid-day contemplation or napping. But aboard ship, Jess had more than enough time to spend in thought or sleep.

As the crew gathered once more for a meal, Jessamyn suspected they would hear news of a revised mission. She was not disappointed.

The Captain expressed her confidence in the new plan to take on both missions. Jess noted with a mixture of relief and slight disappointment that she would spend her entire time on Earth waiting with Crusty alongside the Red Galleon so that they could return rations to Mars in the event the satellite-hacking mission should not proceed according to plan.

Crusty, who rarely spoke more than two words together, shocked everyone by breaking the silence after the Captain's new plan was announced. "Glad to hear we'll be killing two birds with one stone. We owe that much to the memory of the good folks lost on the Red Dawn."

At the conclusion of that lengthy speech, Crusty stood and went to check the health of an algae he kept in the rations room. After grunting at what he saw, he left with the Captain to begin the "night" shift.

Jess sighed, looking over her assigned role as a "fourbody" while on Earth. "Why can't Terrans stay in one body like regular people," she muttered, standing.

"*Regular* is different on Earth," said Ethan. "Their system has worked for centuries, and, assuredly, they feel that it is normal." He followed his sister, who trailed Harpreet out of the rations room and into the central corridor.

"There's nothing normal about swapping in and out of bodies every eighteen years," said Jess.

"The desire to practice consciousness transfer is difficult for us to understand," agreed Harpreet.

"Their lives are not so different from our own," said her brother. "The divisions of their lives are like ours: early schooling, apprenticeship for an occupation, serving in that occupation, and retirement."

"And mandatory death at seventy-two. Oh wait," said Jess in a voice dripping sarcasm, "We don't do that part. Besides, it's not like you have to swap bodies to do those other things."

"You do not," he agreed.

"Sleep well, Ethan," said Harpreet as she and Jessamyn arrived at their quarters.

Ethan turned back to his room and Jess entered hers, crawling up to her top bunk.

"I don't know how I'm going to impersonate an elderly person, if it comes down to it," said Jess.

"Being old is not so difficult, child. I would not know my own age if I never looked in the mirror," said Harpreet.

Tired, Jessamyn smiled. She didn't have it in her to continue the conversation. She'd found it impossible to sleep last night, so her body felt exhausted now. She brought a hand to her mouth to cover a huge yawn. Looking at her fingers, she wondered who she would be in the body of another person. *Not Jess*, she thought.

How could she possibly separate the part of herself that knew flying in her bones from the part of her that understood it in her head? Crazy. That's what Terrans were. She yawned once more and fell asleep.

~ ~ ~

Life aboard the ship settled into a simple and somewhat dull routine. Earth began to appear brighter, and Jessamyn sometimes thought she could see a blue tint. Her brother continued visiting the observation deck four times a day, Jess joining him each morning before and each evening after their duty shift. The systematic visits, especially those made with his sister, provided incalculable relief for Ethan. He admitted that he often felt an unpleasant sensation that the walls were pressing in on him, but when Jess questioned him about it, he insisted he would survive. His sister worked hard at believing him, ever watchful for telltale signs that all was not well. Ethan certainly performed his tasks with efficiency, running systems checks several times a day that would have made his sister cross-eyed with boredom.

"Ship still holding together?" Jess asked her brother one morning as he completed a report.

"I believe so," said Ethan. "Although I have detected an anomalous reading in the observation deck."

Jess snorted. "The window's tired of you, Eth. This is its way of saying, give it a rest already." She grinned at her brother. Privately, she was proud of him for finding a way to manage his claustrophobia.

Ethan didn't reply but stared intently at a series of readings. His fingers flew across the screen and he frowned. "The observation deck appears to be drawing oxygen from other parts of the ship."

The smile faded off Jessamyn's face. "You serious?" She left her post at navigation and stood behind her brother as he scrolled through a series of numbers.

"There," she said, pointing to a reading.

"Yes," said her brother. "I believe this may indicate a small leak."

"Small leaks don't stay small out here, Eth. How long has this been going on?"

He retrieved a set of readings from the prior day. "Nothing yesterday."

"It could still be nothing, today, too, I suppose," said Jess.

Ethan, shaking his head as if uncertain, checked his chrono-tattoo.

"You thinking what I'm thinking? Wake up Crusty?" asked his sister.

"The payload specialist will have entered REM sleep at this hour."

Jess rolled her eyes. "Crusty would want to be woken, trust me. And don't do that. Don't go all Kipper on me with the names."

"Payload specialist is his designation."

Jessamyn groaned, then tapped the screen. "Refresh those readings on the ob-deck."

Ethan startled visibly at what he saw.

"*Holy Ares*," murmured Jessamyn. "Is it me or did those numbers just take a big jump in the wrong direction?"

"I believe we must interrupt the payload specialist's sleep cycle," said Ethan.

But Jessamyn was already on the ship's comm, hollering for Crusty to wake up *now*.

They met him in the hall that connected Crusty and Ethan's shared quarters with the rest of the ship. Crusty was already pulling up readings on a screen beside the ob-deck.

"That ain't good," said Crusty, shaking his head.

"Can you fix it?" asked Jess.

"Fixing things is what Crusty does," said Ethan when the payload specialist didn't answer.

The gruff mechanic strode back down to his quarters, grabbed his diagnostic wafer, returned, and hit the seal door opening to the ob-deck.

"Wake the Captain," said Crusty as the door slid shut.

Moving forward along the narrow hall, Jessamyn got Kipper up, sending her back to the mechanic.

Harpreet would want to know, too, thought Jessamyn, pausing at the quarters she shared with the old raider.

By the time Harpreet and Jessamyn returned to the ob-deck, Ethan was performing a suit-check for Crusty. The walk-out suits aboard the Galleon met outer-space standards, and protocol for their use included a systems check prior to and after any use.

"Does Crusty expect to use that thing?" Jess asked her brother in a quiet murmur.

"Yes," replied Ethan.

"Where's Kipper?" asked Harpreet.

Ethan explained that the Captain had returned to the bridge to examine the readings. "And Crusty has suggested that we should all move to the forward portion of the ship."

Jessamyn and Harpreet left for the bridge while Ethan finished checking the suit for Crusty. A few minutes later, Ethan joined his sister, Harpreet, and Kipper.

"What does Crusty think?" asked Jess when her brother returned.

"He is a man of few words," replied Ethan.

Jess guffawed. "Says the man of few words."

Kipper spoke. "You caught this early, Communications Specialist Jaarda and First Officer Jaarda. I commend you both."

"*Thanks* would do just fine," muttered Jess.

"Did you have something to say to your captain?" asked Kipper.

Jess bit her tongue, holding back the things she would have preferred to articulate. Instead she said, "It was Ethan who noticed the readings, Captain, sir."

Kipper nodded in response.

Crusty's voice came through the ship's comm. "Captain, I have one confirmed leak along the starboard hull. Requesting permission to go outside and get a better look."

"Permission granted," said Kipper. "I'm bringing down the inner seal door on the ob-deck as a precaution."

"Just what I was about to recommend," said Crusty. "Though it won't stop a bad leak. That seal door ain't no confinement barrier."

For the next twenty-five minutes, the crew listened to the sound of Crusty's breathing, punctuated with occasional exclamations of "Huh," and "I'll be." When he reentered through the aft airlock, they heard him muttering a series of unpleasant wishes regarding Terrans and their technology.

"I slapped a piece of hull-seal on the outside," Crusty reported on the comm. "The sons-of-bugs made all kinds of work for me when we get planet-side."

"And the prognosis?" asked Kipper.

The mechanic grunted. "Hull-seal's only good so many days, ain't it? I'm mixing up some omni-poxy right now for the inner seal. That oughta hold her together."

The crew sighed in collective relief.

After a moment, Kipper spoke. "I am declaring the ob-deck off-limits for the duration of our flight."

Jess gasped. "You can't do that." She glanced anxiously at her brother.

Kipper stared coldly at Jessamyn for several seconds. "Don't give me another reason to confine you to quarters, Jaarda." She turned to Ethan and Harpreet. "Wake me at once if there is further degradation to the ship's hull."

Jess followed Kipper down the hall. "I'm sorry I said it that way. Kip—Captain, wait, please."

Kipper paused, one hand on the door to her quarters. "First Officer?"

"It's my brother," said Jess. "You can't seal off the ob-deck. Ethan needs to go there to keep his . . . his autonomic nervous system balanced."

"Duly noted," said the Captain, turning to her door.

Jess grabbed Kipper's shoulder to keep her from leaving. "Crusty's fixes always work. Please. If you don't let Eth stand and stare out at the stars four times a day, he'll shrivel. He won't be able—"

"That's enough, Jaarda," said Kipper, removing Jess's hand.

"—he won't be able to make the kind of discoveries he made today. I know my bro—"

"I said that's enough, First Officer. Are you incapable of recognizing an imperative when your captain issues one?"

Jess stood, caught between shame and panic. "I know how to obey an order, sir."

"My order stands. For the safety of this crew, the ob-deck will remain sealed." And with that, Kipper punched her door button and left Jessamyn standing alone in the hall.

Harpreet, standing at the far end of the hall, had seen at least some part of the interaction.

"*Ares and Aphrodite!* She makes me *crazy*," Jess said, her voice angry and low.

"No, Jessamyn, child. You do that to yourself. The Captain is not answerable for your responses. You are."

"But, this isn't even about me! It's about Ethan. He needs to spend time on the ob-deck every six hours. It's how he's keeping it together."

Harpreet touched Jessamyn's face softly. "Daughter, your brother is a remarkable young man. Perhaps it is time for you to let him fight his own battles. Did you hear him demanding that the Captain change her mind?"

Jess thought about it for a moment, then asked, "You think I get in my brother's way?"

"I think your brother would have spoken up if he felt the loss of his time upon the observation deck would impair his performance."

Jessamyn frowned. "I want him to succeed so badly. To prove to himself that he can live any life he chooses."

Harpreet smiled. "Then allow him to prove this to himself."

Jessamyn placed a hand over her eyes and slowly shook her head. "I only want to help, but I don't have the first clue, do I?"

"It is always that way with those we hold closest, child. Give your brother some room and see what he does on his own."

Jess laughed half-heartedly. "Give him some room. Yeah, that ought to be obvious enough, huh?"

Further down the hall, Jess saw Crusty exiting the ob-deck, sealing the door behind him. He removed his helmet and took a long, deep breath.

Jess straightened her back and lifted her chin. "Crusty," she called. "You want a hand with your suit-check?"

"I'm fine," he said, shuffling toward the rations room, removing his gloves. "I'll check it come morning. Evening. Whatever."

"Good night, daughter," said Harpreet, returning to the sleep quarters they shared.

"Good night," said Jess. "And thanks."

Returning to the bridge, Jessamyn seated herself back at navigation. "So I guess everything's going to be fine," she said to Ethan.

"Everything will be well," replied her brother.

He couldn't have been more wrong.

10

CALLIBRATED TO SHATTER

At the end of her shift, Jessamyn felt as if she'd completed twenty-four and not twelve hours on duty.

"I will never complain about boredom on the bridge again," she said as she sat between Harpreet and her brother.

"Boring over drama any day," mumbled Crusty from across the room.

"Crusty obtained some vid footage of the outside of our ship," said Harpreet, passing a computing wafer to Jessamyn.

Jess winced upon viewing the long ugly scarring along the starboard side of the Galleon. "Poor old girl," she said, her voice a mere whisper. Tracing her fingers along the image of the scar, Jess shivered. It was a grim reminder of the destruction of the Red Dawn.

"'Nother two minutes was all they needed," said Crusty. The dark flash of anger in his eyes told Jess he felt the same way about the ship as did she. "You did good, kid, getting the Galleon out of range."

The Captain entered, looking bleary-eyed, and the conversation turned to their mission. With only four days remaining in transit, many details remained to be hammered out, reconsidered, and otherwise determined upon. Jess tried to focus upon her ration, but the images from Crusty's vid danced before her eyes still. She realized anew how fortunate they were to have suffered only damage to the observation deck.

The meal ended, bringing with it the moment when Ethan would remember he couldn't visit the ob-deck before retiring. Jess followed him with her eyes as he rose and said good night to the crew, but would not allow herself to trail behind him, ask if he was okay, feel sorry for him.

Instead of turning aft to his room, officially the captain's quarters, Ethan strode forward to check something on the bridge. Kipper's giving up of the ship's largest quarters to Crusty and Ethan had surprised everyone, Jessamyn most of all, but she felt certain the additional space was helpful to her brother.

Turning to Crusty at her side, Jess asked, "Will you be able to fix the ob-deck leak on Earth?"

The payload specialist shrugged. "Likely, I can."

Crusty was standoffish to a degree that made Ethan look friendly and accommodating. But it was plain enough why MCC had chosen him: he could fix anything. It was rumored that you could set him out on the planitia with only a methanol/oxygen fuel-cell system suit and a reverse-water-gas-shift reactor, and in a week he would be not only alive, but living in a structure he'd built from dirt and ice by turning these into metals, glass, and other useful items.

It was rumored, but no one had dared him to do it. He didn't invite or welcome conversation.

"Well," said Jessamyn, "If you need someone for grunt work, I'm at your disposal. I won't have much else to do."

Crusty grunted.

Harpreet smiled at them both, but whether it was because Jessamyn's attempts at conversation amused or pleased her, Jess couldn't tell.

"I'll be on the bridge, Payload Specialist," said Kipper, rising to depart.

"If Ethan's on the bridge still, would you tell him I'm calling it a night?" Jess asked. Catching Harpreet's gentle eye upon her, Jess restrained herself from adding *but he can wake me up if he needs me.*

The Captain nodded curtly.

Harpreet smiled, and this time Jess felt sure what it meant: *Well done, daughter.*

Crusty, bent over the used walk-out suit for a thorough systems-check, called after Jess as she rose to leave. "Thanks for the offer to help. You're like your ma, you know."

Jessamyn flushed and smiled. Usually people remarked upon her similarity to her granddad, which was fine, but this was a welcome change. Turning forward to her quarters, she tried to remember what she knew about her mom's acquaintance with the gruff mechanic. She had just entered her room and pressed the hatch button to close behind her when she heard Crusty's voice again.

"Bells of *Hades*!" he swore.

Jess caught the utterance as her door slid shut. She paused, then punched the hatch button to re-open her door. It pulled back just in time to reveal Crusty, racing for the bridge, shouting on the ship's comm to the Captain.

"Shut down the whole mid-section!"

Harpreet, trailing in Crusty's footsteps, stopped to speak to Jessamyn. "It's the ob-deck leak. The patches didn't take, and the seal-doors aren't to airlock specification. He's going to have to seal off the back end of the ship."

Jess looked down the hall. She could already hear the grind of the emergency airlock seals. "My brother!"

"Is he not on the bridge, child?"

Jessamyn was already dashing along the hall to make sure. She called out, "Ethan? Eth? You on the bridge?"

Reaching the front of the ship, she looked to her brother's seat at the communications panel. He wasn't there.

"Where's Ethan?" cried Jess. "Stop the isolation protocol!"

"Belay that," shouted Kipper.

"No," Jess shouted, "You have to stop—"

Kipper bellowed, "Get off my bridge, First Officer."

Harpreet, examining a screen, spoke softly to Jessamyn. "It cannot be stopped, daughter. The hull breach is venting air into space at a terrible pace."

"My brother!" cried Jessamyn.

"Payload Specialist, seal the aft sleep quarters as well," called Kipper. "Mombasu, get her off my bridge, *now*!"

The order was unnecessary; Jessamyn was already running, hurling herself at the emergency bulkhead, calling her brother's name. Harpreet grabbed Jess, threw her to the ground, and used her own weight to pin Jessamyn.

"You cannot cross the seal!" said Harpreet.

Jess struggled—a mad, wild thing desperate for freedom.

Harpreet shouted, "Listen: the Captain has ordered the bulkhead on the far side to be closed as well. If I allowed you to pass, you would suffocate, sealed between doors."

The bulkhead's set of airlock doors bolted into place, shuddering the floor beneath Jess's pounding heart. Harpreet shifted off of her, allowing Jessamyn to move. But Jess lay still.

"He's trapped," she whispered.

"He's safe from the breach," replied Harpreet. "He is in his quarters and he is safe."

Crusty pounded down the hall, a leak detector in his outstretched hand. He ran the device along the seams of the bulkhead. "We have a lock-seal on this side, Captain," he said into the comm-link.

Kipper strode down the hall as well, calling into her own comm-link. "Communications Specialist Jaarda, do you have a secure seal on your side?"

Jess dug her nails into her palms as she heard her brother's voice. "The airlock doors have followed the protocol for confinement mode. I detect no leaks."

"How are your oh-two levels?" she asked.

"I am checking," replied Ethan.

Jess held her breath.

"Oxygen levels in the aft portion of the ship are stable," said Ethan.

"Good," said the Captain. "But I still want you to suit up immediately. We're going to evaluate the possibility of bringing you through the aft airlock, past the ob-deck, and through the mid airlock. Do you copy?"

Crusty spoke to Jessamyn. "The doors to the ob-deck aren't airtight, but they're shut, and that should be enough to get your brother past 'em."

Jessamyn's voice, when she found it, was so low as to be almost inaudible. "He has no suit."

Crusty swore.

Kipper turned. "What in *Hades* is wrong now?"

"It's the walk-out suit, Captain," said Crusty. "I left it in the rations room. I hadn't finished checking it, Sir."

There was only one walk-out suit assigned to the aft quarters—the quarters intended to house a captain. In the hushed moment that followed, Jess cursed herself for not having foreseen this.

"'Fraid he's stuck," said Crusty.

"I'll take him a suit," said Jessamyn. "Suit me up and I'll carry an additional suit to Ethan."

Kipper hesitated. "Your idea has been noted, Jaarda. Crusty, I want you on the bridge. You, too, Mombasu." She strode along the hall.

"I'll suit up," Jessamyn called after her.

Kipper whirled to face her. "I have issued no such directive. You will confine yourself to quarters, Jaarda. No one is going through those airlocks until Crusty *and* Mombasu confirm it is one-hundred percent certain such an attempt will not place Specialist Jaarda or yourself in additional danger."

Jess bristled, ready to shout down her captain, disobey direct orders, and otherwise do anything necessary to rescue her brother.

But Ethan spoke first. "I believe they will concur that the safest course of action would be for me to remain here. I have air and water."

Jess opened her mouth to speak, but found she had nothing to say and closed it again.

Kipper spoke to Ethan as she continued her march to the bridge. "Specialist Jaarda, I've got the payload specialist and Harpreet running checks for me right now. We'll get you out if we can."

Her back against the wall, Jess slowly shrank to the floor, knees up in her chest, hands loose at her sides. She wouldn't be sleeping tonight.

Remembering the earpiece that allowed her to communicate privately with her brother, Jess jerked her head to one side, activating the device.

"Hey, Eth," she said as she heard his *beep* in response to her hail.

"Jessamyn."

"You okay?"

"I am in excellent health. I have water and oxygen."

"Check your pockets," said Jess. "I've seen how you stuff your rations away 'for later.'"

She heard a rustling noise as he searched.

"Jessamyn is correct. I have food as well. That is fortunate."

Yeah, thought Jess. *This whole thing's just one big piece of fortunate.* Aloud she asked, "What are you going to do?" She felt her fingernails as they dug into her palms.

"I will rest."

Jess sighed in frustration. "That's not what I meant."

"What did Jessamyn intend to inquire after?"

"You're in a *small room*, Eth. What's your plan for dealing with that?"

"Thanks to the generosity of Captain Kipling, I am in the largest quarters normally reserved for a captain."

"Yeah," said Jess. She itched to ask for more, to demand that her brother present a five-step plan, but then she remembered what Harpreet had said. *Allow him to prove things to himself.* She sighed.

"Okay, so, um, call me if you get bored," she said.

"It is unlikely boredom will be a problem. I require sleep. When I awake, I have a wafer-computer to read. I have occupations to forestall boredom."

But what about forestalling claustrophobia? She felt her nails digging into her palms again and took a slow breath, unclenching her fists.

Her brother was an adult. A remarkable adult. It was time she started treating him that way.

"Goodnight," she said. "Call me if you need, you know, anything."

"Goodnight."

"Hey, Eth?"

"Jessamyn?"

"Would you leave your audio earpiece turned on?"

There was a pause before he answered. "Very well."

"Thanks, Eth. Goodnight."

Her brother, having uttered the phrase once, did not repeat it a second time. Before long, Jess heard the regular sound of her brother's sleep-breathing. It lulled her, reminding her of the nights she'd spent sleeping on his floor before launch. Without intending to sleep at all that night, Jess fell fast asleep. When she awoke the next morning, hearing nothing from the audio device, she thought at first that her brother was sleeping still. Then she remembered the device was supposed to shut down when she slept. Shaking her head to the right, she reactivated her link to Ethan. To the sound of her brother humming to himself.

She sat up at once. For most people, humming was an activity carried out when they felt especially happy. Her father hummed while working. Her brother, however, hummed—at one unvarying pitch—only when severely distressed.

"Ethan?"

He paused and then resumed his flat hum.

"Hey, Eth. You don't sound so good."

The humming stopped again. There was a quiet pause before Ethan spoke. "I am coping."

"Um, yeah," said Jessamyn.

"The Captain informs me—" Her brother paused again. "The Captain informs me it is too dangerous to cross through the sealed portion of the ship, and I concur."

Jess's heart contracted and she punched her firm mattress.

"Okay," she said. "Okay. So, um, three days to go, huh, Eth?"

He didn't respond.

"Come on, Eth, you got to talk to me here."

"Speech is challenging at this time," said Ethan.

"Sure. Of course."

"I have endured only one panic attack, however."

Hunched over on the edge of her bunk, Jess ground her palms against her knees.

"One's better than ten, huh?" She squeezed her eyes shut tight. What a stupid thing to say. "How about I tell you a story?"

"Yes."

Jessamyn launched into a tale about a dragon guarding a treasure. The crazier tales accomplished two things: they gave her brother something to focus upon during the time it took her to tell them, and it gave him a series of logical fallacies to pick apart when she had finished.

Jess glanced at her chrono-tattoo as she drew to the tale's close. The bright red glow told her she needed to join the others for morning ration and then begin her duty shift.

"That tale was ridiculous, Jessamyn."

"Yeah, I know. Good one, huh?"

"If by 'good' you mean 'improbable,' then, yes," said her brother.

Jess laughed. He was being funny. Funny was good. "I need you to do something for me, Eth. You get out your wafer and type up all of the things that make that story impossible, okay? *All* of them."

She heard her brother's soft breathing.

"That would be a time-consuming pastime," he said. "Jessamyn tells highly unlikely stories."

"You work on it."

Ethan's interactions with his sister on the second day were brief. Jess noted that Kipper had trimmed a few hundred kilometers here and there during her duty shift. The Captain's kindness—or perhaps desperation—encouraged Jess to do the same. At the end of her own duty shift, Jessamyn's brain ached from the hundred calculations she'd run and re-run to shave off a few thousand kilometers with minute course adjustments.

Earth grew closer and larger, but by his third day of confinement, Ethan stopped talking at all, humming at a monotone pitch exactly calibrated to shatter his sister's heart.

Jessamyn left her audio comm permanently turned on in case he should call for her. Off-duty, Jessamyn could focus upon her brother exclusively. But she had felt him each day passing beyond help, locked in a tiny prison of the mind with boundaries more definite than those of the quarters in which he now lived. Jess spoke to him constantly, told stories when she could, and begged him to hang on, *please just hang on*.

When Kipper discovered Ethan had become non-responsive, she began to talk of changing the mission once more. Jessamyn scowled and told Ethan increasingly improbable stories, but secretly she feared Kipper was right. And even if her brother recovered entirely, would he do so in time to complete the hacking mission? Or had he traveled all this way only to suffer, only to fail?

11

SKY TOO BLUE

Jessamyn allowed that some might call the spinning blue and white planet below them beautiful. But dread filled her heart as she contemplated Earth from the Galleon's bridge. Where were the warm reds and golds that whispered *home*? To her, the planet appeared a chill and hostile place, fit dwelling for those who had destroyed the Red Dawn and her brother's peace of mind. She felt now that her Earthward yearnings had been childish dreams—gossamer things which fluttered away before the cold reality of the planet beneath her.

Terrans had grown complacent through the years, no longer patrolling the skies for Marsians. Most believed Mars Colonial had long since perished, and if members of the Terran government knew otherwise, they kept it to themselves, speaking of the Mars Project only in the past tense. Now, the Terran government kept a lazy eye out for any of their own people tempted to break the regulations in place against flights more than 300 kilometers above Earth.

Nonetheless, for a century, Mars had paid for the secret maintenance of blind spots within Terran surveillance, and Jess followed the coordinates from MCC more carefully than she'd ever followed orders before. If she burned through the atmosphere at the wrong angle or wrong speed or if she deviated from the specified path by even a half-kilometer, the Red Galleon would be visible on Terran monitors. And there was always the very real danger that an amateur astronomer might notice and report them.

Her fingers flying across the navigation panel before her, Jess caught sight of the European continental mass. She adjusted her ship into geosynchronous orbit above the blue planet. In a few minutes, she would have the final landing pattern calculated and the Galleon would continue its descent.

A small smile crept along Jessamyn's face. In spite of the loss of the Red Dawn, in spite of her brother's sufferings, Jess couldn't help but feel a rush of pride as she guided the Red Galleon down to Earth exactly like the great raiders before her had done.

"Commencing final descent on my Mark: *three, two, one, Mark!*" she called.

Easing the ship through Earth's dense atmosphere felt different from coming in to land on Mars where one second you were surrounded by black space and the next you were touching the rocky surface. But the ship and Jessamyn worked well together.

"That's right, my beauty, nice and easy," murmured Jess. She gave the ship one final series of commands and then she was free to gaze at the surface beneath her.

"Nearly there, Ethan."

His hum, a constant in her ears, faltered for a moment and then resumed.

The now-large island of Britain slid off the view screen to reveal a smaller island off to the northwest: her destination—the tiny, ash-covered Isle of Skye.

Falling into this world, the crew was silent, hushed by the strange colors, or maybe the solemnity of their charge to save Mars. Even the Galleon quieted before the final noisy vertical landing on the green-and-ash-colored surface that had played home to Mars's ancestors.

A cloud of grey-blue volcanic ash billowed around the ship.

We made it, thought Jess. Aloud she said, "Captain, the Red Galleon has landed."

She wanted to rip off her helmet and race for the sealed doors separating her from her brother, but there were protocols to follow, systems-checks to run; and besides, she couldn't take him outside until the ash settled.

The Isle of Skye, just off the west coast of Scotland, endured regular dustings of volcanic detritus from Iceland's two dozen active volcanoes. The nearby volcanic activity made the remote Scottish island an undesirable location to most, but a quite perfect location for the clandestine activity of Clan Wallace, maintainers of the black market trade with Mars.

Jess rushed through her duties as Harpreet, beside her, attempted communication with their Terran contact. It would have been Ethan's job, had he been on the bridge. Jess was glad the task hadn't fallen to her; her skill set with communications systems consisted of the ability to shut them down when she wanted to.

While completing her tasks, Jess heard a voice on the receiving end. Clear. Crisp. An oddly accented, *Hello?*

Harpreet followed a simple script. "I wish to speak to Brian Wallace."

"Aye, ye've found him, then, haven't ye?"

"We're here about the sheep," said Harpreet.

"Bloody right on time, aren't ye?" replied Wallace.

Jess glowed briefly with pride in her precise landing.

"I'll code the gate to let ye pass," continued Wallace. "Take the second left and ye'll see me place." The call was disconnected.

Crusty spoke over the ship's comm. "Captain, the confinement barriers are down mid- and aft-ship."

Jess jumped from her seat. "Permission to leave the bridge, Captain?"

"Permission granted," said Kipper.

Jess wobbled down the hall. The ship's artificial gravity was off now that the Galleon had landed and Earth's gravity pulled, insistent, although Jessamyn didn't have the inclination to give it much thought. Pounding upon the button to open her brother's door, she called his name. The door receded and Jess rushed to her brother's side.

He didn't look good. Ethan had folded his body together until he occupied only a small corner of the already small quarters. Knees pulled up in front of his chest, Ethan had wrapped his arms around his legs. His eyes stared into the darkness under his bunk, but Jess didn't think he was seeing whatever was down there. He hummed a single deep note, pausing only for the briefest of periods when he required breath.

He didn't move his eyes to look at his sister.

"Ethan, I'm here. I'm going to tell you the story about the girl who stole a kingdom." Jess kept her voice low, in hopes he would quit humming so as to hear her better.

Only toward the end of the story did the humming cease. Though still lost in a place of anguish, Ethan had calmed enough to simply breathe, without the accompaniment of his monotone hum. It wasn't as good as standing and walking, and it was a far cry from talking or working at a console, but it represented a start.

"We made it to Earth," said Jessamyn. "And you're going to make it, too, Ethan."

She heard her brother whisper a single word: "Water."

Her mind struggled for the connection. "Yeah, Eth. The water planet. We made it."

"Water," he repeated.

Her brother's lips were cracked and swollen. Jess reached for an unopened water packet lying beside him and, fumbling with the closure, brought it to her brother's mouth. He swallowed and nodded his head a mere fraction of a centimeter.

"Good," he whispered.

"I know you feel stuck, Ethan, but there's a whole world outside this ship. You want to see that, right?"

He nodded, barely.

"The colors here are *crazy*, I'm telling you. Everything's blue and green. No yellow. No red. No brown."

Ethan nodded.

It took another half-hour of murmuring to her brother about Earth's wonders to get him to rise from his crouched fetal position. But Jess saw a light in his eyes replacing the dull glazed look they'd had when she'd entered his room.

"Okay, look, Eth, there's clothes you've got to change into. And I'm not helping you with that, 'cause . . . just . . .gross! You want Crusty to give you a hand?" she asked, indicating his jumpsuit.

"Send Crusty," whispered Ethan.

She stepped out and called for the gruff mechanic.

"Ah, Jessamyn," said Harpreet, who had changed into her Terran outfit of black pants and a black shirt. "The Captain would appreciate a word with the two of us."

Jess followed Harpreet to the rations room.

"Status report on Communications Specialist Jaarda?" demanded the Captain.

Jess felt her face flushing with anger. "My brother's not a machine with a re-set function."

Kipper exhaled loudly and Harpreet stepped in. "Yes, but the Captain does need to know if your brother can do what he came here to do."

"I can only say that when he's been like this in the past, once we got him home, he recovered quickly. In a day or so," replied Jess.

Kipper frowned.

"If I might make a suggestion," said Harpreet, "Perhaps the best way to approach things would be to move forward as if he will make a full recovery. We have come a very long way to abandon our planet's hope of a freer future."

"Indeed," said Kipper. "Very well. First Officer, you will do whatever is necessary to promote your brother's recovery."

As if I'd do anything else, thought Jessamyn. She felt a scowl forming but forced herself to maintain a neutral expression.

"Aye-aye, sir," she replied.

There followed a hurried half-hour scramble to descend to the bowels of the ship where an amphibious Terran transport had been stored for the past eighteen annums. The crew piled aboard, a hatch was opened allowing them to drive out of the Red Galleon, and the five Mars Raiders rumbled out onto a field of what resembled blue-grey snow.

Kipper had directed Jessamyn to keep close to Ethan, who was humming again, and this meant Jess got out of driving and could look about her on the five ash-blanketed kilometers to Brian Wallace's dwelling. Jess startled at something green peering up through the coat of grey.

"Grass," she murmured. "There's grass, Ethan!"

Her brother broke off mid-hum to look but gave no verbal acknowledgement.

"Still thirsty?" she asked him. He shook his head once to the right—the briefest of answers.

Jess frowned. His color looked off, but maybe that was because Earth had such odd light. The sky—the very *air*—was too blue.

"I shot him full of rehydrant," murmured Crusty. "He'll pull through fine."

Jess smiled at the mechanic, grateful.

Glancing outside once more, she startled as a dozen faces turned toward their passing vehicle. "What on *Ares* are those?"

Ethan spoke. "Amend your phrasing."

Jess looked to her brother.

Crusty chuckled. "Bet he means, you should ask, 'What on *Earth?*'"

Harpreet turned from her position in the front, beside Kipper. "The answer to either question is that they are hybridized goats designed to survive in this climate," she said. "The Wallace family keeps a large herd as their cover, claiming to be farmers."

Several dozen golden eyes, rimmed in black, stared at the passing vehicle. Then the heads turned back to crop grass, and the creatures, colored the same blue-grey as their surrounding, seemed to vanish.

"I wonder what their fur would feel like, huh, Eth?" Jess now wished she'd thought to ask about walking the five kilometers to Brian Wallace's cottage. They drove over a low rise. On the opposite side was an entire field of *green* sloping down to meet the ash-grey field before Brian Wallace's tiny dwelling.

Jessamyn blinked, uncertain her eyes truly saw what she thought she saw. "Oh, stop!" she cried. The field of green was so unexpected, so lovely. She felt certain she could bring her brother back inside his own skin if he would only step outside.

Alarmed, Kipper applied a braking system that caused everyone to lurch.

Crusty's head and shoulders fell forward. As he lifted himself, he muttered, "*Bells of Hades*, we're *heavy* on Earth."

"What is it, First Officer?" asked Kipper.

In answer, Jessamyn opened her door and escaped out into the fresh air of Earth. "Ohhh," she cried. "It's so . . . *wet*!" Laughter burbled up from deep inside and she giggled like a child.

"Jaarda, return to the vehicle at once," called Kipper.

Jessamyn heard the order, but only barely. Even *sound* carried differently through Terran air. She felt the tremendous tug of gravity calling her earthward and yielded, sinking to her knees so that she could *touch* the blades of green growth blanketing the hillside. *Oh*, she sighed again, this time to herself. She ran her fingers across the tips of grass. Bent one strand over between forefinger and thumb. A drop of moisture clung to the backside. *Oh, oh, oh.*

“Officer Jaarda, I order you to return *at once*!” called Kipper.

Jessamyn looked back to the transport and saw her brother, his brows furrowed.

Ignoring her commanding officer, Jess asked Ethan, “Do you want to get out?”

Harpreet murmured quietly to Kipper, and Jess heard her brother’s name.

Jess told her body to stand, but was surprised at the effort the simple motion required. Moving back to the transport, she offered Ethan her hand, but he shook his head.

“Ethan, it’s . . . unreal,” whispered Jess as she returned to his side in the vehicle. “Like a dream.”

“A good dream,” replied her brother, his voice rough-sounding from lack of use.

Jess closed the door and the vehicle advanced once more.

Straining to look as far away as she could see, Jess searched for the horizon line.

“The sky is blue here,” she said. “That’s so weird.”

Harpreet’s light laughter filled the transport. “Your eyes must grow accustomed to a myriad of differences. The horizon will feel too far . . . the colors strange . . . so many adjustments . . .” Harpreet fell silent, her mouth curving slightly upward as she remembered her last visit, perhaps.

As they drew close to Brian Wallace's dwelling, a black-and-white blur rushed toward them. The front door of the building opened and Brian Wallace himself whistled. The blur—a dog, Jessamyn was sure of it—returned to the house, disappearing inside with its owner.

"That dog's gait is shortened by Earth's gravitational pull," said Ethan.

Jess grinned at her brother's lengthy observation. Interest in the world outside was an excellent sign. Of course, he was still humming off and on. *He'll be fine*, she told herself, longing to grab her brother's hand and squeeze it. But he would hate it, so she didn't.

They parked beside the tiny whitewashed cottage of Brian Wallace. Jess looked nervously at her brother after she exited, waiting to see if he would follow.

He set one foot and then the other upon the wet surface of Earth. His face calmed, the furrow between his brows smoothed. Jess realized with a pang that Ethan had acquired his First Wrinkle during his lonely ordeal.

He stood outside the vehicle, then took a step and smiled softly.

"I like Earth," he said.

Jess closed her eyes in a moment's gratitude.

12

WHAT IT FELT LIKE

It was an anxious moment for four out of five crew members—Harpreet alone had encountered a Terran before.

The front door swung open and their contact emerged into the alcove before his dwelling. The dog was nowhere to be seen.

The first words of Brian Wallace, representative of the Clan Wallace, struck Jessamyn as extremely odd. "Ye'll want to be leaving yer great boots just here." He pointed to one of two built-in benches on either side of the door. Both benches—colored white like his home—had a series of shoe prints painted in black upon the stone floor of the alcove. The shoe prints were grouped in pairs of two: left and right.

Harpreet, smiling pleasantly, removed one shoe and placed it carefully upon the painted image. Raising an eyebrow significantly to the rest of the crew, she indicated that they should do the same. Only once all five Marsians had removed their footwear did Wallace move to allow them inside.

His front door, instead of sliding into the wall to admit them, swung into the room. *No need for airlocks*, thought Jessamyn. An odd smell greeted her nostrils. After a moment, she recognized it as the smell of damp rock, like one of her mother's labs in New Houston where they grew experimental algae in hypertufa. She looked about her for the origin of the odor. Instead of hypertufa containers, Jess noticed shiny pots—ceramic, she thought—containing plant life.

Crusty was already bent in examination of an exotic bloom.

"Is this what you eat?" asked Jessamyn, approaching the white-and-magenta flower on its tall green stalk.

"Don't touch!" cried Wallace, crossing the room to prevent Jess from fingering the plant. "Orchids, ye know. Very fussy. Fragile in this climate."

Placing himself firmly in front of the flower, he attempted a smile. It looked very much like a worried frown.

"Not for eating, though, no," said Wallace. "Ornamental."

"Imagine that," she murmured. It was difficult to conceive of a world where water existed in such abundance that it could be wasted upon plants merely *decorative*.

Hearing a noise from outside, Jessamyn glanced up. In Wallace's home, the windows were single-paned and sound traveled right through. Jess noted a dust storm picking up speed—it would be a bad storm, she thought, hearing the first small pebbles kicking up and hitting the windows. Then, experiencing a momentary disorientation, she realized that on Earth, that sound wouldn't come from a dust storm. *So what was it?*

Jessamyn crossed to the closest window and beheld her first rainfall. Like tiny bits of glass falling from the sky, drops of rain pelted down. She gazed at the angled descent of the water, enchanted, and turned for the door so that she could *feel* the rain.

"Ask first," grunted Crusty beside her.

Jess's fists clenched, but she followed his advice. "Permission to exit the building *with Ethan* and observe rainfall, Captain?" she asked politely.

Harpreet stood beside Kipper, murmuring.

"Oh, very well," said the Captain. "But I want you two back in *ten* minutes."

Jess raced outside, shoved her feet back inside her Earth-style footgear, and dashed into the falling rain. Her brother followed suit. Their Terran garments offered protection from the deluge, but drops struck the backs of their hands and scalps. Instinctively fearful of any cold sensation out of doors, Jess felt a brief panic, drawing her hands back inside her sleeves. On Mars, such exposure would have meant frostbite, at the least. Of course, this was *Earth.*

Laughing at herself, she turned to her brother. "Nothing's cold here, Eth!" It wasn't exactly true. The rain *did* feel cold as it struck her, but unfathomably, wondrously, it couldn't harm her.

"Remember the day I touched the pump?" she asked her brother.

Ethan gave a brief nod in response.

Their mother had sent her and Ethan outside on a rare, warm day when the temperature hovered a handful of degrees below freezing. Jess had waited until Ethan got interested in something besides his little sister, and then she'd slipped off one of her outer gloves and pressed a minimally-protected forefinger to the pump handle.

"Everyone said it would freeze you so fast you wouldn't even feel it," she said. "And then they'd have to cut your finger off."

"Why did Jessamyn do it?" asked her brother.

Another complete sentence, thought Jess. And sometime in the last minute, Ethan had stopped humming.

"I wanted to know what it felt like," she said, shrugging. She recalled the burning sensation, how it had *almost* felt nice.

"I told you to replace your glove," said Ethan. "That was the first time you defied me."

"But not the last, eh, brother of mine?" She giggled. "*Mom*," she said, imitating her brother, "*Make Jessie put her gloves back on*."

"You should have complied," Ethan said.

Jess, examining the sense-dead spot on her finger, had to agree.

They continued walking through the rainfall as it grew heavier.

The sensation of being rained upon was entirely novel. It reminded Jess a bit of being tickled. When a gust of wind swished past, she had the impression that the temperature dropped suddenly. But just as quickly, it passed. Of course she had read that wind passing over moisture created the feeling of temperature change, but actually experiencing it was wondrous.

Peeling off her jacket, Jess turned into the storm and ran, laughing as drops struck her face and arms and soaked through her shirt. She paused atop a small hill, her heart pounding with the effort of climbing. Below, her brother had stopped, clearly weakened by his last few days. She bounded back down to where he stood gazing at something upon the ground.

He pointed to the object as she drew close. It was a marvel of tiny fibers, stretching outward in spokes from a central circle.

"The web of an arachnid," said her brother.

Jess watched it quiver as a gust of wind passed by them. Tiny beads of water clung to the conjunctions of one thread where it met another. It looked to her as if the weight of the water or the pressure of the wind ought to dissolve the slight strands. Jessamyn had never seen anything at once so delicate and strong.

"Beautiful," she murmured.

They stood for a minute, admiring the spider's handiwork until Ethan pointed to his wrist tattoo.

"It has been nine minutes and five seconds," said her brother.

"I wish I'd brought a wafer to take pictures," said Jess, gazing with regret at the web.

"Store the image in your mind," said Ethan.

She smiled and together they tromped back through the muck of wetted ash and grass. Shedding their footwear once again, the siblings prepared to reenter Brian Wallace's dwelling.

But something was wrong with Ethan. He stood before the door, making no attempt to enter.

Jessamyn moved to where she could observe her brother's face, expressionless as usual, but there was something beyond his normal bland visage; his gaze, where it rested on the door, seemed troubled. Jess heard the humming resume, starting as a low rumble and building to the sustained single note that said Ethan suffered distress.

He doesn't want to go back inside, thought Jess. "Eyebrows," she said softly.

Ethan brought a hand to his forehead, located a brow, and ran his fingers over and over the short hairs.

"Good, Eth," said Jessamyn. "Now I want you to count down from ninety-eight to zero by sevens. When you reach zero, we'll open the door and go inside."

The humming came to a stop. "Ninety-eight," said Ethan, "Ninety-one. Eighty-four. Seventy. No. That was incorrect."

The mistake struck Jessamyn's ears like shattering glass. Her brother never made mistakes with numbers.

Ethan exhaled slowly, his chin dropping to his chest. Then he raised his head and began over. "Ninety-eight. Ninety-one. Eighty-four. Seventy-seven."

Jessamyn realized at "seventy" that her lungs were aching—she'd held her breath too long. Inhaling deeply of Earth's moist air, she listened as her brother finished the count correctly.

Upon reaching *zero*, Ethan grasped the door handle. But he didn't open the door. Jess felt a dozen small muscles around her mouth and forehead as they tightened.

"Eth? It's time to go back inside."

Very quietly Ethan began to hum once more.

No, thought Jessamyn, racking her brain for another idea. *The dog.*

"Ethan, Brian Wallace has a dog." She watched her brother carefully. His hand tightened upon the doorknob. "Would you like to see it?"

Ethan answered by pushing the door open and stepping inside. Jess sighed in relief as she followed him.

Inside, everyone gazed at a vid-screen from which a woman spoke, her deep voice lovely and completely free of the rasp normal for Marsians. She said, "We will prevail," as if in conclusion, and Wallace flicked the image off.

"I don't trust that woman," he muttered, shuffling toward another room.

Jess stared at the vid-screen. "This is Marsian-made, isn't it?"

"Oh, aye," replied Wallace. "You recognize the symbols, then? No one on Earth can understand it, outside the Family Wallace." He laughed as if this amused him.

Harpreet spoke. "The computer aids Brian Wallace in communicating with the Galleon during our stay."

Jess nodded. Having seen how much ash the ship kicked up when it touched down, Jessamyn understood the need to separate Wallace's home from the landing site. Readily-available communication was a necessity.

"Mr. Wallace?" Jessamyn glanced over to see her brother staring at his feet. He hadn't started humming again, at least. "Would it be possible for Ethan to meet your dog?"

Brian's wide face broke into a generous grin. "Oh, aye. She's a friendly one. Didn't think Mars-folk were much for dogs." He gave a short, sharp whistle and a blur of black-and-white rushed into the room.

Once Wallace had introduced Ethan to his dog, the Terran disappeared into what Jess decided was a rations room before returning with a tray bearing a covered vessel that exuded dust as he set it upon a low table.

No, Jess realized with delight, *that's steam, not dust.* It was tea. Jessamyn smiled at Harpreet.

"Who was that woman?" asked Kipper. "On the broadcast?"

Wallace grunted as he poured out mugs of dark tea. "Och, that's Lucca Brezhnaya, that is. Politician. I don't trust her. Not at all. She's up to naught that's good." He shook his head gloomily and poured an ivory-colored liquid into his tea. "Anyone else, a wee drop of goat milk? There's sugar, too, somewhere . . ."

The crew declined the additions.

"The tea is delicious," said Harpreet.

Brian continued between sips of tea. "Lucca's the one who brought in the Red Squadron. Bloody nuisance, they are. Any other branch of security, ye can buy them off. But don't even think of trying that with the Red Squadron. Don't know what she's paying them with, but they're bloody incorruptible." Wallace shook his head as though this were a terrible shame. "Still, if ye're dead set on visiting Budapest, it's best ye know these things ahead of time."

"I'm afraid we must travel to Budapest," said Harpreet. "And you will be able to provide us with the type of identity chips we require?" she asked.

"Oh, aye. The ones identifying ye as a single family are no trouble at all. I can do those me own self. But I'll be calling in some favors to land ye the security clearance ye're asking for with the other set of chips." Wallace paused, tapping both thumbs lightly on the table. "Ye do realize that double-chipping's illegal?"

Harpreet nodded. "It is our understanding that forced scans are also illegal."

Wallace shrugged, removing an outer layer of clothing. Jessamyn realized with surprise that Wallace was a very round individual. She had assumed his outer garment contributed to his bulk. It did not. She had never seen anyone so . . . enlarged.

"Aye, it's illegal, but with the attacks today . . ." Wallace sighed, shaking his head.

"What attacks?" asked Jessamyn.

"Ah," replied Harpreet. "You missed the broadcast while you were out of doors."

“It’s those bloody inciters,” said Wallace. “Terrorists, they are.” He leaned in toward Jess, conspiratorially. “Gone and blown up one of the main transfer hospitals.”

“Someone has attacked a consciousness-transfer hospital?” Ethan asked, looking up from Wallace’s dog.

“A main one for Western Europe,” replied Wallace. “In Paris, it was. I reckon ye couldn’t have picked a better day to fly down through our atmosphere, what with all eyes turned to the breaking news.”

“Will this make our additional mission more . . . difficult?” asked Ethan.

Jess thought she saw a quick wordless exchange between Harpreet and the Captain. Were they having second thoughts about the mission?

“It is impossible to be certain,” Harpreet said aloud. “But Wallace is correct in surmising that the Terran government’s preoccupation with inciters made it easier for us to arrive undetected. Perhaps our other task will be simplified as well.”

“Or maybe they’ll take additional precautions that will make our job impossible,” said Kipper, glancing nervously at Ethan.

“With regard to those security clearances,” said Wallace, “They’re going to cost extra.” He leaned back, smiling.

Harpreet suggested that they discuss the price while the rest of the crew begin exchanging the ship's holding bays of tellurium for ration bars.

"Bays one through six," Harpreet murmured.

Jess, her brother, Kipper, and Crusty took the transport vehicle back to the Red Galleon. While the party had been inside, rain had washed several sloping hillsides clear of ash.

"The color is amazing," admitted Jess. She didn't want to like Earth. But her father had been correct about her sense of wonder. The beautiful, the new, the strange—these acted upon her as surely as scent and light, pressure and sound.

"Green looks fake," muttered Crusty.

"Mars will look like this one day," said Kipper.

The crew of four arrived at the Galleon and unloaded bars of pressed tellurium into a shelter the Wallace family had erected a century ago, refilling the emptying holds with precious ration bars. After a couple of hours had passed, Wallace and Harpreet joined the group, riding on an odd hovering craft. It looked to Jess like the top of a table, with low sides.

"What is that?" she asked.

Crusty was already staring at the unusual form of transportation as if eager to take it apart and find out how it worked.

"A most exhilarating ride," said Harpreet as she descended.

"Hovercart," explained Wallace. "Meant for hauling things about. Me brother's lad makes them. I must have two dozen lying about. Darned things are always getting buried beneath the ash. Suppose I should have offered ye the use of a few . . ."

Crusty stood to one side of the hovercart, running his hands over the controls so that the tiny craft moved up and down, forward and to the side.

Brian Wallace smiled, nodded, and murmured something to Harpreet.

"Actually, my friends," began Harpreet, "We will be emptying bays seven and eight as well in order to compensate our friend Mr. Wallace for his additional trouble. So we will have the opportunity to utilize the hover-crafts."

Wallace rustled up another pair of carts, and the work was soon finished. Jessamyn, noting how much more quickly things moved by hovercart, felt irritated that Wallace hadn't suggested the devices sooner. But Crusty pointed out the exercise worked as a good replacement for shipboard calisthenics.

"Humph," grunted Jess as they shifted the final load.

"Ye'll be wanting supper, now," said Wallace once they'd finished. "It's goat stew, carrots, and potatoes." He looked at the confused faces before him. "Unless ye prefer ration bars? I have a stash somewhere in the cottage."

"Ration bars would be lovely," said Harpreet.

Jess stopped herself from saying aloud that she thought goat stew, carrots, and potatoes would be lovely. They'd been warned back at MCC that their stomachs wouldn't tolerate rich Terran food very well. For a moment, she regretted the additional mission before them. On a regular raid for rations only, they'd have been free to simply leave Earth. They could have eaten whatever they liked and suffered bellyaches on their flight home.

Wallace hopped aboard one of his strange carts, and Kipper drove the raiders back in their own transport for a shared evening ration. The earlier storm appeared to have moved on, and Jess could see the horizon clearly. The edge of the world felt too remote, Earth too large a world. But it was when she risked a brief direct look at Sol that she gasped aloud.

"The sun's *huge* from here," said Jess.

"Do not look at the sun," warned her brother.

Jess rolled her eyes and bumped his shoulder. "I only looked for a second. I'm not an idiot."

"You are not," he agreed. "But you take unnecessary risks."

Jessamyn flushed and threw an annoyed glance at her brother. He looked tired and she realized she felt very tired herself. They'd been up all night—the hours aboard ship had been set to coordinate to a morning landing upon the Isle of Skye. Aboard the Galleon,

Ethan and Jess would have just risen for their shift. She'd missed an entire night's rest.

She watched the over-large sun dipping behind a hill. The flares of oranges and yellows reminded her of home and she closed her eyes. She didn't awaken until much later. Someone must have carried her inside, because she found herself resting in a soft chair beside Brian Wallace's rations table. A familiar copper-wrapped bar sat at an empty place—*mine*—she realized, and an unfamiliar scent filled her nostrils. *Goat stew*, she thought. It looked remarkably unappealing, except perhaps for the bright orange bits. It smelled wonderful, however, and Jess wished she could try it.

She attuned herself to the conversation, which seemed to be a discussion of the route to their next destination: Budapest, Earth's capitol city. In fact, it seemed they were discussing having Jessamyn accompany them there.

"It's not true, of course, that firsties have a better chance at a good apprenticeship simply by taking their exams in the capitol," Brian was saying, "But it's one of those myths that won't die. Hope springs eternal, as the saying goes."

"We have that saying as well," said Ethan.

Brian laughed, a merry sound. "Aye, well, ye'd have to, living on the ball of dirt and ice like ye do!"

Jessamyn saw Kipper scowling and, for once, found herself in agreement.

Harpreet spoke quickly. "And yourself? Do you have plans to leave your island of ash and rain?"

"The early retirement's a blessing, indeed," replied Wallace. "No one's happier than me own self that ye lot showed a few years early. I've got me eye on a patch of land in the Great Victoria Desert in Australia where me goats and I could be quite happy." He frowned, turning to look at his orchid. "Don't know that the flowers will be too pleased about the move. I've a greenhouse full of 'em. But a greenhouse in the desert . . . seems a bit implausible, eh?"

Crusty cleared his throat. "Not necessarily."

"He speaks," said Wallace, laughing.

"Can I see the greenhouse?" Crusty asked.

Once the two departed, Kipper turned to Jessamyn. "A decision has been made that you will accompany us to Budapest in order to better assure your brother's continued recovery."

"Brian Wallace has suggested we travel under the pretense that you are attending your apprenticeship examination," said Harpreet. "It gives us an unassailable excuse for travel to Earth's capitol city."

Jessamyn saw something in the angle of her brother's body that told her he wasn't at peace. Was the smallness of the room bothering him, or was it the arrangements under discussion that he didn't like? She wanted to ask him, but not in front of Kipper. Besides, she had another more important question. "We need two people to get the Galleon back to Mars. If something goes wrong, I mean. Crusty can't make that voyage alone. Why take all four of us to Budapest?"

Harpreet began to explain. "We feel that it would be best for your brother if you journeyed with him. And once we arrive, of course, the Captain has been trained to assist your brother—"

Kipper exhaled noisily. "Which means the four of us go because MCC saddled this crew with a hacking expert who apparently needs babysitting." She marched to the door and stepped outside, slamming the door behind her.

The room was silent. Jessamyn felt heat building along her neck and face. She rose, spitting mad, to give Kipper a piece of her mind.

"Jessamyn," said her brother, "No good can come of an interaction with the Captain at this time."

Jess turned, her face flaming. "She—she—Eth, she *insulted* you!"

"She bears a great weight as captain for the success of this mission," replied Ethan. "Also, the insult was directed toward me and not toward Jessamyn."

Jess looked from her brother's face to Harpreet's. She could hear Harpreet's thoughts as clearly as if the old woman had spoken them aloud: *Let your brother look out for himself.*

Furious, she strode around the tiny front room, wishing the items inside were hers to kick and break.

Finally, the fatigue brought on by Earth's heavier gravity brought her to a standstill and she returned to the rations table to sit.

"My question is still perfectly valid," said Jess. "Harpreet, why don't you stay behind instead of me?"

"For two reasons," said Ethan. "Though your presence on the journey to and from Budapest will promote my well-being, I believe that, should you attempt to fulfill Harpreet's role as lookout during the mission, I would be concerned for your safety to the degree that it would be a distraction from my task."

Jess recognized immediately that what Ethan said was true. He wouldn't focus on hacking if he had her to worry about—"big brother" was too ingrained a part of his identity.

"Also," continued Ethan, "You do not have Harpreet's skills as a negotiator should we find ourselves . . . detained."

Jessamyn frowned. Her brother's rationale was, as usual, sound. "Okay, then. Crusty stays here alone. I go with you to the satellite control center."

"The plan is to conceal you and the transport beneath a cloaking-tarp," said Harpreet.

"The tarp should render your discovery highly improbable," said Ethan, sounding as if he were trying to convince himself. He looked like he might add something, but in the end he remained silent.

"Sounds *fine*," Jess said. She hated it when her brother worried about her.

From outside the house, Jessamyn heard Crusty and Wallace speaking.

"Mighty convenient, not having to keep your greenhouse pressurized," Crusty said. Looking around, he frowned. "Where's Kip?"

Harpreet replied, "She discovered a need for fresh air."

"*Bells of Hades*," chuckled Crusty. "Plenty of that here."

The crew spent the night scattered on the floor of Brian Wallace's living room. Jess was the last to wake the next day. Outside, she saw a sky impossibly blue and dotted with white clouds. A strong smell, vaguely sulfuric, drew Jess to the room Wallace called "kitchen." She stared curiously at Wallace's cooking *egg*, a golden orb set within a white orb.

"A lovely morning for travel," said Wallace, smiling as she entered.

It's really happening, Jessamyn thought. They were about to pit themselves against the murderers who had killed Lobster and the others. Who were they to move against such dreadful power? A recently catatonic hacker, a bookworm-pilot, a captain with a serious attitude problem, and Mars's most friendly citizen. Assaulting a Terran satellite control facility. It was insanity. Her stomach seemed to drop through the floor.

The vaguely sulfuric odor of Brian Wallace's breakfast made Jess feel nauseous. Turning, she fled outside.

13

COLLECTING

In the end, they left later than intended. Crusty had insisted upon giving their amphibious craft a thorough going-over.

"I don't see why we can't use a flying craft," grumbled Jess as Brian Wallace prepared a midday ration.

"Flight is monitored whereas ground travel is not," explained Harpreet.

Jess snorted. She had no very fine estimation of Terran government to begin with, and *interference with flight* didn't improve that opinion one bit.

A cousin of Wallace's arrived with precious scan chips which would provide the raiders with the Terran identities they would need. Ethan, who'd been quiet all morning, perked up to ask questions about the chips and their subcutaneous insertion, one into either wrist.

"Ye'll only want to offer one hand at a time, obviously," remarked Brian Wallace. "Fortunately, there exists considerable disagreement upon which hand ought to be chipped. Ye can offer either, as suits at the time."

Harpreet offered a phrase to help the crew remember which scan chip went with which identity.

Left for family, right for escape, Jess repeated to herself, hoping she wouldn't have cause to use either identity. She'd never been good with rights and lefts, despite her ability to pilot her way home in a dust storm without instruments. *Left for family, right for escape.*

Wallace shook each of their hands farewell in turn but hugged Harpreet. "Thank ye for the generosity ye've shown," he said. "I'll nae forget ye." Jess thought he might be blinking back tears.

Once they'd begun driving away from Wallace's home, Kipper spoke sharply to Harpreet. "I hope, Negotiator, that you have not increased the expectations for future transactions with Terrans."

Jess snapped back, "If we get this right, there won't *be* any future transactions." To herself, she added that if they got it wrong, there wouldn't be any future transactions either.

Harpreet answered calmly. "Mr. Wallace has sufficient incentive to keep his excellent bargain secret from others. If he tells, he will have to part with a larger percentage."

"Harpreet is as generous as a dog," said Ethan.

"*Harpreet* understands human nature," said the old raider. Laughing, she added, "But I certainly try to be like a dog, child."

Their route led them off the small island of Skye and onto the larger island of Great Britain. Jess hadn't been sure the amphibious craft would keep them above water, but they arrived on the shores of the Scottish highlands unharmed. They came to the border of a wilderness preserve Wallace had spoken of and had their first opportunity to test the scan chips, as passage through the preserve cost credits.

"Would you like a receipt?" asked the attendant, after removing credits for travel from Harpreet's wrist-chip.

"No," said Kipper.

"*Yes*," said Jessamyn, holding her hand out to receive the piece of plastic. "And we'll take any other . . . publications you might have on the ecosystem of the area," Jess added.

Harpreet paid for three small plastic cards which were apparently intended to be read on a computer that most transports came equipped with.

"No stick-reader, eh?" said the attendant, looking at the vehicle. "I haven't seen one of these old Dashers since I was in first-body! Don't worry—the cards will work on your stick-reader at home. The one on the Scottish Highlands Recovery program is very good, and you can only buy it at this entrance. Enjoy your visit to the wetlands reserve."

Jessamyn passed the receipt and video sticks to her brother. "Time to start in on a Terran collection, eh?"

The journey through the reserve was unexceptional. A recent eruption on Iceland had left the area covered in a layer of fine ash. Noting that her brother seemed relaxed as he studied his collectibles, Jessamyn allowed herself to feel hopeful for the mission.

Beside her, Ethan had figured out a way to make his wafer-computer read one of the sticks, and a video of the Scottish Highlands Recovery program began playing on the screen. Jess saw artist's renderings of what the area would look like when the volcanoes were done erupting. She smiled. It reminded her of terraforming vids she'd seen in school as a child.

They continued southward under heavy cloud cover—a phenomenon Harpreet recalled with delight. As the day wore on, though, a brilliant flash stirred Jessamyn from her drowsy state—the sun had sunk below the clouds, lending a mellow gold to the bottoms of the clouds for the last hours of daylight. The amphibious craft crossed a stretch of sea called *The Channel* and Jess amused herself watching the light shimmer and glint upon the waves.

When the sun set a few hours later, Jessamyn's stomach had begun to hunger.

"Sunset means rations, right?" Her stomach punctuated the question with an impressive growl.

Kipper nodded at Harpreet who retrieved the box of rations Wallace had insisted upon giving the crew.

"Goodness," said Harpreet. "He's given us a full box of one hundred rations."

"If all Terrans are the size of Wallace," said Ethan, "Then they would have higher caloric requirements to maintain their bodily weight."

"Ugh!" said Kipper. "Something's wrong with this bar. It tastes dreadful."

"No," said Harpreet. "It is a fresher box than the one Wallace offered us from his kitchen. You three young ones won't remember the last time a fresh batch came to Mars. The taste is more pronounced before they've had a chance to age."

Jessamyn read the ingredients listed on the box, like she'd done a thousand times back home: desiccated liver, butter oil, coconut oil, palm oil, whey, sprouted kamut, dried sauerkraut, acerola powder, and a string of minerals. This time as she read, she wondered if her mother's agricultural program would allow them to grow these exotic-sounding foods in her lifetime.

Marsian terraforming had succeeded in so many ways already. Mars had a thin but permanent atmosphere now, and temperatures were rising every orbit thanks to a greenhouse effect. Jessamyn's teachers had stressed how quickly Mars would change by the time Jess had grown up. "It's the first two centuries that were the hardest. The next twenty annums will see miracles, children." The promise of miracles had been what started Jess reading: she had wanted to know what Mars would be like when she grew up.

Finishing her ration, Jess passed the wrapper to Ethan.

He shook his head *no*.

"I have collected a large number of objects already," he told his sister. From his pocket he withdrew several items: an entrance ticket, an exit receipt, the video cards, a receipt for fuel purchased in a place called "Calais," and something that Jess thought looked like a hunk of dog fur.

"What's that?" asked Jess.

"Thistle down," said Ethan. "A form of plant life."

"Huh," said Jess.

"Ethan," called Kipper, "Can you check your wafer and see if we're expecting a halt up ahead?"

The stream of vehicles which they were following did, indeed, seem to be slowing. Another kilometer proved this was the case. Traffic crept forward at a fraction of their former speed.

"We should have requested a vehicle that wasn't ground-only," murmured Jess. "This is ridiculous."

"Remember your identities," said Harpreet.

"Is this dangerous?" whispered Jess to her brother.

"On Earth, a slowing of vehicles can indicate that security forces are investigating or interrogating travelers," replied Ethan.

Jess shrank down in her seat. She didn't want to be investigated. *Left for family, right for escape*, she told herself again.

An aircraft flew lazily down the line of transports. It shone a floodlight upon the vehicle three ahead of the raiders. Then two ahead. One ahead. The floodlight came to rest on their transport. The aircraft hovered slowly beside them before landing on the shoulder of the road.

Three armored guards stepped out, weapons drawn, and approached the Marsians.

14

GUMPTION

"Everyone will please remember that we are a family on our way to Budapest where we plan to drop off our first-body daughter for her apprenticeship examination tomorrow morning," said Harpreet. Her voice, calm, had the effect of calming others.

But when one of the officers tapped a weapon against Kipper's window, Jessamyn failed to repress her gasp of shock. Ethan ran a finger along his brows.

"What's the meaning of this interruption?" asked Kipper, sliding her window so that she could speak with the person aiming a weapon at her. "My granddaughter has her firstie exams early tomorrow morning. We have no time to waste."

In that brief moment, Jess felt proud of her captain. Kipper had gumption.

"Step out of the vehicle, ma'am," said the officer. "Hands where I can see them. Slowly."

A second officer pushed his head into the vehicle. "Where's your stick reader?" he barked at the three inside.

"There is no stick reader in this craft," said Ethan.

The officer stepped out and conferred with his team. "Their vehicle's from the last century," he said. "Like you said, perfect for avoiding a stick-scan."

Jessamyn and the others could only pick up bits of the other officer's reply. There was something about ". . . automatically suspicious" and "thorough search of the vehicle," neither of which sounded good.

"The fourbody outside tells me you're the head of household," said an officer who had just opened the door beside Harpreet.

"That would be me," said Harpreet.

"Where have you driven today?"

"Oh, my," said Harpreet. "We began our day visiting the Scottish Wetlands Reserve. Then we drove south, past London, and crossed the channel between Dover and Calais, and we've been on the motorway ever since."

"With no stick reader to prove it," said the officer.

"I'm afraid not, Officer," said Harpreet.

Beside Jessamyn, Ethan pointed to his wafer computer. There had been an inciter bombing in London only a few hours earlier.

"What time did you say you passed through London?"

"I didn't say," replied Harpreet. "But I believe it must have been just four o'clock. The children complained when we didn't stop for tea. We're in a hurry, you see. It's my daughter's exam tomorrow. In the capitol. So, we'd appreciate anything you can do to speed us along." She flicked her left wrist.

It could have been nothing, that casual gesture of Harpreet's hand. Merely a nervous shake. But Jessamyn remembered Wallace describing how to initiate a bribe by wiggling your chipped-wrist.

The officer grabbed Harpreet's wrist in a violent motion. "How can you even think about bribery after what's happened in London? I should arrest you right now."

Jess held her breath, but Harpreet remained calm.

"If I had the credits to bribe a fine officer such as yourself," said Harpreet, "Do you really think I'd be driving this vehicle?" She smiled warmly.

The officer dropped Harpreet's wrist and stepped around to the far side of the vehicle to speak with his fellows.

Ethan's fingers flew across his wafer as he enabled it to voice-capture the conversation outside. Jess leaned in to read it in transcript form.

Male officer: *The head of household claims the family are on their way to exams and that they passed through London at approximately 4:00 this afternoon.*

Female officer: *I've got the same story from the fourbody who was driving. But they're in an untraceable vehicle. It looks suspicious.*

Male officer: *I don't know. My Opa drives one of these old amphibs. This family doesn't seem the type.*

Female officer: *They never do. I say we send them in for further questions.*

Male officer: *I concur. Let's scan them in.*

Ethan passed his wafer to Jess, opening the door to step out.

"*Halt!*" cried the male officer. "Hands where I can see them!"

Ethan held his hands out in front of him, palms up. "I have proof that we have been to the places of which my mother spoke," he said. "Within my shirt pocket."

"Freeze!" commanded the female officer. "Gabor, check his pockets." To Ethan, she barked a short, "Keep your hands up."

Gabor removed the contents of Ethan's pockets, containing items he had "collected" during the day's journey.

The female officer asked, "Well?"

Gabor answered, "This corroborates everything the head of house *and* the fourbody claimed." He shook his head. "Ma'am," he said to Harpreet, "I think you lost track of what time zone you're in. This says you left Britain prior to 3:00 p.m."

"You will forgive me," said Harpreet. "We are all a bit turned around from our travels."

The female officer spoke. "You have date stamps I can check?"

"Several," said Gabor. "This fuel receipt says they were in Calais at 4:03 p.m. They certainly didn't blow up a hospital in London at 4:30 p.m."

"Very well," the female officer said to Gabor. "Place a twenty-four hour tracker on the vehicle, and let's move on to the next one."

Gabor placed a small device upon the front window, and Kipper was permitted to return to the driver's seat.

Jessamyn, observing her brother, saw anxiety written in his posture as he contemplated returning to the confines of the small craft.

Ethan spoke to Gabor, beside him. "If we are innocent, why use the tracking device? And if we were not innocent, could we not simply disable it?"

Jessamyn froze. *Stop talking*, Jess thought. *Just stop talking!*

"That's my grandson, always curious," said Kipper, laughing lightly.

"Young man, you couldn't disable it without understanding a whole lot more about radio-frequency encryption than someone like yourself. And the tracker is standard. Nothing personal, son. Now get inside before your family leaves without you."

As Gabor walked to Harpreet's side of the vehicle, Jess whispered to her brother, "I need you to get back inside, Eth. You can tell me about your collected items, okay?" She breathed a sigh of relief when, after a brief hesitation, he complied.

"Ma'am," said Gabor at Harpreet's window, "You're free to continue to Budapest. Good luck to you," he said, nodding to Jess. "My daughter's testing tomorrow as well. Guess that makes you birthday buddies."

"Guess so," murmured Jess.

"Officer," said Harpreet, resting a hand upon his armored arm, "Thank you for the job you are doing. I'm certain it is unpleasant and thankless work."

Through his face-shield, Jess could see Gabor frown and then soften. "You say your daughter's taking her exam in Budapest?"

"Yes," replied Harpreet. Jess nodded in the back seat.

"Here," he said. "Let me see your daughter's wrist real quick." He held out one of the small plastic sticks Terrans seemed so fond of.

Jessamyn panicked, momentarily unable to remember which wrist to offer. Her brother tapped her *left* hand.

Gabor spoke quickly. "We bought a pass for the awards banquet, but my daughter won't be going. With everything that's happened today, she wasn't in the mood for a party. Someone ought to get some use out of it. It cost a fortune."

"How kind of you," said Harpreet. "Here, darling."

Jess held her left wrist-chip out to the officer. He passed the stick over her chip. Something glowed briefly under her skin.

"You must allow me to compensate you," said Harpreet.

"No, no," said Gabor. "How often do you think I've been thanked for doing my job in sixteen years? Not once. Your gratitude is compensation enough." He turned to Jess. "You go and have a fabulous time, young woman."

"Absolutely," said Jess as Kipper revved the vehicle.

"Gabor, we're on the clock here," said the female officer.

"Good luck," said Gabor, waving them ahead.

The road before them was empty now, and Kipper pulled forward into the dark.

15

REAL SILK

Ethan surprised everyone by suggesting that Jessamyn leave the group prior to their arrival at the Terran satellite communication facility.

"Not going to happen," said Jessamyn. "I came to make sure you can do your job and I intend to see it through."

Her brother spoke again. "I have recovered sufficiently from my confinement to perform my task. However, I find that I am distressed at the thought of Jessamyn's safety. I believe it would be difficult for me to concentrate on hacking ancient Terran code while knowing her to be in harm's way."

"Don't be ridiculous," said Jess. "We've been in harm's way every minute since we boarded the Galleon."

"I have been researching the customs surrounding first-body apprenticeship examinations," said Ethan, ignoring his sister's retort. "Budapest throws the largest awards banquet. The opportunity to purchase admission is earned through a merit system. Jessamyn has been given a ticket and I believe the awards banquet would be a remarkably safe place."

"Humph," said Jess.

"The party lasts all night and the examination is held in the upper portion of the same building the following morning," concluded her brother.

"That's a ridiculous way to prepare for an important exam," muttered Jess.

"We are attempting an important task, and we are under-rested," Ethan countered.

Kipper glanced back at Ethan. "Your suggestion to increase your sister's safety has merit. First Officer, is it your conclusion that your brother has made a full recovery?"

Jess, out of the Captain's range of vision, rolled her eyes and muttered. "He just disabled the tracking device those Terrans placed on the front window."

"Indeed?" Kipper sounded impressed. "Harpreet, what is your recommendation?"

"Ethan has watched over his sister her entire life. If he feels her presence would compromise his productivity, I suggest we do as he asks. A Terran banquet is certainly a safer location than a cloaked transport, should we encounter . . . difficulties." Harpreet paused to smile at Jess. "And daughter, I must implore you, for my sake, to sample a raspberry at the banquet."

"Very well. First Officer," said Kipper, "You will await us at the banquet."

And so Jessamyn found it a settled thing: she would remove herself from the rest of the crew, maintaining communication through the audio device of Ethan's invention. She felt disgruntled at being set aside during the real action. Then she remembered a conversation around Brian Wallace's table. She recalled how her brother had seemed to be trying to *convince* himself that she would be safe under the cloaking tarp. *He's been worrying about this all along*, she realized. Her brother didn't need additional worries. She smiled softly. She was doing what Harpreet said she needed to do: to consider a situation from someone else's point of view.

Budapest sprawled, a vast city on either side of the Danube River. The boundaries of the capitol had doubled several times over in the centuries since colonists first left for Mars. The city center maintained some of its antique beauty, the ancient buildings in warm browns, golds, and pinks that felt restful to Jess's eyes after the blue-greys and greens of Scotland.

As they drew closer to the exam building where Jessamyn would depart from her crew, she found herself recalling her father's final words to her before she'd said goodbye on Mars: *Remember to use all your senses, Jess.* Her sense of taste had been vastly underutilized so far. She smiled; she would rectify that omission tonight.

Kipper brought their vehicle to a halt beside the award banquet building, a sunset-colored building ornamented with crumbling statuary, several stories tall and some eight kilometers distant from the crew's mission. Half an awkward hug from Harpreet, a nod from Kipper. And then, against her better judgment, Jess leaned over and hugged her brother.

"I'll be in range of what the ear implants can handle, right?" she whispered.

"Yes," replied her brother. Tense.

She released him from the hug and he relaxed.

"I will contact you when we have completed the task," he said.

"See you all in a few hours, then," she said, exiting next to a long row of hover-bikes available for rent.

Slipping into the back of a queue for admission, she watched her chrono-tattoo move from red to orange: Ethan was already half a kilometer away. The line snaked forward. She flicked her wrist to turn the tattoo on again. Green. Two kilometers. Jessamyn could hear music belting from inside the building. It sounded lively and not unpleasant. Another wrist flick. Blue. Many kilometers.

Behind her, several girls laughed. Jess felt hairs rise along her neck, certain they were discussing her. She turned back and glared at them.

The first-body girls stared at her in silence, then tittered again.

Jess turned to the front. *Terrans.*

A boy in front of her cleared his throat and addressed her. "You should've had it removed."

"Pardon?" asked Jess.

He touched his wrist. "Your tattoo. You'll lose a couple credits toward your twobody for marking your current body."

"Oh," said Jess.

"Why didn't your parents make you remove it?" asked the boy.

The line advanced and Jess—to avoid answering—pointed forward, indicating the boy should move. They shuffled ahead.

"I'm sorry," said the boy, turning back again. "That was rude of me. Tattoo removal is outrageously overpriced for first-bodies."

Jess, lacking a frame of reference from which to respond, kept silent. She found his accent fascinating and subtly shifted the shape of her mouth wondering how to match his "o's" and "i's".

"I'm Pavel," he said. "In case, you know . . ." He trailed off as if Jess should know the remainder of the sentence.

"In case what?" she asked.

"Oh," he said, a look of surprise flitting across his face. "It's only that . . . well, a lot of people know my name already because of the election campaigning."

"Sorry," said Jess. "I don't recognize you." She thought she'd done a good job matching his long vowel sounds.

He flashed a row of white teeth, then hid them again, amused. "So, I say 'I'm Pavel,' and you say—."

"Jessamyn," she heard herself replying.

"I would have worn black, too," he said, gesturing at Jess's garments. "But Aunt Lucca's a hard woman to say no to." He laughed as if Jessamyn would get the joke.

Her blank stare told him she didn't.

"Never mind," he said, sobering. "Did you lose someone you knew in today's attacks?"

Jess shook her head slightly. *He thinks I'm grieving*, she thought, recalling Earth-stories where people dressed in black to mourn death.

"You're showing solidarity, then," said Pavel, nodding approval. "I should have packed a change of clothes. This—" he indicated his midnight blue garb. "This is one hundred percent Lucca Brezhnaya."

"Hmm," said Jessamyn, nodding. She thought the name sounded familiar. Maybe from a book she'd read?

Immediately ahead, Jess saw the reason for the line's slow progression. A group of three women assessed the attendees' appearance before allowing them to scan inside the building.

"Good luck with the outfit," said Pavel, seeing where Jess's gaze rested. "You could try explaining your reasons. Solidarity with the victims is running high tonight, my aunt says."

He crossed to stand before the trio of inspectors. Each gave a curt nod "yes," and Pavel gained admittance.

"See you later, Jessamyn," said Pavel.

Not likely, thought Jess.

She approached the group of arbitrators. All three women shook their heads *no* at the same time. One took Jess by the upper arm and jostled her to the entrance, murmuring, "I'm sorry for your loss, but the dress code has not been relaxed. Someone will help you with a change of clothes just inside. Look for a gentleman in red. Bright red. Talk to him about renting an outfit, dear."

Jessamyn glanced back before passing through the narrow entrance door. She wanted to turn and run.

Inside her Terran shoes, her toes curled and uncurled. *Run.*

No, she told herself. Staring down at both wrists, she chose the left one containing her admission, scanned it, and passed inside the building.

The music proved much, much louder now than it had been outside. It wasn't in a style she recognized, though that was hardly surprising. Colonists had destroyed Terran recordings, and a good deal of Terran art, during the war fifty orbits earlier. Jessamyn had to admit the Earth-music at the banquet stirred her. It shook the floor, hummed through her breastbone, steady like a pulse. She looked for the man in red, but he found her first, grabbing her upper arm like the woman outside had done. It was irritating.

"Size minus six?" he asked as he steered her to a counter.

"What?" asked Jess, shouting to be heard over the music.

"Your dress size. Minus six? Minus eight?" He let go her arm. "They'll help you find something . . . appropriate." He gazed at her from head to toe, shaking his head in disapproval. Then he was gone.

"Your wrist, sugar?" said a woman from behind the counter.

Jess repeated her *left/right* mantra and held out the correct wrist.

"Hmm, tall *and* thin. Not a lot to choose from in your size," said the woman. Her hands tapped the counter separating them and it lit up with images of dresses. "Black-and-white means we don't have it, full color means we have it in your size."

Jess nodded. She stared at the counter as it came aglow with a row of six gowns. Six very ridiculous-looking gowns. Fortunately all were grayed out. *Not available,* she said to herself.

"Hurry up, honey," said the woman behind the counter. "The speaker address starts at 9:00 whether you're dressed or not." As the woman finished speaking, she swiped her hand across the counter, revealing for Jess a new set of dress pictures. "I can help the next guest over here," she said, moving to the far side of the counter.

Jess passed her hand across the counter, moving past one page and another and another. The gowns were equally repulsive or bizarre, but she hadn't seen any in color yet. Then three slid into place before her in color. They reminded her of gowns from a book of Terran fairy tales she'd loved once. The dresses might have enchanted her when she was five or six years old, but she couldn't imagine encasing herself in those layers of . . . whatever the gauzy material was. Another page with two more gowns. One had no sleeves or shoulder-covering. *How does that stay put?* She scrolled again.

END-END-END read the panel before her. She pushed backward. Between two gowns that reminded her of illustrations from the long-discarded fairytale books, she saw something she might actually wear. *It's called a* sari, some part of her remembered. She'd read a sprawling saga set in India with a heroine who'd appeared on the cover wearing the long, pleated skirt and abbreviated bodice of a *sari.* Harpreet had given her the book.

The short-sleeved top which bared a hint of belly would have been vastly impractical on Mars; the flowing, long skirt would be a nuisance, impossible with a walk-out suit. *Here's to new experiences*, Jess thought, shaking her head slightly. She raised her left wrist once again and held it over a box that read "Select Me!"

Looking up, she waited to see what she was supposed to do next.

"Move on, syrup," said the woman behind the counter to Jess. "To your left."

Glancing left, Jessamyn saw a small glass door lighting up. Behind it lay an orange length of fabric. She reached for it.

"Dressing rooms to the right, sugar," said the woman behind the counter.

Taking the package, Jessamyn suddenly remembered the pages-long description of how the heroine had dressed herself in a *sari.* She wasn't at all certain she'd be able to turn the length of fabric into something meant to be seen in public.

But inside the dressing room, she discovered several elderly Terrans waiting to help girls with their gowns. "We've got a *sari* here," called one of the women. "The skinny redhead."

A wrinkled and white haired woman shuffled toward Jess. "I can do a *sari*," said the old woman. She grinned at Jessamyn. "This would be a lot easier if my fingers weren't so arthritic." She laughed. "Just you wait. Tomorrow's going to be a big shock, I can tell you."

Jessamyn stood uncertainly and then realized the woman was referring to Jess's presumably-imminent re-bodying.

"Go on, then, undress," said the old woman.

Jess didn't want to undress. She wanted to be ready to leave as soon as Ethan contacted her. She stared at her black top and trousers.

"What's wrong?" asked the old woman. "You want to wear the *sari* over your shirt and pants?"

"Yes, please," replied Jessamyn.

"Suit yourself," said the old woman. "Come closer. You can move quicker than me. For now." She cackled again. "I'm going to do a quick spray-shrink," she said, removing a canister from a pocket.

When Jessamyn looked puzzled, the old woman said, "It'll wear off by morning. Don't worry."

With that, the woman spritzed Jess's top and trousers. She felt a mild tingle and gaped as her garments contracted to form a second ink-black skin.

"There," said the wrinkled woman, nodding in approval.

Next, Jessamyn was pushed, prodded, and spun round a few times. The fabric of the *sari*, when it drifted past her cheek once, felt warm and soft and light as sunshine.

"Wow," Jess whispered, running her fingers over the pleated length at her waist.

"Silk," said the old woman. "*Real* silk. No expense spared for those of you invited to the Awards Banquet. I almost got in, myself. It was easier though, fifteen years ago. Don't know how you kids manage all those volunteer hours and lessons and the rest of it."

"Mmm," said Jessamyn, nodding. "Getting here was no easy feat."

"Your generation will be running things when I make fourbody, so I'm glad to see the increase in civic contributions, I can tell you," said the old woman.

Jess realized with a shock that the woman wasn't old at all—that she was maybe the age of Jess's own mother. A shudder of aversion ran through Jess. Body-swapping was *real* here—not just an imagined thing.

"You're done. Go have a look." The not-really-old woman smiled, revealing a few missing teeth. "Oh, no. Wait-wait-wait!" The woman shuffled off to a counter, pushed the lid off of a small, thin box, and removed something Jess couldn't quite see.

Holding her arms apart, as though pantomiming the carrying of an object, the woman approached Jessamyn. Jess caught a glitter of something that looked like the spider's web she had seen with Ethan. She felt a light tickle as the something was draped over her head and fluttered to rest upon her shoulder.

"Mmm, yes. That does it. Make sure you find a mirror out there in the banquet hall. The web comes alive under low lighting," said the woman, wheeling an oblong mirror in front of Jess so that she could see herself.

She looked . . . not like Jessamyn. Back home, she'd avoided wearing orange (popular for hiding dirt stains) because of her red hair. But she looked really good in the flame-colored *sari*, she realized with a tiny smile.

She took a small step forward. *Swish-swish*—the silk whispered against her, more a thing of liquid or air than the solid fabrics Jess knew from home. Another step—*swish-swish*—it was marvelous.

"Deposit the gown before you leave for exams," said the woman who had dressed her. "Or they'll garnish your first day's wages. First week's wages, with that much real silk."

Jessamyn smiled her thanks, wondering if she was supposed to pay the woman, when a bell sounded in the hall outside.

"Hurry up or you'll miss the graduation address!" cackled the old woman.

No paying, then. Jess took a deep breath, gathered the soft layers in front of her, lifted them a few centimeters, and stepped into the hallway.

16

A ROPE TUG OF SADNESS

She followed a group of brightly costumed eighteen-year-olds up a broad marble staircase as they pushed into a large and dark room. The room wasn't merely large—by Marsian standards, it was enormous. Strangest of all to Jessamyn was the high ceiling; it made the Crystal Pavilion seem dumpy and squat. *The air required to fill such a room would be* . . . Jess stopped herself, laughing inside. Breathable air was everywhere on Earth. They could make their ceilings as high as they liked without regard to the cost of filling them with breathable air.

Upon the distant ceiling, star-like pulses winked on and off to the beat of the music. The lighting inside was subdued and Jess thought the small points of light were meant to imitate a vast night sky. Everywhere, she saw decorative plants and trees. A girl beside her plucked something from a nearby tree. A *pear*? The girl took a couple of bites and then tossed the fruit into a large receptacle before reaching for another one.

Jess stared at the girl, stared at the receptacle. It was full of things that smelled strongly. Two more girls drifted past, swathed in cloud-like fabric, and dumped half-full drinking vessels into the receptacle.

Waste, thought Jess. *The container is for waste.* She stared in amazement as guest after guest tossed half-full plates or uneaten pieces of fruit into the large container. Appalled, Jess moved away from the waste receptacle.

Swish-swish-swish whispered her *sari* as she trailed along the walls of the great room. Her eyes caught movement and she looked up, catching sight of herself in a mirror. She gasped. The "spider's web" glistened on her skin, countless jewels held within the silken strands. Beneath the soft lights of the banquet room, the orange-colored silk had turned the burnt-rust of a Marsian sunset.

A bell sounded and the "mirror" disappeared. Upon every wall, Jessamyn now saw repeated the image of a woman she recognized from the broadcast at Brian Wallace's. It was the woman Wallace didn't trust.

"Welcome," boomed the politician's deep voice. "Welcome and congratulations on this, the eve of your eighteenth birthdays."

More interested in finding food, Jess tuned out the speaker's voice. As the politician upon the walls wished everyone good luck, Jess found a queue for a long series of tables laden with foods she'd only seen in pictures. Hundreds of scents wafted upon the air, and she could identify none of them.

Stomach-ache or not, she was *so* going to eat Terran food.

Ahead of her in the queue, a group of boys took disks from a stack as they approached the rations table. They placed food upon the disks. Upon the *plates*, Jessamyn corrected herself. Plates weren't in use on Mars, but Jess could see they would come in very handy for the sort of rations spread before her. She watched the others picking and choosing from amongst the varied offerings. Placards glowed before each food, identifying it with a name.

Realizing her throat felt parched, Jess reached for a small cup marked "honey," which she felt fairly certain was a Terran beverage. Then she took several leaves of a curly, dark green vegetable that resembled an overgrown algae. It was unlabeled, which made Jessamyn think it must be popular enough that it didn't need a placard. Atop the leaves of dark green nestled a variety of small items labeled "mixed berries." Jess took one of each type, hoping, for Harpreet's sake, that one of them was a raspberry. A girl behind her piled twenty or thirty of the round blue-colored ones onto an already-full plate.

Jess's own plate looked very empty in comparison. And she was holding up the line with her indecision. She took several steps forward, pausing at "butter." She placed a stack of the yellow-y slices on one side of her plate.

"Way to live it up your last night," said one of the girls clustered in line behind her.

Jessamyn smiled and continued past plates of strange-smelling steaming dishes. There was a delay beside a food called "pizza." Jess remembered *pizza* from a series of detective novels she'd read over and over when she was ten. There seemed to be several varieties, but she kept looking until she discovered one labeled "pepperoni." That had been the detective's favorite. She took a triangle-shaped portion.

Behind her, she heard whispers. "She took one raspberry. Look—*one*!"

"Must be how she stays thin. Look at her."

"If she turns sideways, she'll disappear!"

Jessamyn turned around. "I'm *thin*, not deaf," she said, glaring at the trio of whispering girls. Remembering Harpreet's request, she asked, in a gentler voice, "So, which one's the raspberry?"

Two of the girls had covered their mouths, eyes wide. The third pointed to the red berry on Jess's plate.

"Thanks," said Jessamyn.

She left the food line, even though the laden tables continued on into the distance. She already had more food than she was sure she could finish. "Waste must be contagious," she murmured, grasping a handful of *sari* so that she could cross the crowded room more swiftly. The setting brought to mind her first day at school—the hushed awkwardness of being surrounded by complete strangers.

Well, she was here, and she had a plate of Terran rations, and she was going to consume pizza of pepperoni. Crossing to a tall window, she found a corner where she could sequester herself behind a column. The window looked out over a large rectangular body of water. *A pool*, her mind told her. So many things she'd only read of or seen in pictures, and now she saw them in reality. A smile grew on her face. She would collect experiences so that she could pass them out through the annums like Harpreet's tea.

Jessamyn reached for the *raspberry* and passed it cautiously beyond her lips. It felt dry and velvety upon her tongue. Crushing it against the roof of her mouth, she felt herself puckering. The unfamiliar combination of sweet and tart made her shudder once. Such flavor in so small an item! It was wondrous. She swallowed and noticed how the scent of the fruit lingered in her nasal passages and upon her tongue.

On Mars, she would have drawn out the experience of *raspberry*-ness. Would have rested with closed eyes to concentrate on its subtleties. Would have replayed the experience in her mind. But she had limited time and a large plate of rations to finish before her brother and crew returned.

She reached for a fingerful of butter. *Wet*, she thought, *Slippery*. She took another mouthful, trying to focus on the flavor. *Delicious*. Then, she noticed in annoyance a heated discussion happening on the other side of *her* column. Taking another mouthful of butter, she paid attention to the rate at which her mouth converted it from semi-solid to liquid. The great thing about butter, she decided, was that you didn't have to chew it at all. It was a very . . . *restful* ration.

Behind her, the discussion between a boy and a girl had become an argument.

"Why can't you see the flaws in the system for what they are? *Flaws!*" The girl's voice undercut the music.

"All systems have flaws," replied the boy. "Ours has remarkably few. And there are ways to express dissent that don't involve killing innocent people."

Jess picked up the vessel of honey, feeling thirsty after several mouthfuls of butter.

"You've never lived a day in the real world," snapped the girl. "For most of us, expressing dissent, as you call it, is simply another way to lose next-body credits. When have you ever spoken out against this government or its practices?"

The boy was silent. Jess hoped the arguing pair would move on.

"Oh, *shizer!*" said the girl. "Are you going to report me as an inciter-sympathetic?"

The boy sighed with exasperation. "Of course not. You're entitled to whatever view you like, however misguided."

"*Thank* you," said the girl.

"Look, if I don't speak out, it's not because I'm afraid something bad would happen to me. It's because the system *works*. But if that changes, I'll be the first in front of the news-cams, telling the world what I think."

The girl made a snorting kind of laugh. "Your aunt or one of her minions would make sure the segment never posted."

The two fell silent, during which time Jess decided *honey* was not a beverage. At least, not a particularly thirst-quenching one. She wanted to go find a wet ration, but she'd have to walk past the arguing pair, and she didn't want them chasing after her, making her swear to keep their secrets.

The boy was speaking again. "Lucca's not like that. You don't know her like I do," he said. "But look at what you *do* know: her government's first act eight years ago was to bolster the Freedom to Speak edicts."

The girl gave a joyless laugh. "Those edicts are to make it easier to catch and punish inciters and sympathizers."

"Listen," said the boy. "I'm the last person to say my aunt is an easy person to live with. We argue almost every day. But you're wrong about the edicts. And you're wrong about the system. It prevents untold suffering. It keeps poverty and crime at levels previous generations only *dreamed* of. We're about to celebrate a century without war. Doesn't that count for something?"

The girl laughed again. "There's a war. Wake up, Brezhnaya. What do you think the inciters are playing at?"

Brezhnaya. Lucca Brezhnaya. Jessamyn's mouth formed a tiny *o.* The boy in line had mentioned an overbearing "Aunt Lucca." Jess realized she was overhearing Pavel. Who was important on this planet, apparently. Now she *really* didn't want to draw attention to herself. Grabbing her *sari*, she pulled it slowly back and out of the view of those on the far side of the column.

"I'm sorry you feel that way," said the boy. "Do you want to tell the banquet officials or shall I?"

"Tell them what?" asked the girl. Jess heard fear in her voice.

"About the midnight kiss?"

"Oh," said the girl. "*That.*"

"Kissing doesn't seem reasonable given our . . . differences in views."

"No," said the girl. "I mean, yes. But I don't want to lose credits over it."

Pavel sighed. "You won't. The system doesn't work like that, whatever nonsense you've heard to the contrary. I'll message the officials that I'm not feeling well. They can go with the next pair on their list," said Pavel. "Unless you still want the honor, but with someone else?"

"No," the girl replied. "It's not an honor I covet. Goodbye, Pavel. And good luck. A starry-eyed dreamer like you—you'll need it."

Jess heard clicking heels as the girl departed.

"Good luck to you, too," called Pavel. Then, softly, Jess heard him murmur, "Better starry-eyed than bitter."

In her stomach, and somewhere behind her forehead, Jessamyn felt odd. She decided the odd feelings were unpleasant and possibly related to her sense of balance. Was she having an adverse reaction to gravity? *Think about the rations,* she told herself, picking up a small, blue berry. The tart sensation felt refreshing after so much butter. She picked up a piece of the green, leafy food.

And so, when Pavel slipped around to the back side of the column, nearly seating himself in Jess's lap, he observed that the girl in orange was *eating* decorative green kale.

"Oh," he said. "I didn't realize anyone was here."

Their eyes met and Jessamyn set the dark leaf back on her plate. "I promise I won't repeat that conversation. If you're worried," she said.

"Um, no," said Pavel. "Not worried about that. Oh—you're the girl from outside."

"That's me," she agreed. She took another bite of the leafy green. It seemed to combat the uncomfortable sensations in her head and belly.

"Is that . . . good?" asked Pavel.

"Yeah," she said, holding one up. "Have one of mine. I took too much food, I think."

Pavel took the offered piece of kale. "It's only decorative, you know. Not meant for eating. At least, I've never seen anyone else eat . . . kale."

Jessamyn felt her face turning red. "It's a delicacy where I come from."

"I didn't mean to offend," said Pavel. "Nice job wearing black under your dress, by the way. Oh. Was that offensive, too?"

"Why would it be?"

"Guess you missed the start of my last conversation." He looked down over the pool outside. "I tried telling her that I admired her choice to wear a black evening gown and that I thought the banquet should have been a bit more subdued in light of the bombings today and things pretty much went downhill from there."

"Sounded like it," said Jess.

"Yeah. We were supposed to lead off the midnight kiss. I thought maybe we should get to know each other. So I introduced myself, and, well, you heard how that went." He shrugged. "Stupid of me."

"Stupid to get to know someone before kissing? Or stupid of you to introduce yourself?" Jess asked. "'Cause you're pretty much repeating the second offense."

Pavel laughed. "No, I meant the first. I'm glad I don't have to do the kiss." He looked at Jess out of the corner of his eyes. "Seeing as you and I will probably never meet again, I have something to admit: I haven't kissed a girl since I was eight. Believe me, I'm relieved to get out of doing it so publicly." He placed his arm, bent, high on the large window before them. He sighed loudly and leaned his head against his forearm. "Tell you what I won't miss tomorrow evening: no one will recognize me as Lucca Brezhnaya's nephew. For awhile, at least."

Jessamyn shuddered as she heard how easily he talked about shedding his own body.

"How's the pizza?" Pavel asked, still gazing down at the pool.

"I was saving it for last," said Jess. Since it was the only thing left on her plate, she took a bite, chewed, and then paused, her taste buds ablaze. How could anyone, she wondered, give proper attention to so many sensations? Nor were the flavors confined to her mouth. She found that drawing breath brought additional pleasure. She sniffed the scent of pizza. Intoxicating! She took repeated small breaths until she grew light-headed. "That is the best thing I have ever tasted," she said at last.

"What, you've never had pizza?" asked Pavel.

"I've never tried pizza of pepperoni before," said Jess, gulping down another bite, larger than the first.

"No kidding?" Pavel laughed. "Hey, you want to get out of here?"

Jessamyn considered the question, but the pizza was so good, so distracting. She took another bite, chewing and swallowing swiftly.

"Just down to the pool? They made a little sandy beach area—the sand's heated, even. It'll be quiet," said Pavel. "When you're done eating, I mean." He watched as she continued inhaling the pizza. "Unless you were planning to just eat pizza all night?"

"Oh, um, no," she replied. "Just this one pizza." It happened suddenly—she was no longer enjoying the myriad flavors. In fact, she felt odd. Placing the remaining pizza in the waste receptacle was unthinkable, so she decided to be done with it as quickly as possible. As she swallowed the last bite, the unpleasant sensation behind her forehead and in her stomach increased.

"Outside sounds good, actually." The air quality was poor inside, even by Marsian standards. "Lead on," she said, placing one hand protectively over her stomach.

"You feeling okay?" asked Pavel.

Jess shook her head *no*. Then she realized head motion was a very bad idea at the moment.

"Come on. Let's get you some fresh air," Pavel said, walking toward a large window that parted as they approached it. "If you need to be, uh, sick, you'll have more privacy outside."

Sick, thought Jessamyn. *That's what's wrong with me.* The advice to avoid Terran food now seemed imminently sensible. She would never, ever, disregard Harpreet's counsel again. They rode down in an elevator. The slow ride and slight jolt at the bottom did little to improve conditions in Jessamyn's stomach.

She stumbled toward what looked like Marsian soil. She sat, sinking her fingers into the pale grains. It wasn't frozen—it felt warm—another Terran miracle. How would she remember half of what she'd experienced this day?

"Better?" asked Pavel.

"Working on it," said Jess.

"Give it a minute." Pavel turned to stare at her, as if wanting to say something more.

Jessamyn frowned. "What?"

"Listen, I'm not an idiot. You've spoken, like, twelve words to me. Obviously you want me to leave. And I will as soon as your color returns. I've never seen anyone so pale outside a hospital."

"You haven't?" Jessamyn wondered if he knew that Marsians with light skin tended to be paler than Terrans with light skin. She wished she looked like Harpreet.

Pavel took her wrist in his hand and held a finger over the small blue veining on the inner side.

Here it was—another Terran grabbing her arm without asking. But Pavel's touch was light and warm and kind. "What are you doing?" whispered Jess.

"Hold on," he said, frowning in concentration. Several seconds passed. "Checking your pulse. You're within a normal range."

Jessamyn looked at him in surprise. "You checked my pulse without a pulse-reader?"

"Sure," he said. "It's easy."

"We always use pulse-readers back on . . . back home," Jess said, flushing slightly.

"I've done my volunteer months in hospitals the past five years. Pulse-readers are broken half the time, I swear." He grinned broadly, revealing very white teeth. The two front teeth overlapped slightly, reminding her of Ethan's. "By the way, I think you just doubled the number of words you've spoken to me. So either you're feeling better, or you changed your mind about ignoring me."

"I wasn't ignoring you," said Jess. "You simply . . . talk a lot."

Pavel laughed. "Are you always this friendly?"

"Not as a rule."

The light had been growing steadily brighter since they'd stepped outside. Pavel looked up and just behind them. "Full moon," he said, pointing overhead to where the moon had just cleared the top of the building at their backs. "It's supposed to be good luck for exams. Better than the midnight kiss, even."

Jess smiled at the odd Terran beliefs. Then, twisting, she followed Pavel's gesturing hand.

"Oh," whispered Jess. "Oh, *Hades*, that's beautiful!"

"Better get an eyeful tonight," murmured Pavel. "Loss of night vision is the most common complaint among twobodies."

I'd better get an eyeful tonight, because by dawn, I'll be counting down a launch, thought Jessamyn.

"What are you hoping for?" asked Pavel.

Jessamyn wondered briefly if "hoping on the full moon" was a Terran custom like wishing on a shooting star back home.

"For your apprenticeship?" Pavel added.

"Oh, um, for tomorrow?" How could it hurt to give an answer, she wondered. "I want to be a pilot."

"*Really*?"

Jess frowned. "Yes. Is there something wrong with that?"

Pavel laughed, threw a small pebble into the pool before them. "No. I'm a licensed pilot myself."

"What do you fly?" asked Jessamyn.

"You name it, I've probably flown it," said Pavel. "I took every level they offer, so I'm good right up to 300 kilometers above Earth."

As they discussed the merits of various crafts Jess had only read about, she had to remember to keep back certain pieces of her familiarity with flying. She could tell her knowledge impressed Pavel as it was.

"Tell you what I'd do if I weren't interested in medicine," said Pavel. "I'd sign on for satellite-trash harvesting just so I could fly the high-orbit runs." He leaned back on his elbows, gazing at the heavens. "Not that Aunt Lucca would ever allow that."

"Why not? She's not the one taking your exam, is she?"

Pavel grunted. "You can bet she'd like to." He grimaced. "She's got her mind set on me following a medical course so I can be elected Head of Global Consciousness Transfer someday." He sighed, burying his hands deep in the sand and bringing them slowly out.

Jess watched the sand trail off his long fingers. He had what her dad would call surgeon's hands. Of course, he wouldn't have them tomorrow once he transferred into a new body. The thought made Jessamyn sad, although she didn't know why it should.

She leaned back, nestling into the warm sand, turning to face Pavel. "Is that what you want? To be a politician?"

"I want to help people. Heal the sick. I guess I'd be okay in a transfer hospital if I could do the recovery therapy part. I've assisted at a few transfers already for my volunteer hours. Tomorrow, I'll be new-bodied at New Kelen, where I volunteered. It will be interesting to experience the change from the point of view of a patient."

"Interesting," said Jess, feeling an uncomfortable twist in her stomach. "Yeah."

They lay silent for several minutes. As Jess looked at clusters of stars overhead, she wondered how much of what she saw was satellite trash, how much actual gaseous giants across the galaxy.

'In a couple of minutes," said Pavel, "The New Terra Space Station should pass overhead."

"I thought space exploration was banned," said Jess, feeling confused.

"A hundred and eighteen years ago. But the space stations still circles. Hardly anyone remembers it's up there."

"You do."

"Yeah. I've got . . . reasons." Pavel was quiet for a few minutes, then raised a finger. "That's it. See?" Another silent half-minute as he followed the bright spot across the sky with his finger.

"I see it!" said Jessamyn.

"My parents died up there," said Pavel, his voice dropping low.

"I thought—" Jess paused, curious, but not wanting to give away her ignorance of Terran law. "Wouldn't that have been illegal—going to visit the space station?"

"It was. *Is*," said Pavel, correcting himself. "They took risks. They paid for those risks with their lives."

"I'm sorry." Jessamyn tried to imagine life without her parents. She couldn't. "Has your aunt been a good . . . surrogate parent?"

Pavel grinned lazily. "That's a very expensive question. If I had a credit for every time a reporter asked me that, I could build my own illegal space station."

Jessamyn flushed and turned away, murmuring, "Sorry."

"No, it's okay." He twisted onto his side to face her. "Hey." Nudging one of her feet with one of his own, he said softly, "I'm the one who should apologize. I just implied you'd sell my answers for credits."

"Of course I wouldn't," Jess snapped.

"I know. Forgive me."

She raised her eyes to meet his—so earnest, so dark and lovely—and she felt herself softening inside. "I only meant to say," she murmured, "That I don't know how you survived growing up without your parents."

A furrow grew between Pavel's brows. "I had them my first ten years. And Lucca's okay. She tries hard, anyway. We're just . . . we're very different from one another. Even though we believe in a lot of the same things. I don't know if that makes any sense at all."

"It does," Jess replied. "You should see how different my brother is from me. But we get along great."

"Hmm. Yeah, that's the thing. I don't think anyone would say Lucca and I get along well. We argue a lot. Junk harvest is a perfect example. She *says* she'd never want to see me go into something like that because of how my parents died up there. But really, that's not why. Really, she hopes I'll get a more prestigious apprenticeship, because that will reflect well on her. I mean, Lucca doesn't want her nephew taking an apprenticeship that actually accepts *volunteers*."

He glanced quickly at Jessamyn. "I don't mean to imply that I look down on trash harvesting. I think it would be a great job."

"I'm not offended," said Jess. "Even if I were planning to volunteer for it."

Pavel smiled, relieved. "Well, my aunt's attitude towards junk harvesting is a perfect example of where we don't see eye-to-eye. Her public policies are fine—but privately, she's a bit of a snob."

"I've met someone like that," said Jess, thinking of Kipper. Although, at the moment, she was having a hard time feeling hostility toward the Captain. Every time she remembered Ethan's mission, her stomach sloshed and she felt a downward *whoosh*, like riding the elevator, which left a hollowness behind. She wished one of the crew had remained with her. Even Kipper.

"You're quiet again," said Pavel, after a couple of minutes passed without either of them speaking. "Do you want to go back inside to the party? They'll be bringing out desserts now that it's almost midnight."

The idea of further food (and she was fairly certain *desserts* meant food) made her feel ill. Better to remain outside, with Pavel and conversation to distract her from unwanted worry. "I'm fine here," said Jessamyn. "I want to enjoy the night sky one last time."

Pavel sighed contentedly. "Me, too."

It was true, Jessamyn realized—she was exactly where she would choose to be, lying on her back, breathing out-of-door air, staring into the heavens.

"That moon is amazing," she said. "It's like someone cut out a piece of mirror and hung it in the sky."

"I wish it were still legal to fly to the moon," said Pavel. "If I were in my aunt's shoes, that's a law I'd bring before parliament."

"It must've been amazing, back in the day," said Jess.

"Can you imagine being Neil Armstrong? Or Roberta Zubrin-Trujillo? That was the golden age, Jess. I mean, I know there were wars and poverty and life was awful for so many people, but can you imagine being the first person to set foot on the Moon? Or Mars?"

Jess smiled.

"Tell you what. I'll run for Head of Consciousness Transfer when I'm a threebody, then, once my political career takes off, I'll see about re-opening the Terra-Luna shuttle runs. And you can be a shuttle pilot. Deal?"

"Sounds great," said Jess. "But what about you, don't you want to pilot, too?"

"Shuttles? Nah, where's the fun in that? I'll hold out for a flight to Mars."

Jess turned sharply to face Pavel, her brow furrowing.

"Just kidding," he said. "Anyway, it would be too sad. For me, at least." He paused to brush sand off his chin.

"You can see Mars over there," he said, pointing. "It's as close as it's going to be for over a year, which makes it bright. I wonder how long the last survivors hung on for, anyway?"

Jess held her breath. This wasn't a conversation she wanted to fake her way through.

"There's Arcturus," said Pavel. He pointed to a bright stellar cluster. "Did you know ancient peoples used that star for navigation? One group traveled all the way from Tahiti to Hawaii with only that single star in view to keep their course true. Can you imagine that? Weeks in a boat on the sea, guided by the heavens?"

Jessamyn could imagine it in some detail, if you substituted "ship in space" for "boat on sea," but she kept her thoughts to herself.

Another bell sounded from inside the hall and Pavel sat up, checking a device which flashed a readout of the local time.

"Almost midnight," he said.

Jess couldn't remember what time her body—still accustomed to ship time—thought it was now. "Do we have to go back inside?" she asked. "For the kiss or whatever?"

Pavel shook his head.

"Good," said Jessamyn, settling back into the sand.

"Hey, Jessamyn, can I tell you something?"

Jess looked at him. "Isn't that what you've been doing all night?"

Pavel's eyes looked bright, animated. Jess waited but he didn't speak.

"What?" she asked, finally.

Licking his lips once, he spoke. "So, I know it's a load of shizer, what they say about the midnight kiss being good luck." He paused and took a deep breath, then spoke very quickly. "But if I'd met you this year at school, well, I'm pretty sure my last kiss would have been a lot more recent than the one when I turned eight, assuming you'd said okay, because obviously I wouldn't have just grabbed you in the halls, even though I would have wanted to very much." He laughed and covered his eyes with one hand. "I *cannot* believe I said that out loud."

"You want us to kiss?" Now Jess laughed, too, shaking her head at Pavel, his face half hidden under his hand. Then, more quietly, she asked another way: "*You* want to kiss *me*?"

"Pretty much since I saw you standing there in line, all dressed in black," he said, looking at her through parted fingers. His hand dropped away from his face and he met her gaze.

Her skin tingled like it had when the woman doused her with spray-shrink. She thought she liked the feeling, this time. She smiled at Pavel's dark eyes, turned upon her. She fingered her *sari*, slippery against her skin.

"I'm shallow," groaned Pavel. "Go ahead. Hate me."

"I don't hate you," said Jess. She thought about New Orbit countdowns back home where Marsians kissed at midnight for good luck. As a child, Jess had always hidden behind Ethan, covering her eyes against the thousand kisses. Last New Orbit, she'd watched. It hadn't looked all that bad.

"I've never kissed a boy," she whispered. "Not when I was eight. Not ever."

A tiny smile broke upon Pavel's face. "I don't think that one counted for me."

"Come closer," said Jessamyn. As she shifted toward Pavel, burnt-orange silk cascaded from over her shoulder making a *sh-sh-sh* sound.

Pavel gathered a handful of the silk where it had settled between them. The *sari* whispered susurrations once more as Pavel tried to arrange it correctly over Jess's shoulder. "It's as soft as parachute-silk," he said, voice quiet with wonder.

"It *is* silk," said Jess. "At least that's what they told me."

They were very close now and Jess detected on Pavel's breath things he'd eaten at the banquet. *Nice* things, she noted. A shout went up from inside the Banquet Hall.

"The countdown," murmured Pavel.

Jessamyn scented the moisture humming between them. *Remember this*, she told herself. *Pavel, the moon, the moisture-laden air.* Hundreds of voices chanted *five-four-three—*

"I probably suck at this," Pavel whispered.

Distantly, from inside the hall, a clamor rose.

"Hush," said Jessamyn. As she shifted to meet his mouth, her dress whispered s*hhh*.

Jess's heart beat faster than it should have for so small an effort, the pressing of her lips against Pavel's. *This is what* sweet *tastes like*, she thought. And then she stopped thinking and simply felt the kiss: silk-soft, honey-sweet, Earth-moist.

They pulled apart, eyes flickering down. Then, in turn, their two pairs of eyes darted back to take in the *other* before them—lips warmed red, cheeks flushed, eyes shining. Pavel laughed first, and then Jessamyn did, and they passed happy echoes back and forth until both sighed and laid their heads back upon the sand. Overhead the stars wheeled in an ancient dance.

"Do you know any constellations?" Jess asked Pavel, running her fingers in a sweeping motion across the sky. She wondered if they would be called by the same names as back home.

"Sure," Pavel said. "But the moon's so bright that most of the constellations are hard to see. Can you find Mars?"

"I hope so." Jess couldn't help herself—she giggled.

"What's so funny?"

"Nothing," she said. "Keep going. Mars."

The side of Pavel's mouth quirked and he showed her how to draw an imaginary line from where Mars sat over to a bright star in the Milky way. From there, he began outlining constellations: *Bootes*, *Cygnus*, *Ursa Major* and *Ursa Minor*. "Mom used to tell me this story about that bright star in *Cygnus*. Well, she told me lots of stories, but I asked for this one often because she would only tell it outside. Which meant prolonging the time before I had to go to bed." He chuckled at the memory.

"Tell it to me, already," said Jess, smiling.

"Okay. It's a Chinese story about two lovers—*Niulong* and *Zhinü*. *Niulong* was a herder of cattle, and mortal, while *Zhinü* was the daughter of the goddess of heaven. They fell in love and married secretly, having two children. For years, they lived happily together on Earth, but when the girl's goddess-mother found out, she punished them by placing the two on opposite sides of the Milky Way."

"That's a sad story," murmured Jessamyn, her eyes on Pavel's lips. She wondered if *Zhinü* found *Niulong's* kisses sweet and soft.

"Wait, that's not the end," said Pavel. "The goddess of heaven felt sorry for them after awhile. Or maybe popular opinion was against her. Either way, she made it so that, once a year, the pair could reunite. Magical magpies flock to the heavens and create a bridge for the lovers across the Milky Way."

Jess thought how much she would enjoy telling the *improbable* story to her brother.

"See the bright star at *Cygnus's* tail? That's Deneb. The Chinese say that's where the bridge can be found. And down there and there," here Pavel pointed out two bright stars astride the Milky Way, "You can see *Zhinü* and *Niulong*."

Jessamyn frowned, thinking about Zhinü's mother. "What's it like, living with a powerful woman as your guardian?"

Pavel shook his head. "I couldn't possibly do your question justice in the next couple of hours."

"How much time do we have left?" She felt a rope-tug of sadness with Pavel on the other end of it.

Pavel checked and smiled. "Enough time for a few life-with-Aunt-Lucca stories. They won't start calling for us until nine in the morning."

Jess yawned. "It's a stupid idea, making everyone stay up late the night before such an important exam."

"The food at the banquet is enhanced to increase concentration," said Pavel. "Didn't you catch that in the brochure?"

"No," said Jess. That would account for the gluttony, she thought. Eat more so you can score higher. She yawned again. She should have eaten more, obviously.

"Okay, let me think," said Pavel, chuckling. "So, when it comes to Aunt Lucca, the biggest difference I'm aware of between me and my peers is that I have a lot more unsupervised time. Lucca's a busy woman. We don't sleep on the same continent, most nights when she's campaigning. You know how in that story *Zhinü* gets away with being married and having a couple of kids and her mom doesn't catch on for *years*?"

"Yeah, that was completely unrealistic."

"No," replied Pavel. "I totally get that. If I'd been inclined to, I could've gotten away with all kinds of stuff."

"Oh," said Jess. "I see. And you never once took advantage of that?"

Pavel's mouth curved upward. "Well, I didn't say that, did I? Flying's a good example. You've probably heard how Lucca wants to pass legislation that restricts first-bodies from flying anything that goes faster than the speed of sound."

"Boring," murmured Jess.

"I know." Pavel laughed. "So, when I got my first license, Lucca gave me a motor pool pass and forgot to place restrictions on it. It's a classic example of her parenting style."

"Oh," said Jess, laughing. "So she's giving speeches about—"

"First-body safety," Pavel said, completing Jess's thought. "And I'm listening while I fly sub-orbitals."

"How very wayward of you."

Pavel shrugged. "Yeah, I know. But all the statistics about first-body crashes are based on a group who haven't had the kind of training I've had."

"Does your aunt know you've been licensed—" Jess paused to make sure she said it the way Pavel had. "Licensed up to 300 kilometers in space?"

"She never asked," said Pavel. "But she paid the bills for the tuition."

"Or her administrative assistant paid them."

"Probably," grunted Pavel.

"Does she . . . do you think she cares about your safety?" Then, more quietly, "Does she love you?"

Pavel sat up. "In her way." He brushed sand off his fingers. "In the space of a year, I lost both my parents and then the uncle who cared for me. Lucca took me in even though she'd just been elected Chancellor. She did little things to help make my new life with her easier, like finding out what kinds of books and games I liked, fixing up my room exactly like my parents had it, giving me flying lessons when I asked. She did other things, too. My parents' bodies were unrecoverable, but in the case of my uncle, Lucca made sure the re-body went to someone in her cabinet, so that I'd still be able to see him from time to time. Not everyone would have gone the extra mile like that."

Jess shuddered. The *last* thing she'd want if her loved ones died was to see someone else walking around inside their bodies. She scrambled for a change of subject. "What was it like—your first flight where you broke the sound barrier?"

Pavel shook his head. "Scary as anything. But don't let that stop you from trying it someday. That first time up, I caught seven sunrises before the refuel alert forced me back down."

Jessamyn smiled. Catching serial sunrises was one of her favorite pastimes back home. "What's the best place you've ever flown?"

"The great southwestern desert in North America. It's beautiful. Have you seen it?"

"No," murmured Jess. "Never been."

"My parents used to take me every year. I think I was six the first time. I remember watching the sun rising on the flat horizon. It had no color and Mom said how that was because the air lacked contaminants. That was the thing about the desert. How clean it felt. And how it smelled: pure. Fresh. Like every breath I took cleaned out my lungs.

"I had figured a desert would have no color. All washed out like the sky at sunrise. But the desert has so much color, Jessamyn. Every shade of tan and brown and pink that you can imagine, all there in the dirt. Close-up, at your feet, it only looks sand-colored. But when you look out, there are these little hills and they look like someone's been trying different paints, figuring out what color would look best."

Jess's eyes drifted shut and she imagined Mars at sunrise, looking just like Pavel described the North American desert.

"Am I boring you?" asked Pavel.

Jess's eyes flew open. "No," she said. "I've seen pictures of that desert, but it looked like everything was brown."

"They do that to discourage tourism, I think," said Pavel, laughing.

"Keep going," said Jess. "I'm closing my eyes so I can imagine it."

Pavel sighed and continued. "So, yeah, a million shades of tans and golds, like the colors at the heart of Budapest."

"Mmm," Jess murmured.

"I saw cactus for the first time on that trip. I had no idea what it was. It looked like a cluster of pipes sticking out of the ground. I asked my Dad what it could be and he said what he always said." Pavel laughed softly. "'*Let's go find out.*' So we took off and when we got close, something very weird happened: I swear I could *smell* the moisture collected deep inside."

Pavel looked over at Jess. "I *am* boring you to death."

"No," mumbled Jess, her eyes closed. "The desert sounds beautiful the way you describe it."

"Yeah. It's so pure. The worst part was always coming home and trying to sleep—it was like there were too many smells at home. I would grab one of my shirts from camping and sleep with it pressed into my face every night until finally it would lose that clean desert smell."

Pavel looked over at Jessamyn. Her mouth had parted slightly and she looked like she was sleeping. Stretching out on the sand beside her, he placed himself so he could see the next time the New Terra Space Station passed by.

Jess slept, dreaming of home: the deserts of frozen sand and soil in a thousand shades of orange-y brown, until, just before dawn, her brother's voice, terror-filled, awakened her.

17

THE YOU I MET LAST NIGHT

Inside her ear-implant, Jessamyn recognized her brother's voice. "Orbitals down! Orbitals down!"

As he uttered the code phrase selected to indicate mission failure, Jess heard the fear in her brother's voice.

"Follow your tattoo!" Ethan whispered. "Now!" He cut the connection.

Jessamyn found she was already sitting upright beside a sleeping Pavel. To the east, the sky remained dark, but the stars had nearly all vanished. Morning was near. Her tattoo glowed a deep purple and she tapped it to get directions. Ethan was over eight kilometers away. She needed to find transport, *now*. Remembering the row of hover-bikes for rent, Jess rose, shedding her *sari*.

As the fabric slipped into a pile of burnt-orange, a few grains of sand spilled across Pavel. His hands twitched and he opened his eyes.

"Hey," he said, a lazy smile upon his face.

"My brother's in trouble," said Jessamyn. "I need to go."

"Go where? Testing starts in five hours."

"Yeah," said Jess, walking briskly toward the front of the building. *Left hand family, right hand escape*, she repeated to herself.

"Jessamyn. Wait up, Jessamyn!" Pavel jogged alongside her.

It irked her to see how much more quickly he could run. The Terran gravity felt as if it were trying to draw her down inside the Earth's core.

"Did you hear me? Five hours, Jessamyn. If you no-show, you get a manual labor sentence. In, like, Antarctica!"

"Doesn't matter." Jess was *so* done pretending she was here for an exam.

"You're telling me you don't care if you spend the next eighteen years of your life swinging an ice pick in an arthritis-ridden body?"

"Exactly," she said. "Goodbye, Pavel."

She stared at the row of rental bikes, looking for anything that resembled a place to scan her wrist-chip.

"Jessamyn, don't be crazy. Message your parents. Let them deal with it."

Hades, thought Jessamyn. Ethan hadn't said anything about the rest of the crew. Were they all in danger?

Pavel placed himself before a box with writing on it, and Jess glimpsed the rental instructions she'd been looking for.

"Message your parents."

"I can't. Move out of my way."

Pavel stood his ground, arms crossed.

"I said, *move*!" Jess thrust her arms at his chest with a force that would have toppled most Marsians. On Mars, at least.

"Why can't you let someone else deal with your brother?" asked Pavel, laughing at her clumsy attempt.

"I can't tell you," said Jess, swiping her left wrist.

The box made a buzzing noise and a panel flashed a "CHIP DENIED" message.

"Holy *Ares*," muttered Jess, swiping her right wrist instead.

"PLEASE CHOOSE A TRANSPORT" flashed across the panel this time and Jess ran down the row looking for something fast. None of them looked like great candidates. Maybe Pavel would know.

"Which one's the fastest?" she asked. "Please. My parents can't help. They're too far away."

Pavel's mouth shrank into a frown. "Take my bike. It's faster than any of those."

"Really? Where is it?"

Pavel walked away from the motor pool row to another, smaller group of bikes. Placing his thumb over a scanner, he started the engine. Jess hopped aboard.

"Thank you," she murmured, scrutinizing the dash for gears, braking, acceleration.

"I'm going with you," said Pavel.

"No. Absolutely not."

"Jessamyn, tell me what's going on. It's like you're a totally different person all of a sudden." His grip, as he placed a hand on her forearm, felt strong.

"I've told you everything. My brother's in danger. Now let me go," she said, trying to shake his hand off her.

"It's my bike—I'm going with you."

I don't have time for this, Jess thought. "Fine," she heard herself agreeing, "But I drive."

He shrugged, hopped on behind her, and linked his arms around her waist. "Careful," he said. "It's been modified to be faster than most Series 400s."

Jessamyn accelerated and turned onto the main street, following her chrono-tattoo. The hover-bike *was* fast.

"When we get to my brother," she hollered over her shoulder, "You have to promise to leave. Take your bike and get out of there."

"Your brother's in bad trouble?"

"Promise you'll go," said Jess.

She slowed for a traffic indicator, uncertain what the consequences would be for reckless driving, and not wanting to find out. The engine whined softly as they waited, and Jess decided to pump Pavel for information, something she wished she'd done last night. It had been a fool's use of time, conversing about stars and deserts.

"Where's the municipal hoverport?" she asked.

"My bike's not fast enough?" he asked as she sped forward.

"It's fine," she said. "Do you know which city-zone the hoverport is in?

"What's your brother got himself mixed up in?"

Jess worried that she was spooking Pavel.

"If my brother has injuries, I want better options than waiting for emergency services to respond."

"If your brother's injured, I've got a med kit under the bike seat. I can stop bleeding, set bones, whatever he needs."

Jessamyn chewed her lower lip, worrying she'd never get rid of Pavel. She wished she could risk calling Ethan to learn more about his situation but she couldn't 'til she got rid of Pavel. She continued following her tattoo's directions, feeling more and more anxious as it transformed from green to yellow to orange. *Just hold on another minute, Eth*, she thought.

"Do you know where the nearest hoverport is or not?" She was less than a half-kilometer from Ethan's location. Jess blinked her right eye three times, causing the membrane in her eye to shift into place to reveal cloaking fabrics in operation. She prayed they'd cloak-tarped the Terran transport. *There it was*! Sitting in a parking lot behind a rusted-out truck.

"Jessamyn," said Pavel. "That last barrier we passed through? People can't normally drive through that."

"They can't?" asked Jess.

"No, of course not. This facility is under high security. The only reason you got through is that my bike is registered to Lucca Brezhnaya. What is your brother involved with?"

"I'm not sure," replied Jessamyn, bringing the bike to a halt. She swung her legs out. *Hades*, she weighed so much on Earth. She looked Pavel in the eye. "But I know he's in trouble and I have to try to help. Please, go. *Now*."

Jess glanced down at her tattoo, glowing deep red. Seven minutes had passed since he'd called. She needed to find her brother *now* whether Pavel stuck around or not. She thought of something.

"If you don't leave, I'm messaging emergency services that you're kidnapping me," said Jessamyn.

"*What?*"

"Because you're worried I'll earn your apprenticeship."

"You're joking," said Pavel. Jess saw an angry look flash across his face.

"I'm counting down from five."

"Jess—"

"Five. Four. Three."

"Message me and let me know you're okay," he said, flicking his wrist over the spot where her scan chip lay. Jessamyn had no idea how to "message" Pavel, but she wasn't planning to in any case. "There was no need to threaten me," he said coldly. "I'm doing this because you *asked.* Because I liked the *you* I met last night."

Pavel revved the hover-bike and drove off, leaving her alone in the dark.

18

NO LANGUAGE TO EXPRESS

Jessamyn noted that her clothes had returned from their spray-shrunk state to their former size. Reaching into a back pocket, she pulled out a thin black balaclava and gloves. It wasn't as effective as a cloaking fabric, but the black rendered her difficult to see in the pre-dawn gloom. She advanced toward the cloaked transport. Through her glove, the red tattoo glowed softly. Suddenly, her ear implant began transmitting again.

But it wasn't her brother she heard. Voices, electronically altered, filtered through the device in her ear. Ethan was with others, it seemed—but who? Friend or foe? And then, glancing along the building, she saw him. Ethan was being marched and then made to halt facing a wall, legs apart and hands clasped atop his head.

The voices she'd heard weren't Kipper and Harpreet—where were they? And how was she going to free her brother? She glanced at her tattoo, preparing to flick it off. But it was doing something funny. As she crept toward her brother, the red flashed to orange. She paused. What was going on? Had Ethan set her tattoo to lead her somewhere *instead* of to him? What else was there? The transport?

She angled toward the vehicle and the chrono-tattoo glowed cherry red. Another couple of steps and it shifted to a deeper red. She crept up to the side of the transport, hoping to find something that would allow her to rescue Ethan. Lifting the tarp and opening the door silently, she slipped inside.

"Jessamyn, daughter," said Harpreet, seated in the transport. "Thank goodness. Listen carefully. Kipper's been shot. I don't know where they took her. Or if she's alive. Don't use your left chip again. Stick to the right. Do you understand?"

"What about Ethan?" It was all Jess could do to utter her brother's name.

"I'm going to negotiate for his release. If things don't go well, I need you to do two things. Listen to me," said Harpreet, grasping Jessamyn's shoulders. "Set aside your concern for your brother; you cannot save him, but I may be able to."

Harpreet passed Jessamyn a sling-pack meant to sustain team members for up to forty-eight hours solo. Jess couldn't remember half of what was inside the tiny bag, but the simple act of accepting it awakened a part of her that felt bold and alert, like she felt in a cockpit.

"I'm listening," whispered Jess. "What are my orders should you fail?"

"First, cover yourself in the small cloaking wrap." Harpreet handed a flat-folded object to Jessamyn. "It is *extremely* heavy in this gravity. Then, set this transport to auto-destruct using this device." Harpreet placed something small and black into Jess's palm. "We can't have the vehicle traced back to Skye. There's another motor pool two streets back. You would have passed it."

"Yes," said Jess. She'd seen it.

"If I don't succeed, go to the Galleon and get those rations back home."

Jess nodded once, the pilot in her accepting her mission without question. Then the sibling in her struggled to the surface. "Save my brother," she whispered.

Harpreet touched Jess's cheek softly and exited the transport. Jessamyn watched from inside as Harpreet strode toward the small grouping, shoulders back, head carried high. In Jess's ear, a jumble of voices competed for her attention. Her sibling-self ached to follow each word, as if by listening carefully she could expedite her brother's safe return. But the pilot in her focused instead upon the tasks with which Harpreet had charged her. In minutes, the transport would either carry the three of them to safety or need to be destroyed. It all depended upon how skillful a negotiator Harpreet was. Jess spun up the transport's navigation and disabled autopiloting. Then she retrieved the small-vehicle cloak from the seat, settling it on her lap. It weighed more than it ought to have, like Harpreet had said.

Harpreet's clear and cheerful voice echoed in Jess's ear device. "Good day, gentlemen. I understand my son has been the cause of some trouble. Well," she said chuckling, "It wouldn't be the first time he's gotten me out of bed early."

A rush of angry voices, shouted commands. Jess couldn't make out the individual strands of conversation.

"I am sure there will be a *hefty* fine due from me as his mother," said Harpreet, raising her right wrist. "Now, then, which one of you collects fines? Or, considering the large amount I am certain to owe, would it be best to distribute the funds evenly?"

Having readied the vehicle as much as was possible short of starting the noisy drive engine, Jess allowed herself to watch Harpreet and her brother. She saw one of the armored officers take Harpreet's right wrist and scan it. A hopeful smile crept across Jess's face. *Harpreet is* so *good at this*, she thought.

Then the officer grabbed her other wrist and scanned it as well.

"*No!*" Jess murmured. Would they arrest her for double chipping? Or might Harpreet have enough funds to buy the officer's silence regarding her second chip? Jess wondered if she should run out as well, to offer the currency stored on her chip. How much would it take? She didn't know. She hadn't paid close attention to the lessons on bribery.

But, no. Something was wrong. Very wrong. She heard her brother emit a low hum, monotone, sustained. Then she saw a second officer approach Harpreet with a billy club held high. Through her earpiece, Jess heard the sound of the weapon as it connected with her friend's tiny form. Harpreet fell, and Jess cried out silently—*no!*—and in that moment she felt very small, very young, and completely inadequate.

Two officers raised Harpreet—*gentle* Harpreet—forcing her arms up and over their shoulders. Within her ear, Ethan's hum grew into a quiet tune. Her brother *never* hummed anything but one sustained note. But as she listened, she heard him humming a child's ditty. The goodbye song visiting children sang when playtime with the planetary dog ended. *Goodbye, goodbye, next year we'll both have grown, goodbye, goodbye, we leave you now for home.*

Why the goodbye song? What was her brother doing?

He was telling her to leave.

Her eyes stung with tears, hot and sharp.

Yes. It was time to leave. She had a job to do. As she slipped quietly from the vehicle, sling-pack over one shoulder, her eyes caught on something familiar: a plastic container on the back seat. Ethan's collected items, lying atop his wafer-computer. Her heart seemed to split in two and she felt one of the halves float out of her 'til it came to rest beside the carefully arranged items. Tenderly, she retrieved her brother's wafer. She didn't trust herself to gather his collection without tears.

No tears, she commanded herself.

From inside her head, she could hear a single Terran voice. A commanding officer had arrived and the others kept silent before him.

Jess shifted the heavy cloak to cover her as she walked away from the vehicle. *One hundred meters*, she told herself. *Then destroy the transport. Then take the food home.*

Her earpiece relayed a crisp single voice. "That's the pair of them, commander."

Take longer strides, she told herself, bowing under the weight of the cloak that shielded her from the officers.

"Counselor, proclaim the pertinent section of The Bill of Human Rights to the inciters."

Fifty steps to go, Jess told herself.

"All citizens of Earth share certain inalienable rights including the right to live out a span of two-and-seventy years."

Keep going. Thirty steps more. Each step felt harder than the last.

"Read the findings against the prisoners."

Twenty-nine. Twenty-eight, she counted. *Don't look back*. Her weight seemed to increase in an exponential relationship to her distance from her brother.

"Citizens of Earth, you have been found guilty of attempting acts of terror against your fellow citizens and an act of treason against their government."

Don't look back don't look back don't look back.

"Pronounce the sentence," said the commanding officer.

Take another ten steps, she told herself. *And then ten more. Then you're done.*

"You are each required to perform acts of manual labor beneficial to those citizens you have attempted to harm. You will receive reorientation training during the balance of the remaining years of your life. Your current bodies will be entered into general reclamation and you will be assigned geriatric bodies in which to carry out your sentences."

This isn't happening, Jess told herself. But it was. She turned, the weight of her cloak insignificant beside the weight of her sorrow. One hundred meters stretched between her and the transport. She collapsed to the ground, spent.

"Prisoners, turn slowly about."

Jess saw her brother turning, saw Harpreet being turned. Ethan hummed the goodbye song again.

"I'll find you," Jess whispered. He would hear that. Would it give him hope? Courage?

Ethan hummed the goodbye refrain more loudly.

"Officers, *fire*," called the commander.

From inside her earpiece, Jess heard two light popping sounds, like birthday balloons punctured at a party.

Harpreet and Ethan crumpled to the ground.

Jess stared wild-eyed, her face folding into an origami of pain.

Jessamyn, the girl who slept surrounded by words, had no language to express what she felt.

19

JOB TO DO

Dawn stretched across the sky, a sickly white which spread like fungus. Slowly, the greys of night gave way to a world tinted with color. Jessamyn's eyes distinguished red-tones in the guards' armor which, minutes before, had appeared as merely *dark*. A flare of light from their hover-transport confirmed the red of the armored officer carrying her brother's unconscious body.

Jess remembered Brian Wallace's injunction against bribing members of the Red Squadron Forces. Surely Harpreet had remembered it, too. The old pirate had gambled and lost. Jess felt a fierce anger burning its way through layers of numbing pain.

Why hadn't Harpreet tried something *else*? They could have snuck the cloaked vehicle closer and tried a rescue. Harpreet could have approached under cover of the smaller cloak and thrown it over Ethan while Jess distracted the guards. They could have blown up their vehicle—a certain distraction! Surely there were dozens of other scenarios which would have ended better than the one Harpreet had chosen.

Jess shook her head. *It doesn't matter now. You've got a job to do.*

She crouched under the weighty cloak, awaiting the moment when she could detonate her abandoned vehicle. Ethan's earpiece continued to transmit, and she heard confused chatter aboard the departing Red Squadron transport. Eager for a name, a destination, something to tell her where her brother and Harpreet would be taken, she listened, breath held. And then her lungs seemed to compress as she realized she had *no* hope of finding Kipper. Or even knowing if she lived still. It was all wrong, so wrong. It was the destruction of the Red Dawn all over again. She forced herself to take a deep breath, to prove that the weight upon her lungs was a nothing, born of imagination.

From beneath her dark glove, Jess's chrono-tattoo glowed faintly red, mocking her loss of her brother with its refusal to change color as the hover-transport lifted off and crossed the sky, taking him away.

Don't think about it, she ordered herself. *Just destroy the transport.*

Her hand shook as she raised the detonator that would erase any damning evidence pointing to Skye or to Mars. She had no idea whether the device could transmit a signal while the heavy cloaking garment covered her. Deciding not to risk a malfunction, Jess shifted the weighty cloak back so that it lay in stiff folds against the building beside which she crouched. Lifting her black-gloved hand once again, she toggled an "on" switch and tapped a glowing button.

The transport came visible for a split second, lit from inside as the interior blew to pieces. Windows shattered outward and the cloaking tarp billowed, then settled itself back upon the transport, minus the bits which had covered the windows. The vehicle remained difficult to detect. Beside it, a derelict truck rocked gently, as from a gust of strong wind.

Jess stood to leave, folding her own rumpled cloak until it was no larger than a computing wafer. As she tucked it inside the sling-pack between her brother's wafer and a folder of first aid items, she thought she heard a tiny something. A mere ghost of noise. Not hearing anything more, however, she decided the sound must have been one of the many coming from inside her earpiece. Unfortunately, she was wrong.

Strong arms grabbed both of her hands from behind, twisting one arm to the point where she felt sure bones would shatter.

An angry voice whispered beside her ear, “Give me one good reason why you shouldn’t die right now.”

20

THE MOST ELOQUENT PERSUADER

Jessamyn recognized the voice, even colored with anger.

"Pavel?" she whispered.

"One good reason, Jessamyn," he said.

"Let go," she said. "You're hurting my arm."

"Not good enough," he said. "I saw you blow something up. Your brother—you're *inciters*! You don't deserve to live after what you've done."

Pavel punctuated his words by twisting her arm higher behind her back.

"We're not terrorists. It's all a mistake. You have to help me save my family!" She winced as he gripped her arm more tightly. "You have to believe me, Pavel!"

"You want me to believe you over Budapest's Red Squadron Forces?" Pavel swore. "I saw what you did, Jessamyn. Or whatever your real name is. And I saw you were double-chipped, back when you needed a bike. Who does that unless they have something to hide?"

"Jess *is* my real name. And if you saw everything, then you know my brother and my friend are in terrible danger. They didn't do anything wrong. Please believe me."

"So what are you doing on the wrong side of a barrier you shouldn't be able to cross? And what was your brother attempting in a strategic deep-space communications facility?"

Jess's heartbeat increased. "My brother wouldn't harm a leaf of . . . *kale*." She'd been about to say "algae" as Marsians did, but doubted Pavel would have understood.

"What?"

Apparently her substitute word was no better.

"Your security force picked up the wrong people!" Jess cried. "Ethan is gentle. He'd never hurt anyone. And Harpreet . . . she's as generous as a dog."

"Are you taking narcotics?" asked Pavel.

Just then, from inside her earpiece, Jess heard the phrase she'd been praying for—a location: *New Kelen Hospital.*

Pavel spoke again, slowly and clearly. "Here's what's going to happen. I'm going to release one of your arms so I can summon emergency services. If you attempt to escape or fight me in any way, I'll break your arm. Understand?"

"No!" cried Jess. "You can't call them! They'll re-body me. You have no idea what's at stake here. I've got people depending on me. Thousands!"

"So you *are* an inciter?"

"Of course not!" Jessamyn remembered words her father often spoke to her mother: *The truth is the most eloquent persuader of all.* But she couldn't risk the truth.

Pavel grip tightened.

"Ow! That hurts. Release me," Jess pleaded. "Please, you've got to release me."

"You're not very strong, for someone mixed up in this kind of mess," muttered Pavel. He eased his grip, but he didn't let go. "So start talking."

Jess took a deep breath. Now the earpiece was emitting the sounds of several voices and machinery. It would only distract her. She could risk a few minutes not hearing Ethan's surroundings now that she knew where he was. She shook her head sharply to one side, to disable the device.

Unfortunately, Pavel took her action as a hostile move.

Jess heard a sickening crack of bone breaking. She knew it had to be hers, although for a moment after the sound, she didn't feel anything. And then she did. She moaned, long and low, as the pain enveloped every other sense.

She heard Pavel swear and then felt him release her, gently. Her throat continued to produce a moaning she knew wasn't helping anything, but she couldn't make the sound stop. Then she noticed, as if she were outside of her body and observing it, that Pavel had jammed something sharp into her upper arm. The pain from the broken limb dissipated instantly, but a soft fog drifted over her, intensifying the sensation that she'd left her body.

"Does that help the pain?" asked Pavel. He sounded very far away.

Oh, it's Pavel, thought Jessamyn. "Mmm-hmm," she murmured. Her tongue felt thick. She watched through half-closed eyes as Pavel placed something on her dead-feeling arm over the section she knew (in a vague sort of way) had been broken. The something began to wind a white, gauzy membrane around and around her lower arm. It was like watching a video of a caterpillar making a cocoon. Why was Pavel putting her inside a cocoon, she wondered?

"Why?" she murmured. Speech came with great difficulty.

"It's just a bone-set," said Pavel. "Listen, I'm sorry I broke your arm. At least, I think I am. Maybe I shouldn't be. I'm going to give you a stimulant, and then I want you to tell me everything, Jessamyn. One side effect of what I'm giving you is that you will have a harder time telling lies. Don't try. Your pulse and oxygenation levels are terrible, so don't go wasting your energy by lying to me."

Pavel stuck a patch with many hair-fine needles onto her upper arm. She felt the moment the stimulant hit her bloodstream. Alertness returned, and with it, a panicked sense that she should be somewhere.

"New Kelen," she mumbled.

"What?" asked Pavel. "Do you want me to take you to the hospital? Are you ready to confess?"

"No. Yes." Jess shook her head in frustration. "*No*, I don't want to go to the hospital. Unless you'll let me go alone."

"Not a chance, Jessamyn."

She felt a moment's irritation. Or wrongness. She had to correct him. "Call me Jess. Jessamyn's too formal for our friendship."

Where did that come from? She shook her head and took a slow breath in.

"What are you doing here?" Pavel demanded once more.

"I'm not Terran," she heard herself saying. "I'm Marsian. From Mars Colonial. We are trying to grow algae. We have exactly one dog." Jess clapped her good hand over her mouth in shock. It was as though she had no control over her speech: things came trickling out—things that she *knew* she couldn't reveal.

"Nice try," said Pavel. "But you shouldn't struggle against telling the truth. Trust me, your body is in bad shape right now." He seemed to be consulting read-outs from a device he'd attached to her forefinger.

"We came here from Mars to get some items we need." Jess cursed herself for letting slip information she knew she shouldn't share. "What was in that patch?"

"It's *Equidima.* It'll be a lot easier if you stop fighting it and simply tell me the truth," said Pavel.

"I *am* telling the truth," said Jess. "Look in my pack. See if you recognize the manufacturer of *any* of the items in there."

Pavel regarded her suspiciously. "You want me to look through your stuff?" He took the sling-pack. "Maybe this is some passive way of telling me the truth, huh? I've heard of patients responding to Equidima like that. You got explosives in here? Manifestos?"

Jess shook her head in frustration.

Pavel lowered his voice. "I'd really like to help you, Jess, but you picked a bad morning to get mixed up in all this."

"You should go," she said. "I don't want you missing your exam because of me."

"I'm not going anywhere until we get this straightened out," said Pavel.

He'd pulled out Ethan's wafer and it greeted him with a slide show of pictures from home—Jess's heart contracted.

"That's where we live," she said softly. "I'm not lying about Mars."

Pavel looked up, shaking his head. "I'll admit you've got some weird stuff in here. And not weird like I was expecting. A first aid folder? Ration bars? And whatever this metal thing is." He pointed to a flat bar of tellurium.

"It's meant to help me in the event I'm separated from my crew," said Jess. Tears formed and spilled onto her cheeks. "Does this *Equi*-stuff make you . . . cry?" She'd been about to say "waste water."

Pavel's mouth twisted in a frustrated grimace. "Don't cry."

"My readings," said Jess, blinking back the shameful tears. "You said my body's in bad shape."

"Your bone density's terrible, your oh-two levels are off, you're *severely* malnourished. Jess, whatever crowd you've been running with, have you considered that they don't have your best interests at heart?"

"Those readings," said Jess, speaking quickly now, "Would they be consistent with someone who lived her entire life on Mars?"

Pavel's shoulders raised in a small kind of shrug. "Sure, Jessamyn. But we both know that's not what's happening here. Just tell me the truth."

"Run any kind of test you like. Prove I'm lying."

Pavel looked at her, eyes narrowing. "You really believe you're from Mars, huh? Someone's brainwashed you good."

"*Test me.*"

Pavel turned, muttering to himself, something about proving to her she'd never been to Mars, whatever memories she had to the contrary.

As he attached items from his med kit to parts of her body, she tilted her head to reactivate the transmitter. Pavel, preoccupied with his investigation, didn't respond this time.

He spoke, as if to himself. "These readings are . . . wrong. This can't be right." He stared in confusion at his instruments. "Can I . . . do you mind if I take a sample of your blood?"

Jess held her hand out. It felt heavy, even by Earth standards, and it drooped.

Pavel, noticing the sluggish motion, apologized. "There was a muscle retardant in the first shot I gave you. Your arm must feel weak."

"Heavy," said Jess. "Everything's too heavy on your planet. Why would anyone live here?" She knew she was rambling, but the words just kept plunking out, like drops of water melting off an ice sculpture.

"Shizer," said Pavel. "*Shizer!*" He looked at her with suspicion. "These results can't be real," he muttered. "This is impossible."

It was the right moment for Jess to press her advantage. But from inside her earpiece, she could hear two people discussing the "young-body"—her brother's body. They might have a match for him. They want to prep him immediately.

"No!" cried Jess. The sound wrenched from deep inside her, trailing off into an extended wail.

Pavel grabbed her arms again, his instruments clattering onto the pavement. He shouted at her to calm down, but all Jessamyn could hear were the voices dooming her brother.

She turned her face, grief-stricken, to look at Pavel. "They're going to give away my brother's body. What kind of planet is this? How can people do such a thing?"

Pavel's grip upon her arm relaxed. "You're really *Martian*?"

"Mar*sian*, yes. Now, let me go!" Jessamyn's voice rose in pitch, frantic. "They're making a horrible mistake. My brother's innocent!"

Pavel snatched up the array of items surrounding them, stuffing some into Jess's pack, some into his med kit. "I'm giving you a different stimulant," he said. "Some of your pain might come back, but you'll be able to walk. I'm taking you to New Kelen, and I'll call my aunt, see if she can get some kind of . . . interplanetary . . . immunity . . . or something for your brother." He jabbed another sharp into her arm. "This better be real, Jess."

Jessamyn's attention was horribly divided. She heard Pavel's words, and at his mention of "interplanetary," part of her panicked—Marsians couldn't be found in breach of the No Contact Accords. But her audio implant was relaying medical language, and she realized some sort of operation had begun. Her next words come out so softly Pavel barely hear them.

"No. Oh, please, *please*, no."

21

LIFE ON MARS

Jess rose, desperate to get to the New Kelen hospital. Hurriedly, she explained about the device in her ear. "They're doing the procedure! It will kill him, being in someone else's body," she moaned, grabbing Pavel with her good arm to rush him along.

"What are they saying?" asked Pavel. "There's no way they've started the transfer this soon, Jess." He pulled on Jessamyn's hand, his greater strength forcing her to stop. "I know how this works. Trust me." His eyes bored into hers. "I need you to tell me the exact words you're hearing."

Jess listened for a moment. "Something about *stasis* and a big number . . ."

"They're prepping him for stasis while they locate a recipient. Stasis means there's still time. Is he young?"

"Two years older than me."

"Hmm. That's sixteen extra years as a threebody." Pavel frowned. "That's the big number under discussion. They're probably going to enter the extra years in a lottery, which means we've got several hours to straighten things out, okay?"

"Okay," she murmured in response.

Jess's mind felt clearer as the drug wore off, and she began to realize the gravity of the step she'd taken in telling Pavel about Mars. "I never should have told you where I'm from," she whispered.

"We thought everyone on Mars died a century ago." The look in Pavel's eyes shifted. No longer grave, they appeared now wild with elation. "This is huge. Even Lucca will see that. Although, it doesn't look good, your brother coming *here*, of all places. Unless . . . did you need directions to get home? How many of you are there? Why did you come?"

Jess shook her head slowly, trying to decide which questions were the important ones to answer. Which answers would encourage Pavel to help her and keep her visit to Earth secret.

"When I saw those readings from your blood—the peroxide, the accumulation of sulfur derivatives, the absence of normal toxins—Jess! This is incredible! Mars!" He threw both hands up in the air, staring at the sky in disbelief. "You'll be subjected to additional testing before they'll believe it, of course. But, what I can see here . . . it would be impossible to fake even these readings without replacing every bone in your body . . . every blood cell . . ."

"Pavel," Jess placed a hand on his arm. "Pavel, no one else on Earth can know about me. About my crew. My planet is starving. If I can't get home—*now*—while Earth and Mars are close, they will die. All of them."

Pavel brows drew together. "Well, I'm sure that won't be a problem. I mean, Lucca will probably want a representative to go back with you, or maybe an exchange. I don't know. But it's not like they'd stop you from leaving. I don't think."

Jess shook her head. "Mars has broken the No Contact Accords. Repeatedly. I know you're happy to hear there's still life on Mars, but that doesn't mean everyone on your planet would be glad to hear it."

Pavel consulted his timepiece nervously. "I don't think you're here to attack Earth," he murmured.

Jess laughed, her voice pitched high. "Attack? With what? There's so few of us left, the idea is ludicrous."

"Then let me help you. My aunt has influence—"

"You said your aunt and you disagree on important things. It's a risk I cannot—*must not*—take, Pavel. I never would have told you the truth without that drug. It's the most basic command we're given. *No contact.*"

"Jessamyn," said Pavel, his low voice gentle, soft as her banquet gown. He placed a hand upon her face, ran his thumb across her lower lip. "No contact?" He smiled, clearly recalling the moment his mouth had touched hers. "What are you doing here, girl from Mars?"

Jessamyn's color rose as she remembered their kiss. "I'm here to save my planet." Then, even quieter, "Will you help me?"

"You want me to help you by . . . by doing nothing?"

Jess nodded. "Please. Please keep my secret."

Pavel squinted, staring east at the sunrise. "I don't know how Lucca would react," he admitted. "I'd like to think she would act with compassion, but there have been times . . . Maybe you should go, like you said, without me calling Lucca. Hey, you had some kind of camouflage. I saw you take it off and fold it up."

"Yes," said Jessamyn. "Hard to see, though not undetectable."

"That could be useful," said Pavel. "Jessamyn—you're sure you want to try rescuing your brother on your own?"

She knew she shouldn't. She couldn't. Saving her planet *had* to come first. But she heard the words tumbling out: "I have to try."

"He'll be guarded. He's—his *body* is valuable. You should wait until 2:00 this afternoon. There will be a shift change and you'll have a better shot at . . . whatever you're planning. Don't tell me what it is. I'm hopeless under Equidima." He shoved his med kit into Jess's sling pack. "You might need this. There are stim-patches in there that will bring your brother out of stasis. You'll need two. They're marked *Primatum*. This is crazy, you know? What identity do you have in your right chip?"

"Um," Jess stared at her two wrists. "Retired fourbody."

"Good. Lots of fourbodies volunteer at New Kelen. Check in through the back entrance. Here—hold out your wrist. I'm going to transfer my hospital entry clearance to you. " He extended his arm over hers. "Hopefully it doesn't expire today."

"Thank you," murmured Jess.

"Get into volunteer scrubs and then do whatever you're planning to do. The video cams are broken in the bay of physician-only elevators. That can be a good place for you to hide out for awhile."

Jess nodded and her brow wrinkled.

"Ah, *shizer*, Jess. This is insane." Pavel took her hand in his. "Let me call my aunt. Let me help."

She shook her head, gazing at her hand—so pale—enclosed within his.

Then she withdrew her hand, saying, "You could give me a lift to that motor pool two blocks away. Anything else—I'm afraid it wouldn't be helpful. I can't gamble my planet's safety. And you've got your exam."

Pavel's lips pulled tight; she saw how his mind was torn.

"You've done all anyone could," she said. "Thank you for everything."

"Everything except the broken arm," said Pavel, flushing.

"I'm sure you'll be a great physician," said Jessamyn.

The two climbed on Pavel's bike, Jess as the passenger this time. She folded her cocooned arm awkwardly around his waist, catching it with her good arm. Her eyes pressed closed with the small heartbreak of holding so close that from which she must divide herself.

"Oh, hey," said Pavel. "You can remove the cast this evening. Any time after 8:00 p.m. Until then, your left wrist won't scan at all."

Jessamyn laughed, a tiny sort of noise in the quiet flush of dawn. "You do realize that the last thing I need right now is for that chip to be readable? Double-chipping? Not good. Plus, my left chip could link me to the events here."

"Oh. Yeah. So, nice coincidence, huh? If I had to injure you, at least I picked the correct arm."

Jess recalled the words of Secretary General Mei Lo, millions of kilometers away: *I don't believe in coincidences, Jessamyn.*

"Some coincidence," she murmured.

They reached the motor pool.

"The hoverport is right there at the hospital, by the way," said Pavel. "You can rent just about anything."

"Thank you. I won't forget you, Pavel," said Jessamyn. She leaned in, leaving a breath of a kiss upon his cheek, and was gone.

Pavel waited until he saw Jessamyn speeding away on a 300 series hover-bike. "What are you planning, Jess?" he muttered to himself. Then he turned his own bike around and headed for what he knew by rights should be the most important event of his life: his first-body exams. Except everything felt different now. The kiss of the girl from the ice planet burned on his cheek. *The Mars Colony had survived.*

How was it even possible? But she'd said they were starving. A strange resolve began filtering its way through Pavel. For years, he'd thought he wanted to be a doctor, to help people. Apart from piloting, it was all he'd ever wanted. *But what if he could help those who lived on another planet?*

With that dawning idea, Pavel formed a new plan for taking the test. He couldn't answer questions the same way he would have done yesterday, the way that would lead him to become a physician. The solar system had shifted since he had met Jessamyn, and Pavel had shifted as well, tumbling wildly in its wake.

22

FLOOR TWELVE

Jessamyn sped toward New Kelen Hospital. The audio comm in her ear was clear of voices once more; she heard only whirring noises and periodic beeps, which meant her brother must be alone. She took that to be good. Already near central Budapest, it took her mere minutes to reach the hospital.

The task before her, instead of terrifying her, seemed to bring all emotions to a new level of calm. She'd broken the most important rule of the mission, however influenced by the drug, and yet the person who'd heard the truth had trusted her, had let her go. Pavel, far from turning her over to the authorities, had *helped* her. She felt as though she could take on a squadron of red-clad officers.

She recognized the cool and settled feeling in her belly. It was how she felt when flying into a dangerous situation. Where others panicked, Jessamyn's mind cleared and her determination increased. She would rescue her brother, somehow, and take the Galleon back to Mars.

She found the employees' parking lot and left her borrowed craft in a long row of similar vehicles. The morning air was warm and sweet-smelling and Jess found herself casting her eyes about, looking for the source of the scent. She saw scrubby plants with blooms of white and violet. A large sign informed her she was entering an herb garden. She saw a few yawning workers pausing several feet short of the building doors to scan their wrists, which caused a low gate to open for them. Like her, all wore black, and Jessamyn felt certain it must be in recognition of yesterday's losses—the workers grieving the deaths of their fellows in London and Paris. Proceeding to the scanning station, Jess felt her heart begin to race.

This better work, she thought, holding out her right wrist.

A red light flashed at the scan-site. The barrier remained in place.

Hades and Ares! Pavel's clearance must have expired today, after all.

The barrier was low and she could probably jump over it. But a wall of windows faced her, which meant someone could easily notice. She turned back, casually, hoping to make it look as though she'd changed her mind about going in for now.

She saw another woman seating herself upon a marble bench beside a low row of purple-spiked flowers.

"G'morning," said the woman.

"G'morning," said Jessamyn. She'd done well, pronouncing and intoning the greeting correctly.

"You volunteering today?" asked the seated woman.

"Yes," replied Jessamyn.

"Thought so. They told me I couldn't scan in until 6:00 a.m. on the dot," said the woman. "I'm Dana. I'm new."

Jess nodded, realizing the woman probably thought she was a regular. She decided not to offer her name.

Dana didn't wait for it, addressing Jessamyn again. "I just felt like I had to do something, after watching the news all day yesterday. Anyway, retirement's overrated." She laughed.

Jess realized the woman was a fourbody, healthy and youthful, like herself.

"How'd you do that?" asked the woman, gesturing to Jessamyn's cast.

"Hover-bike accident," Jess replied. The lie came quickly, easily. Her belly purred, cool and ready for anything.

"New fourbody, huh?" The woman smiled, shaking her head. "You'll learn. We all go a little crazy making the final transition. But your new body's not indestructible."

"Lesson learned," said Jess, attempting light laughter. "Say, I wonder if you'd let me in on your scan? Mine won't read through this." She lifted her cast.

"Of course, honey," said the woman. "Guess that's a hint for me to get off my gorgeous young posterior." She giggled.

Jess smiled and followed her, passing through the barrier without further problem. Her earpiece continued its whirs and beeps.

Jess passed a sign reading *New Volunteer Registration* and said goodbye to Dana.

Glancing rapidly about her surroundings, Jess moved as though confident of her destination. An alcove marked "clean gowns" caught her attention. Someone had taped a notice which read "Absolutely No Soiled Gowns" beside the alcove. She smiled. This was way too easy. She grabbed a clean gown and layered it over her black garb. *You look official,* she said to a reflection of herself as she passed a window on her way to the *physician's only* bay of elevators.

She garnered a few stares, but no one spoke to her. As she approached the elevators, she slowed, allowing someone with a working chip to precede her. She took the time to read the descriptions of the floors, looking for something that would take her to . . . *Consciousness Transfer*. Floor Twelve.

As doctors entered and exited the elevator, Jess caught a scent so familiar, so *homelike*. Peroxide, she realized. They must use it for its hygienic value. Mars's high levels of the chemical stood in the way of greenhouse success, according to her mother. It had been one of the things Pavel noticed in her blood. She felt a wave of homesickness.

Arms crossed, eyes to the floor so as to discourage interaction, Jessamyn gathered information about the hospital from her corner of the elevator. Unfortunately, it appeared she would have to ride up and down until someone scanned for the floor she wanted. Well, Pavel had said she had hours, encouraging her to wait until 2:00 p.m. She could wait. Unless she heard something in her ear that indicated action was required.

She took advantage of the empty elevator to examine the patches Pavel had slipped to her from his med kit, locating the two he'd said would awaken Ethan from stasis. She was going to need her brother's hacking wizardry to get them out of the secured hospital. Ethan would know what to do, she told herself, although for a brief moment, she felt a twinge of longing for Harpreet and, yes, even for Kipper. Jess had never felt more alone.

No one had planned for a means of communication between raiders, who typically stayed together. Oh, she would have plenty of suggestions for the Academy board of directors when they reached home.

Ten minutes passed in the elevator. Twenty. No new sounds from Ethan's location. Finally a group of men and women requested the twelfth floor.

They entered deep in discussion of yesterday's tragic bombings. As Jessamyn listened, she realized they were discussing *Harpreet and Ethan*!

"One of them was a kid still in his original body," said a graying doctor, "His age indicates he should have transferred two years ago."

"Terrorists don't follow the rules," said a female physician. "Those extra years will go for a premium. How's the reassignment going to be decided? Lottery?"

The graying doctor grunted. "I can tell you one thing: it won't be anyone we know. Go ahead and enter the lottery if you want, but mark my words. It will be a business tycoon or politician, most likely."

"What about the other one?" asked the woman.

"Arthritic, threebody age, only a few extra years, but also appears to have stayed in her first-body. With the arthritis, the extra years won't have the appeal. My guess is they ship her off to the work-camp with no re-body at all. Completely off record, obviously."

"Hmm," intoned the woman.

A new group entered the elevator.

"It all comes down to security," said the loudest of the new group. "You can't let people wander around a hospital like they'd wander around a public park."

One of the new women to enter the elevator stared at Jessamyn. Jess, trying to melt farther into her corner, avoided eye contact.

The elevator settled on floor twelve. *I'm coming, Ethan.* Her heart beat a little faster.

"Ma'am?" The woman who had been staring at Jessamyn spoke.

Jess ignored the question, hoping she addressing another physician.

"Ma'am," said the woman, more firmly this time.

Three physicians remained in the elevator. Jess tried to exit, but they blocked her. Everyone stared at Jessamyn. Everyone who, moments ago, had been discussing hospital security.

23

IT WAS MADNESS

Pavel couldn't rid his thoughts of the phrases repeating in his mind.

You shouldn't have let her go. You shouldn't. You shouldn't have let her go.

What she hoped to do began to sound more and more impossible as he thought it through. It was madness. But Jess had something about her, some attitude, that made you believe she could do the impossible.

What if he followed her? Apart from asking for Lucca's assistance, could he help, he wondered? What could he offer? He was a mere first-body with some piloting know-how and some medical know-how and no idea how to help someone steal a body from a hospital. And then there was the small problem of his exam. Exams weren't reschedulable. Not even for Lucca Brezhnaya's nephew. Not that he would accept that kind of favoritism. If there was one thing *always* true of Pavel, it was that he despised special treatment. Pavel loved liberty, fraternity, and equality: the three pillars upon which Terran government rested.

If he went back to help Jess, missing his exam, he'd be picked up off the street and re-bodied for a life in mining. It was whispered that was what happened to no-shows. This was the kind of rumor Lucca and her government would have encouraged to make sure eighteen-year-olds didn't skip exams and try to pass themselves off as retired fourbodies. Not that you could pretend for long, thought Pavel. As soon as anyone scanned you, you'd be in deep *shize*.

Which Jessamyn would also be in if he tried to help by calling his aunt, he reluctantly admitted to himself. He knew Lucca too well. She wouldn't care about Jess or Marsians—she would seek a way to turn the rediscovery of living Marsians into a Terran advantage. No, he had no way to help Jessamyn.

There was only one place for Pavel right now, however little he might like it. And that place was sitting at a screen answering approximately one-hundred sixty-nine questions to establish an apprenticeship match.

Pavel shook his head and gunned his bike engine.

24

CHIP SCAN

Jessamyn held her head high, glared imperiously at the three detaining her. Instinct told her playing *bold* like Kipper had done with the officers would pay off much better than trying to run. "Can I help you?" Jess asked. "Is there a problem?"

The woman's lips pursed. "These elevators are reserved for physicians."

"They always over-medicate fracture patients," murmured one of the graying men to the other. "The ones in her age bracket whine a lot."

Jess whipped her head his direction realizing the gown which she had taken for *doctor*-clothing must be *patient*-clothing. "There's nothing wrong with my hearing, young man. And I assure you I am not overmedicated. I was informed this elevator would take me to floor twelve for cast removal."

"You want the *second* floor. You should have been given an escort," said the woman.

"I declined an escort," said Jessamyn.

"I'll take her to second-floor reception," said the lab-coated man who'd been lecturing the others on security. "And I'll give them a piece of my mind regarding wandering patients."

"That won't be necessary," said Jessamyn.

But the doctor had already scanned the call button for floor two. He then placed a heavy hand upon Jessamyn's shoulder as the doors slid silently shut. Jess felt all the folly of not bothering to confirm that she'd chosen the correct gown for her disguise.

Speaking to himself the physician muttered, "This is exactly the sort of ineptitude that led to yesterday's tragedies."

As the elevator plunged, so did Jess's heart, feeling heavier with every added floor away from her brother.

The doctor led her into a large room. A glance across the room revealed people dressed like herself, many staring into the distance, eyes vacant. Some slept. Jess felt uneasy in the large and open space with its over-tall Terran ceiling. The chairs were broken into small groupings making her think of a cluster of rooms that should have walls but didn't. Potted plants were scattered with the careless abandon of those dwelling on a water-planet. It was an utterly alien setting, precisely calculated to add to her unease.

The physician, pulling Jess with him to the front of a queue, demanded to see the floor manager. Beeps, whirs, and blips sounded from the nurses' station, echoing the noise inside Jessamyn's earpiece.

"And get someone from security over here," added the doctor. "I want a chip scan on this fourbody."

She felt dread lodge in her stomach—how would she rescue Eth if she couldn't get free herself? Jessamyn swallowed. She could only solve one problem at a time; it was the same as flying an uncooperative craft. *One problem at a time.*

Several people in the room were now casting unfriendly glares at the line-cutting physician, and Jess took advantage of their collective ill will to demand that he unhand her. To her amazement, he complied.

A woman approached Jess from behind the nurse's station. "I'm Nurse Yoko," she said to Jess, smiling. "I'm just going to get your vitals."

"Does that require my consent?" asked Jess.

Still smiling, Nurse Yoko replied. "Yes, dear, of course."

"I'm withholding it, then," said Jess. "No consent. No vitals."

The nurse looked puzzled. "I guess we can wait a minute. Let's start with who you are and what you're here for today, then, shall we? Cast removal, is it?"

"Obviously," said Jessamyn. "I need some fresh air, if you'll excuse me."

The nurse gently blocked Jess's exit path. "I'm sorry, but there's a physician with twelfth floor clearance who's insisting we get some ID for you first."

At that moment, a member of hospital security arrived beside Jess and the nurse.

Holy Ares, thought Jessamyn. *Here goes.*

"Ma'am, I'm going to need an ID scan," said the security officer.

Jess held her cast-encased arm before the officer. "Be my guest," she said.

The security officer frowned and returned to the desk.

Nurse Yoko said, "You're a lefty, are you? Me, too."

The security officer returned after conferring with the physician. "Who is your doctor, ma'am?" he asked Jess.

She fumbled. "I . . . I can't remember the young man's name."

The nurse spoke in a rapid undertone to the officer. "Memory issues are common among fourbodies." She turned to Jess. "How about we make you comfortable until we can get someone from your family to vouch for your identity?"

"I live alone," said Jess.

"In that case," said the nurse, "I'm afraid we're going to need to set you up somewhere until that cast is ready to come off."

"I'll wait outside, thank you," said Jess, turning to make a break for it.

The security officer was on her instantly, his grip like iron. "You're not going anywhere until we get a confirmation that you belong in this hospital," he said.

"I'm sorry, dear," added the nurse. "But you know what it's been like since the attacks yesterday. Let's just get you some place comfortable. When is your cast due for removal? Do you remember that much?"

Jess felt a bead of sweat sliding down her back, a sensation entirely new and just as entirely unwelcome. "I'm not certain," she said, playing for time. She remembered Pavel's words that the cast could come off in the evening. That meant she had several hours in which to manage her own escape and plan for her brother's.

"All right-y, then," said the nurse. "Let's get you settled in."

The nurse led the security officer, with Jess in tow, down a corridor and into a small examination room.

But when the officer attempted to enter the room, the nurse seemed to swell to twice her size. "No," she said to the secure. "You will wait outside. This is a hospital, not a military zone."

The officer grunted and remained outside the room.

Nurse Yoko apologized. "One day and the whole world's turned upside down. I knew we'd have trouble with secures. You give them a centimeter and they try to take a kilometer. No regard for patient privacy." She smiled at Jess. "Fortunately, this is my floor, and I have a *high* regard for patient privacy."

"Hmmph," grunted Jess. "Thanks."

The nurse fluffed a pillow upon a small bed. "They're asking for permission to monitor in-room conversations, if you can believe it." She shook her head as though this would be the ultimate violation of patient rights. "Can I get you anything? Food? Something to drink?"

"I'm fine," Jess lied.

"Okay, then, I'll be back to check on you as often as I can. You can call for assistance right here," she said, indicating a screen panel. "And if you see the monitor light on your cast switch from red to green, you let me know right away, okay?"

Jess nodded.

The nurse smiled one last time and left, scolding the security officer on the far side of the door as it swung shut with a dull thud. When closed, the door blocked all sound, including Nurse Yoko's berating of the officer.

Jess stared at her surroundings. No window. One door. A basin into which it appeared water might collect. A *sink*, she recalled. And a bed. Jess crawled up on top of the rather high and narrow bed and buried her face in the pillow. It smelled faintly of peroxide, of home. When the tears began a moment later, Jessamyn let them fall. She had failed.

25

DEFERENTIAL TREATMENT

Pavel scanned into the exam-floor lobby alongside two hundred or so others who'd turned eighteen yesterday. A man dressed in a teach-suit approached Pavel, singling him out from the crowd as it shuffled forward.

"Mr. Brezhnaya-Bouchard," he said, dipping his head, "If you will step to one side, someone will be right with you to escort you to your exam screen. It is such an honor, sir."

Looking around, Pavel determined that no one else was getting this special treatment. He frowned. When his escort arrived, she chattered about high profile guests providing possible disturbances to other firsties.

"We want to offer everyone an equal chance to do their best in a distraction-free environment. I'm sure you understand." She smiled.

"Sure," muttered Pavel. He might despise the deference, but he had no wish to distract others on such an important day.

His own video screen sat in a smaller room off to one side from the main exam room. From the window next to him, Pavel could look down over the pool beside which he and Jessamyn had traced the constellations last night. He glanced skyward and his resolve hardened. He would take this exam with his new goal in mind: he wanted to help Marsians, and that meant a political career path in civil service, not medicine.

As he sat, trying to think about the exam and not the girl from Mars—*Mars!*—his mind raced, replaying the last twelve hours. He'd always planned to be a doctor, but in the past half-day of his life, everything had changed and now all he could think of was a red-haired girl from another world and how he might bring their two planets together once more.

The video screen in front of him flared to life. A pleasant voice directed him to scan in. He felt an eagerness to answer the questions—to begin the realignment of his new goals with his new future. The first question appeared, asking him what he would be most likely to do in the event he came upon persons requiring assistance. That was easy: *offer assistance while telling others to call emergency services.*

He flexed his fingers and glanced down at the pool once again. A second question appeared, asking him whether the statement, "*I enjoy helping others and I am good at it,*" was true or false for him. Clicking "True," he advanced to the third question which asked him to indicate which of several dozen journals he followed.

Pavel frowned. Why ask questions that could easily be verified? The examiners had access to the minutiae of Pavel's life including where he spent vacations, what tooth cleanser he used, *and* the name of every vid-journal he'd ever subscribed to. He checked the boxes beside *MEDICINE TODAY* and *GENETICS DAILY*.

The fourth question asked Pavel whether, within a surgery room, he could best imagine himself as a surgeon's assistant or as a surgeon. The question seemed innocuous enough, but Pavel didn't like the ways in which each question thus far seemed tilted toward a field in which he no longer had interest.

He selected "surgeon" as more likely to indicate that he saw himself in leadership roles rather than supportive roles.

The fifth question seemed to return the inquiries to more neutral territory: Did Pavel prefer tasks which were repetitive and predictable or those which provided challenge and surprise. He shook his head and chose *challenges and surprises.* But he didn't like the surprise awaiting him on the following screen.

Congratulations. You have been awarded a medical apprenticeship at New Kelen Hospital where you will train for a career in consciousness transfer.

He stared at the screen, first in shock. Then, outrage followed, and he mouthed a single word.

"*Lucca.*"

26

CRIME AGAINST HUMANITY

Jessamyn allowed herself to cry for a long, long while. It was shameful, wasting so much water. But she didn't care. She had no idea how to rescue her brother, much less how to find and rescue Harpreet or the Captain, and she felt alone and completely out of her depth. Jess may have been Mars's best pilot, but she had no training in stealing bodies from a secure facility.

A hospital orderly brought food to her room after an hour had passed. The smells assaulted her and she recognized the creamy scent of butter, but she found she'd lost her appetite for Terran foods. Ignoring the tray of food, she reached into her pocket, grasping the slippery foil wrapper of a nutrient bar. She was feeling the effects of sleep-deprivation, and she knew it would be foolhardy to add *hungry* to the mix.

Peeling back the copper ration-wrapper, she ate mechanically.

The food worked to warm her belly and the walls enclosing her offered comfort as well. Earth was too full of open spaces. She thought maybe she understood her brother a bit better, if in reverse. He reacted poorly to small spaces; she realized a slight level of unease had settled in her simply because she had been denied the comfort of low ceilings since arriving.

She leaned back against the wall. It vibrated slightly—constantly—like the walls of the Galleon. She closed her eyes so that she could arrange her options before her like one of Ethan's collections, but fatigue overwhelmed her, and in the small room—exhausted and insulated from all outside noise—she fell into a profound sleep.

~ ~ ~

Pavel Brezhnaya-Bouchard had never felt so angry. He considered simply never returning home as he haunted Budapest's avenues and alleys for the next several hours. He considered trying to find the girl from Mars—maybe she'd let him leave with her. This idea, he eventually rejected, reasoning that if he went missing, Lucca would call out the Red Squadron to find him. Pavel couldn't risk drawing the Terran military onto Jessamyn's trail. His hours of walking did little to calm him, only increasing his outrage over what his aunt had done. In the end, he hopped back on his hover-bike and sped home in order to rail at his aunt.

Seeing Lucca's palatial residence for the first time as a place he was about to *leave* instead of as a place he called home, he felt a flush of shame for his aunt's extravagance. The ostentatious building served as a perfect example of the basic difference between them: Pavel saw others as his equals; Lucca saw others as her inferiors, to be used in ways that benefited her or her agendas. The palatial dwelling? It reminded others, before they'd even caught sight of the woman who lived inside, that Lucca was wealthy and powerful. It begged the question, "Can you really afford to pit yourself against my will?"

"You can't buy *me*," growled Pavel as he parked his bike beside Lucca's three luxurious travel-sedans.

He stormed inside, shouting for his aunt.

Lucca's butler greeted Pavel. "Good morning, sir. I regret to tell you Chancellor Brezhnaya is sleeping and unavailable. May I offer you congratulations upon completing your examination?"

Pavel didn't respond. Lucca's servants were accustomed to being ignored. But then, despising himself for behaving like *her*, Pavel made a point of answering politely. "Thanks, Zussman."

"Your aunt arrived back from Singapore only two hours ago," said the butler. "She's planned a dinner to celebrate with you when she awakens and will be accompanying you to the hospital this evening *herself*." Zussman smiled. "Will there be anything else, sir?"

"No," said Pavel.

He took the set of stairs leading to his suite of rooms. When he reached them, he scanned his wrist to gain access to a passageway connecting his rooms with his aunt's sleeping quarters. It was something she'd set up years ago, when Pavel suffered nightmares. He hoped his chip would still open the passage. A door panel slid back and he smiled in grim satisfaction. One more example of his aunt's tendency to forget things she'd done for Pavel once they were done.

Lucca Brezhnaya, Prime Chancellor of the Terran Central Government, arranged her morning wake-up calls to imitate the experience of re-bodying. She loved the moment of awakening as a newly thirty-six-year-old, and she'd repeated threebodying a number of times—often enough to have developed the particular habits of a connoisseur. For instance, she liked to begin her awakening—whether to a new day or a new body—to the sound of Tibetan bells. Upon awakening, she kept her eyes closed and flexed her fingers. This was the signal to her attendants to offer bowls of warm rosewater for her hands. The ritual continued with further ablutions until Lucca began her workday. These twenty minutes were stolen, in some sense, from other more profitable activities, but she found the trade-off acceptable.

So, when her nephew stormed into her room three hours before she'd requested the Tibetan bells, she at first assumed she was having a bad dream. Pavel and his parents often featured in her nightmares. She supposed the bad dreams were a sort of punishment for what she'd done. If so, the nightmares were another trade-off she found acceptable for what her actions had bought her.

But this dream was a little *too* real. Lucca sat up in bed and realized Pavel was actually in her room. Was actually shouting at her.

". . . *no* excuse," he said. "And I won't go along with it. I won't. I'll volunteer for work as a satellite harvester."

Oh, thought Lucca. *We're having the conversation now.* She frowned, stretched her long white arms over her head and addressed her nephew. "Who, pray tell, am I to dismiss without references for letting you in at this hour?"

"No one. I used the passageway you set up when I was little."

"Hmm," she said, adding *passage closure* to a mental to-do list. "How did your exam go?"

"Exactly the way you set it up," said Pavel, crossing his arms.

Things tended to go the way she arranged them, Lucca thought, allowing herself a small smile.

"It's unfair to others, it's illegal, and I won't go along with it," he said.

Lucca took a calming breath, reached for a drink of artesian well-water. "Pavel, you're eighteen. It's time you stopped acting like a child." She let the barb sink in. "I've made certain provisions for your future. When you've heard them, I'm sure you'll agree that I've been most generous."

"I don't want your generosity," he said. "I want justice. That exam was a farce. Allow me to retake it, properly, or I swear I'll volunteer to sort space junk."

Lucca smiled. It was not a friendly smile. "*I* will pretend you're not making threats you are powerless to act upon. *You* will listen to what's going to happen. I've ensured you a career that millions would *kill* for. I've done so not because you are my nephew, but because, according to the surgeons and physicians who have worked alongside you, you are one of the most naturally gifted individuals they've encountered."

Pavel looked down. He'd grown accustomed to remarks like this in the past years.

"In fact, it was the current Head of Global Consciousness Transfer who suggested to me that we treat you as a unique case. That it would be depriving Earth's citizens to simply re-body you according to ordinary protocol. You are a prodigy. Like Mozart or Tsing."

Pavel's eyes flicked up. A hundred years ago, Tsing's government had refused to allow her to be re-bodied because of her musical genius. A war had very nearly ensued, but in the end, Tsing had fled to a neighboring country where she insisted upon being properly re-bodied rather than become the cause of global conflict.

Lucca continued. "In your case, as in Tsing's, to separate your mind from your body would be a crime against humanity."

"Tsing re-bodied," said Pavel. "It was the right thing to do then and it's the right thing to do now."

"Oh, grow up, Pavel. Of course Tsing wasn't permitted to re-body. There are times when exceptions must be made. Without Tsing in her original body, there would be no *International Anthem to Peace*."

"Wait," said Pavel, his mind jumping like a malfunctioning hopcraft. "Rosenfeldt wrote the *International Anthem to Peace*. Are you telling me Rosenfeldt was actually *Tsing*?"

"Of course she was Tsing. The new name was a necessary concession to keep the peace. These things must be handled discretely."

"These *things* are illegal!" roared Pavel. "I will *not* break the very law that's kept peace on Earth for—"

Lucca interrupted. "*I* keep the peace on Earth. The system only works because my government makes certain it works. Behind the scenes when necessary. You have no idea what costs must be paid to *keep peace* as you call it."

Pavel, caught between shock and outrage, recoiled as he admitted to himself several uncomfortable truths about his aunt. All his life thus far, he'd seen what he chose to see: a woman who loved the law enough to pursue an exhausting career as a politician. But if Pavel had been honest with himself, he would have admitted it was power she loved and not the law. It had simply been more convenient for him to hide from this truth. Until now.

His aunt was speaking again. "You will remain in your own body until such a time as age begins to affect your ability to treat patients. According to official record, you will be re-bodied. However, in actuality, your apprenticeship begins this afternoon. At New Kelen. Where you will pass yourself off as a fourbody who is very keen on volunteer work."

"No," said Pavel.

"I'm sorry, were you under the impression you could refuse this generous offer?" Lucca's voice was icy, her smile lupine. She crossed to sit at a marble counter before a large mirror and began making up her face.

"Of course I refuse," said Pavel. "There's *nothing* you can say to convince me. It's wrong."

"I wouldn't bother with the 'I'd rather die' part of your speech, if I were you. You don't want to know what I'll do to make sure I get my way on this one, Pavel."

"I'll denounce you," he said softly.

Lucca chose a blood-red lipstick and applied it to her lower lip. "It's good of you to let me know what you've got up your sleeve. I really must return the favor."

She drew the line of red across her upper lip and reached for a blotting tissue. Leaving the impression of her lips upon the cloth, she dropped it casually to the floor where it reminded Pavel of an ugly gaping wound. He'd always hated his aunt's habit of placing messes upon the floor for the staff to clean.

"Pick that up for me," she said.

He saw the action with new eyes now—she meant all who surrounded her to be reminded of their place: at her feet, in a posture of groveling.

"No," he said.

She smiled.

"It doesn't matter, you see, whether you pick it up or not. Someone will, in the end." She paused to let the idea sink in. Pavel was bright and would understand. "However, if I mention to Zussman that Talia has been shirking and leaving messes on the floor, he'll dismiss her."

"You're going to fire Talia if I—"

Lucca's laughter, harsh, cut Pavel off. "They told me you were a lot smarter than the average first-body. This isn't about *Talia*, foolish boy." Lucca paused, admiring her reflection. "No, I'm simply pointing out that when I convey information to someone, that information is always acted upon. What if, for example, I were to discover that the two hundred twenty-four firsties who took their exams this morning *cheated*? Tell me, my law-loving nephew, what would the punishment be for that?"

Pavel's face blanched. "Automatic sentencing to geriatric D-class bodies. Manual labor sentences."

"How lucky for you to have taken the exam in a separate room. Good thing *you* didn't cheat."

"You can't do that to them," said Pavel, his voice a whisper.

Lucca turned, her face powdered white and her mouth like a bloody gash. Meeting her nephew's eye, she spoke. "I can do anything I like."

He was trapped.

"Pavel, my dear, dear boy," said Lucca, her voice suddenly warm. "I'm only doing this for your own good. You *like* to help people. You like to prevent suffering. It's who you are." She held her hands out, as if inviting him to take them.

He stepped back and kept his own arms crossed tightly over his heart.

"Well," she said, "I can see I've upset you. I'm sorry, my dear. You can see that this is all for the best, though, can't you? Humanity benefits, you benefit, over two hundred students benefit . . . It's a win-win."

Win-win, thought Pavel. That was his aunt's campaign platform for re-election. Was this the way she ran her office? He felt sick.

"Think it over, dear boy," said Lucca.

He turned quickly, exiting the way he'd come in. In the years since he'd used the secret corridor to seek comfort from a bad dream, he'd grown large. The narrow passageway pressed upon him, his elbows grazing against one side and then the other as he hurried along the curving route.

Arriving back in his room, he pulled the sheets from his bed, in part because it was an act that felt destructive (and he wanted deeply to destroy something just now) but also because it was a kindness he could perform on poor Talia's behalf.

Echoes of Lucca's threats, the obvious ones and the veiled ones, replayed in his mind. *It doesn't matter, you see, whether you pick it up or not. Someone will, in the end.* Clearly, it didn't matter to her purposes whether or not Pavel agreed to become the next Head of Global Consciousness Transfer. Lucca would select (and use according to her purposes) the successor for the position, even if Pavel refused the job.

He thought of her other threat: to condemn an entire test-group to manual labor sentences if he chose to refuse her. It was criminal. Unthinkable. How could he have so blinded himself to her character? Pavel felt suddenly exhausted. He sank into a squashy and dilapidated armchair he'd kept from his first home. He remembered his father reading stories to him in this chair. Stories where there were good guys and bad guys and no confusion as to which was which. But Pavel felt confused. And hungry. And tired.

His thoughts drifted back to the girl with red hair. Where was she now?

It didn't matter. He couldn't help her. Lucca had him trapped.

His mind retraced the same dead-end paths over and over. *You'll think better with something in your stomach*, he told himself at last. He'd skipped breakfast and lunch and hadn't eaten much last night, either. And he'd skipped sleeping, mostly. Well, he wanted the chance to say goodbye and thank you to Talia. Rising, he crossed to a wall-screen and keyed in an order for food.

A few minutes later, Pavel heard Zussman's obsequious knock at his door. Opening it, Pavel asked where Talia was.

"I'm afraid I had to let her go," said Zussman.

"Why?" demanded Pavel.

"I don't like to say, sir," said Zussman. "Shall we leave it at . . . didn't live up to expectations, sir?"

Pavel stared at the platter of eggs, cold ham and cheeses spread before him. "Thank you, Zuss. I'm sorry I troubled you. I could have come down if I'd known . . ."

"Not at all, sir," said the butler. "Will that be all, sir?"

"Yes."

Dark thoughts clouded Pavel's mind as Zussman closed the door silently.

"She fired Talia for no reason," he murmured, pressing one hand against his forehead.

But he knew the reason. Knew it with certainty. His aunt had fired Talia as a way of showing Pavel that she would follow through on her other threat as well. He stared at the platter of food and found he no longer felt hungry.

Pavel would let Lucca think she'd won, but only until he could come up with a way to outwit her. Gathering the tray, he carried it downstairs where Lucca was completing a conversation—an *angry* conversation—by conference call.

Pavel placed the tray upon the counter, carefully putting away every item himself, waiting for his aunt to remark that the work was beneath him. But she'd evidently decided against engaging in further arguments.

"I'll go to the hospital," he said.

She smiled, but the expression just missed her cold eyes. "There's my bright boy. Doctor Suleiman will be expecting us."

"I'll go *alone*," he said.

Lucca pressed her thin lips together. "Very well."

"And I want you to make sure Talia finds another job. A *good* job. It's important to me that we start this new portion of my life on the right footing."

"Easily done," said his aunt. "You'll find, Pavel, I can be very reasonable. So long as you are reasonable."

Her words sent a chill whispering across the back of his neck as he turned to go.

"Make me proud," she said. The words sounded simple. Pavel knew they weren't. He anticipated her follow-up words before he heard them.

"I'll be keeping an eye on you," she said.

And I on you, thought Pavel.

27

AN EXPERIENCED PHYSICIAN

Jessamyn awoke to a mechanical buzzing sound. After a bleary moment of thinking herself in her snug Galleon quarters, she jolted upright. How long had she slept? As she struggled to read her chrono-tattoo, cold terror filled her belly. She'd lost thirteen hours! She shook her head to the side.

"Ethan!" The earpiece reported the same whirs and beeps as before.

"We're finally awake, are we?" asked a new nurse, bustling into the room. "You slept right through the other times I buzzed your door. Let's just see that arm, shall we?"

Gently, the nurse turned Jessamyn's cocooned arm and pointed to a soft green light. "Monitor says your cast is ready to come off." She smiled brightly, as though this were exceptional news.

"Good," murmured Jessamyn, certain it wasn't at all good.

"Doctor will be here in a minute. Would you like pain medication for the removal?" asked the nurse. "It tends to grab every little hair on your arms when it comes off."

"No," said Jessamyn sharply. "No meds." She needed her wits about her.

"It's the middle of the night," said the nurse. "You're not going to get an experienced doctor on this shift. I strongly suggest an analgesic."

Jessamyn wondered if she could buy some time. "In that case, I'll wait for an experienced physician."

The nurse gave Jessamyn a half-smile. "I'm sorry. Normally that wouldn't be a problem, but once Security gets involved . . ." She shook her head. "From their perspective, it looks highly suspicious, your having no identification, unable to recall your physician's name, no relatives who can vouch for your identity. In this kind of climate, security gets to scan you as soon as it is medically possible."

Jess felt her stomach lurch. She wasn't ready—she hadn't worked out a plan yet.

"The doctor will be with you shortly," said the nurse, walking to the door. "And dearie? Your fourbody is lovely. Now see that you take good care of it." She winked as she left the room.

Jess hopped off the table, opening drawers, cupboards, searching for anything she might use to overpower the physician when he or she arrived. She didn't recognize most of what she saw, and what she did recognize looked useless.

"Gauze," she muttered. "Great. I can *mummify* my doctor."

Then she remembered her pack and grabbed out the med-patches Pavel had given her. She was just reading through the labeling, searching for one marked as a narcotic, when she heard another door-buzz sound.

The door swung open, revealing a young man. Jessamyn gasped when she saw his face.

It was Pavel.

28

THE WORLD SEEMED TO SHRINK

Pavel.

That was her first thought. But it was followed quickly by an absolute revulsion for the practice that landed a new person inside a body that looked so kind, felt so familiar. Her mouth pinched; her face hardened into icy planes.

That is not Pavel, she told herself, *it's his body with someone else inside.* She couldn't look at his face—yesterday the face of a friend in an alien world. Within a space hidden deep inside, she grieved, realizing how very much she would have liked to have been his friend. The boy who would never have the chance to pilot among the stars. The boy who, even now, must be struggling to figure out how to live inside someone else's fifty-four-year-old body while she sat in a room with the body he no longer called his own.

"Did you let them scan you?" asked Pavel's voice.

His exact voice! Jessamyn had expected it would sound different when worn by someone else.

She swallowed. "I'm not ready to have my cast removed. Allow me to go home and I'll retrieve . . . proper identification."

"Jess?" said not-Pavel. "Jess, it's me, Pavel."

She glanced at his name tag.

His eyes flicked to the name as well: *Junior Doctor Yu-Arno*. "Oh, that. It's a complete scam. You were right about not telling my aunt anything."

She maintained her silence. Icy. Wary.

"C'mon, Jess. You've got to talk to me. Are you in trouble? Who do the secures outside think you are?"

Whoever *he* was, he seemed to know who *she* was.

In a whisper, she spoke. "You're not Pavel anymore."

His smile turned grim as he passed one of the silver instruments from the tray over her left arm. "Yeah, well, turns out I am. My aunt fixed the exam. She's . . . She's not who I thought she was." His voice dropped. "I should have seen it years ago."

Jessamyn's cast, cradled against Pavel's arm, responded to the gadget in his other hand. The white layers unwound themselves, pinching each small hair on her arm as the nurse had promised. She winced.

Pavel's eyes filled with concern. "Sorry about the hair-tweezing. I didn't want to medicate you."

"It's nothing," she said. And compared to the pain of seeing Pavel, but not knowing if it *was* Pavel, the pinching on her arm *was* nothing.

"Five questions, Jess. I got my apprenticeship after *five questions* out of a potential nine-hundred. It's like she wasn't even trying to hide what she'd done." Pavel grabbed the last strands from Jessamyn's forearm as the cast fell away. "They cheat the system. Lucca and all her colleagues. They're not transferring me because I'm too *valuable* to them inside this body."

"Prove you're Pavel," said Jessamyn.

"Um. Okay." He licked his lips, stared at the wall behind her. At the floor. At the ceiling. "I loaned you my bike yesterday. A 400 series. You drove it."

Jessamyn shook her head. *Not good enough.*

"*Shizer*, Jess. What do you mean, 'prove I'm me?'"

"Terran Security could be . . . using your body to get information from me. You all think I'm a terrorist trying to blow up this hospital. Don't you." She didn't inflect the last words as a question.

Pavel gazed at Jessamyn's arm, still cradled in his. He ran his free hand gently along her pale, thin arm. "I don't think you're an inciter, Jess. I believed you when you said you came here from . . ." He stopped speaking and formed the name with his mouth, soundlessly: *Mars.*

A tightening in Jessamyn's stomach warned her that this was either very good or very bad. Her own voice a bare whisper, Jess asked a question she thought only the true Pavel could answer. "Tell me what you want to do when you retire."

His mouth curved up on one side. "Last night I told you I wished I could re-open space for travel. Right now, though, all I can think of is how I want to help you. Help your people. Keep you all from starving. That would be a tragedy of—" He paused, searching for the word. "Of . . . *tragic* proportions."

Jess grunted a small laugh.

"You eat butter like it's food," said Pavel, taking her hand in his, "And decorative kale, too. And you kissed me at midnight."

Their eyes met. Jess felt a flutter in her stomach that had nothing to do with escape.

"You had a brother you loved very much," whispered Pavel.

Loved? Jess struggled for breath at his use of the past tense.

"I'm so sorry," murmured Pavel. "I tried to intervene . . . to slow things or delay his transfer . . . but politicians got involved and . . ." He broke off, brows pulled together, gazing at her arm. "Those extra years on his body are too valuable. They're spending time re-mineralizing his bones, replacing his blood, and then they'll release him to someone important. Probably the viceroy, from what I hear. Your brother's under special guard. It's not going to be possible—I'm so sorry."

You will not cry you will not cry you will not cry. And she realized she wouldn't. She couldn't. She was frozen, like Mars's soil. She was made of ice. No tears would melt from her.

"How do I get out of here?" she asked in a low voice. That was all that mattered. Her broken heart was inconsequential. Only getting food back to her starving world mattered now. "Help me escape."

"That's what I'm here for," Pavel said. "Your face is plastered all over screens in the hospital with '*Is this your patient?*' written underneath. As soon as I noticed, I came, saying you were my patient."

Turning, he used his scan chip to open a drawer with wicked looking blades. Blades Jess would have wanted, minutes ago.

"What are you doing?" asked Jess, looking suspiciously at the sharp blade.

"Replacing your chip with one from general reclamation," he said, squeezing a line of green-goo across her wrist, exactly where Brian Wallace had inserted her chip. "Feel this?" he asked, pinching her wrist.

"No," said Jessamyn. "I can't feel anything."

Pavel nodded. "A bunch of us did this when we were twelve. Told you I was a law-breaker," he said, grinning.

Jess didn't return the smile. She couldn't.

"Reclam-chips are only good until the next database update," continued Pavel. "They happen twice a day. You've got one good scan, for sure. We'll use it to get you past the security officer out there, but I wouldn't suggest using it a second time. I'm going to remove your right hand chip as well. You don't want to have two chips if . . . if anything goes wrong."

Jess nodded her permission.

A fine line of red bloomed in the wake of Pavel's knife. He grabbed a swab from the counter which stopped the bleeding. Choosing a pair of micro-tweezers from the tray beside him, he retrieved the chip from the incision site.

"Here it is," said Pavel, removing the dangerous chip that tied her to Harpreet and Ethan and the satellite facility.

Pavel set the reclam-chip on a computer. "Are you still good?" he asked in a low murmur. He ran his fingers along the screen like she'd seen Ethan do a thousand times. The familiarity of the motion sliced like a wound through her chest, and she had to look away.

Pavel grunted in satisfaction and took Jessamyn's wrist once again.

"Why are you helping me?" she asked as he inserted the reclamation chip and sealed her skin.

"Your planet deserves a chance," said Pavel. "I can't trust what my aunt would do with the information that Mars Colonial is alive and well. So that leaves me to help."

There was a something too-casual in the way he said it. Recognition sparked and bounded in Jessamyn's heart: *He's doing it for me.* He just didn't want to admit it aloud. Jess understood. What was the use of putting words to her own feelings for Pavel? Their worlds divided them.

He reached for her right wrist and repeated the removal procedure. Then he grabbed a device Jess thought looked familiar.

"A heat-healer," she said.

"Yeah."

"We used to use them—the first Marsians used them—to remove wrinkles."

"And now you don't?" asked Pavel, erasing the scar from her other wrist.

Jess shook her head. "Wrinkles mean you've survived. And you've got to be smart to survive on Mars." She reached up to the space between her brows, on the bridge of her nose. "I think I'll get my First Wrinkle here. Soon." She pushed away the thought of celebrating the occasion without her brother.

But the thought of Ethan opened a tiny door through which desperate notions crept. Crazy rescue schemes. Impossible ideas. She imagined herself throwing smoke-bombs down corridors. Disabling the power grid for the hospital. Using armor-piercing weapons to take down the secures guarding her brother.

Jessamyn gave herself a mental shake. She didn't know how to do any of those things. She couldn't even pick the right hospital gown for a successful disguise. If she tried to strong-arm herself to her brother's side, she'd end up dead. Or captured. Either way, *Mars would starve* because Crusty couldn't guide the ship back home alone.

She had to leave her brother and the others. They were trapped on Earth, but Jessamyn would be free, thanks to Pavel. She couldn't throw that freedom away. The realization cut deep, deep inside her, sundering what felt like tendon from bone.

You will survive, she told herself. *You must.*

"I was so worried," said Pavel, "When I saw your brother's body still here and no sign of you."

Jessamyn pushed aside the feelings of tenderness Pavel's words awakened within her. Twisting forward, she jumped off the bed and tested her wrist. She couldn't tell that her arm had been hurt earlier. She had a second chance.

"Jessamyn," said Pavel. "Please tell me you know a lost cause when you see it."

He meant *Ethan*, of course. She nodded, her heart fracturing yet again at the thought of leaving her brother. There seemed to be no upper limit to the number of times a heart could be re-broken.

"I'm going home," she said simply.

He fumbled inside a shirt pocket. "Take this," he said, presenting her with a plastic stick. "It's a bit old-fashioned, but it works as good as a scan chip for getting you a transport from the government motor pool. I'm messaging Aunt Lucca that I'm flying down to the Cape of Good Hope this morning. Log a flight plan that direction and then you can change course later."

"The Cape of Good Hope," said Jessamyn, nodding. She liked the way the words sounded—she needed *hope*.

"I don't want to know where you're really going," Pavel added quickly.

Her mouth pulled into half a smile. "Because you're worthless under Equidima."

"Exactly," he said. "I'll see you out of the building."

The two moved toward the door, side by side. Pavel raised his hand to deactivate the door lock, but before he could touch the pad, Jessamyn took his face in her hands and kissed him, hard. All the world seemed to shrink down to the one place where her lips crushed upon his and she wanted to live in the moment forever.

But she pulled away and pointed to the door lock pad, eyes bright with unshed tears.

Outside the room, the security officer on duty was someone new.

"Stop!" he barked. "I need a chip scan on this unidentified person."

Jess's heart sped up.

Pavel, hands on his hips, looked the security officer in the eyes. "My *patient* would be happy to provide that," he said calmly.

As the officer scanned Jessamyn's ID, her heart pounded wildly—she was sure the secure would detain her. But he merely nodded to indicate she could leave now. With Pavel at her side, Jess walked away free. She felt the warmth of Pavel's kiss lingering on her lips. But as she rode the elevator at his side, in silence, the wet-sweet taste of his mouth faded. By the time they reached the exit doors, the kiss seemed a lifetime away. It was something that had happened to a girl Jessamyn knew once.

The pair said their goodbyes in hushed tones and Jess walked into the night, away from the boy she might have loved, if only she could have.

"Wait," called Pavel.

She turned, meeting his gaze.

"Promise me you'll make it," he said, closing the distance between them. "To Mars," he whispered, pointing overhead. "Promise."

Jessamyn nodded, gazing at the bright spot she called home. “I promise.”

She turned once more toward the motor pool.

She had a planet to save.

29

KILIMANJARO

Jessamyn saw the hoverport directly in front of her but had already decided against going through the main entrance which would require her to pass security guards. Instead, she circled to the back end, running her eyes down the rows of vehicles in the transport pool. They had a few of everything on offer, from bikes to newer versions of the amphibious craft her crew had driven to a handful of craft that would fly. The vehicles weren't guarded, so far as Jess could tell.

The only thing separating her from getting airborne was a three-meter fence, constructed as a series of horizontal bars. It looked to Jess as though someone had placed a set of very wide ladders side by side to create a boundary. She knew she couldn't leap over it in Earth's heavy gravity, but ladders could be climbed. It was too easy. Reaching out one hand, she gripped a bar just above her head, preparing to ascend.

It took a moment for the searing heat to register.

In fact, the first sensory input—Jess's first hint that anything bad was happening—was the scent of something burning. But then she felt it. She wrenched her hand off the bar, squelching a howl of pain. Cradling her hand to her chest, she curled to the ground, shuffling a few meters away until she found cover beside a shrub. Had she set off an alarm?

Pain throbbed in her right hand, a steady pulse to mark the seconds and minutes as they ticked past. She drew air in through her teeth in short, shallow breaths. But there were no alarms, and no secures, and gradually Jess came to trust that no one cared that she'd touched the burning boundary.

She opened her sling-pack, searching for her first aid folder. Seeing Pavel's med kit, she pulled it out instead and hunted until she found something white and gooey for burns. The relief was instant, but her hand looked terrible. She found skin-heal strips in Pavel's med kit, including one that was palm-sized. And apparently of a higher quality than the ones from home, she noted, sighing in relief.

She looked at the barrier once more, frowning. Going through the front entrance seemed like the only option after all, but Jess didn't like any choice that included secures.

Tucking the med kit inside her pack, she disturbed a small creature that had hidden in the bushes. It scampered away, running under the fencing until she lost sight of it amongst the vehicles.

"Of course," she murmured. Why go *over* the fence when she could simply go *under* it? She grinned; her thin Marsian frame would allow her to fit where Terrans could not. The bottom rail of the fence sat at least eight centimeters farther from the ground than the gaps between the higher rails. But as she crept nearer, she began to question whether she would really be able to make it. Or rather, if her *head* could make it. Her head was the largest part of her as well as being one she didn't particularly want to fry against the bar.

A memory danced through her mind—her father's laughter, a teasing phrase repeated at her every success: *Don't get a big head, now*!

"I need a hat," she murmured. She'd lost her balaclava, tossing it aside before entering the hospital. She didn't know if her hair would catch fire, but she definitely didn't want to risk it. Earth had so much oxygen—things flamed too easily here. What did she have in her pack that would wrap round her head, preventing a loose hair from igniting the rest of her?

She squatted, examining the space between the bar and the ground. Dragging the side of her face along the paved surface wasn't going to be pleasant. Then she thought of something.

She reached for Pavel's med kit once more. She needed one of those cocoon-like casts around her head—a protective headband. It would at once secure her hair, flatten her ears, and provide protection to part of her face. Tucking the ends of her hair into her snug-fitting neckline, she used Pavel's device to describe an oval around her skull. With a fluttering kind of magic, the device spewed fibers round and round her head. When it stopped, she reached up and felt the strange band. It was hard and smooth.

Jess set her pack on the ground and gave it a small kick under the barrier. It skidded across the pavement, stopping well out of her reach on the far side of the fencing. *I'm committed now*, she thought.

She sighed and began snaking her way under the bar, feet and legs first, until the only thing remaining on the wrong side of the fence was her head. Hearing voices nearby, she froze. Then she realized that the voices were coming from inside her head. From the earpiece. From beside Ethan, as he lay in stasis. She understood only bits and pieces of the conversation. But one thing was certain. Her brother's mind was about to be parted from his body.

"You have a job to do," Jess murmured to herself. That was all that mattered now. She couldn't think about Ethan. She flattened her head against the pavement in preparation to slip the rest of the way inside.

Focus on what you are doing, she told herself. As she slid her head along the pavement, she felt the "cast" bump briefly against the bottom rail of the fence and then she was free. An unpleasant charred smell permeated the air. *The cast*, she realized. It reeked, smoking where it had touched the barrier, but it had prevented her hair from catching fire.

She stood, forcing herself to think about what kind of transport to choose. Reaching down, she grabbed her sling-pack and threw it over one shoulder.

From her earpiece, a voice asked, "*Is the viceroy ready for transfer?*"

"*Ready, doctor,*" came the response.

Jessamyn's eyes stung from smoke. She blinked and raced toward a row of ships she recognized could reach high orbit. Something in her heart reached out toward the escape the spacecraft promised, even though she knew no ship could carry her from her grief. Stopping beside a mid-size craft with thrust rockets and jet engines, she checked to make sure it had hover boosters.

"*Do we have confirmed availability of next-body for the prisoner?*" asked a distant voice.

"*Confirmed,*" replied a low voice.

"*Begin transfer protocol.*"

Jess's breath hitched and she felt for a moment like a Marsian stuck outside their habitat with a busted helmet. *Do this*, she ordered herself. Squaring her shoulders, she swiped Pavel's motor pool stick beside the hatch of a low-orbit aircraft. A set of shallow stairs extended before her, and she ordered herself forward. *You've got a planet to save.* She pressed a large button to seal the hatch and seated herself inside.

"*Doctor, I'm picking up a signal from inside the patient's . . . er, prisoner's body.*"

"*Shizer! Could it be a delayed explosive?*"

"*Negative, doctor. My scanner indicates a transmitting device. For communications only.*"

Jess told herself to concentrate on the dash before her. A screen bloomed to life, glowing softly in the dark. The ship's nav-com asked Jessamyn if she was ready to launch. She punched the systems-go indicator.

A message flashing in red told her to secure her harness.

"*Ares and Aphrodite!*" she swore, snapping the harness in place. But as she did so, something inside her locked into place, settled irrevocably. She was a pilot. This was what she did best.

"*Doctor, shall I alert security regarding the transmitting device?*"

A third voice, deep and resonant, spoke out. "*When you have removed the device, I will take it directly to*

Chancellor Brezhnaya. Red Squadron Forces will wish to evaluate it."

Jessamyn eased the craft out of its berth and onto a short runway. Another message flashed across her screen, requesting a flight plan. She tapped 'Cape of Good Hope' into the insistent monitor, and her itinerary was instantly approved.

As she pulled the craft up into the still-dark sky, she heard hospital personnel congratulating one another on their success. *Don't listen*, she told herself. The doctor's voice, detached and cool during surgery, had a gloating quality to it now.

"*He'll have a hard time blowing up hospitals from inside this body.*"

Jess flinched at the answering laughter.

"*It seems wrong to give the prisoner's new-body an anti-arthritic,*" said a quieter voice.

"*First, do no harm,*" said the doctor. "*Let's get that audio transmitter removed.*"

The craft climbed past three thousand meters, and Jessamyn slammed the ship into autopilot. Jolting her head three times to the side in quick succession, she waited for her own audio earpiece to spiral itself outward and into her waiting hand. She had no wish to hear more. The earpiece no longer linked her to Ethan, only to her loss of him. Small hairs in her outer ear tickled as the device fell loose, reminding her of the day three weeks ago that Ethan had asked her to remove it so he could clean and test it.

"You should have made them for everyone," Jess had said, that day.

"It is too late now," Ethan had replied.

Too late now, repeated Jessamyn's splintered heart.

The memory brought a fresh flow of tears, spilling upon her cheeks as she caught the audio device in the palm of her hand. The stolen aircraft stopped climbing, and Jess pulled free of the safety harness, drying her eyes on her dark shirtsleeve. She threw the transmitter onto the cockpit floor. Her foot crushed it and she heard a satisfying series of cracking noises. Retrieving the broken thing from the floor, she stretched out her arm to deposit it in the ship's refuse.

But something made her hesitate; she remembered how the smashed bit of technology owed its existence to Ethan, and she couldn't throw it out. The device slipped from her fingers onto the ground, and Jessamyn gave way to gulping, gasping sobs, sliding onto the hard flooring of the craft.

The Indian Ocean flashed beneath her—day had broken and early light reflected off a vast expanse of water, turning it silvery-grey, like the carbon dioxide snows of Mars.

Snow.

She thought of Ethan's beloved *Snows of Kilimanjaro.* The great mountain itself lay just to the west of her current position; a broader sweep on her return north would take her past Kilimanjaro—its white snows and golden plains. Wiping her eyes, Jess nodded to herself, taking the pilot's seat once more. She made corrections to her altitude to swing in close for a vid that would serve as a kind of tribute to her brother. Something she could bring home to her family when she walked into their dwelling without Ethan at her side. Her throat spasmed closed at the idea of this homecoming.

Her craft sank lower, running before the sun. Soon she could make out two of Kilimanjaro's volcanic cones. A third came into view as she brushed away the newest tears. She fumbled in her pack for her brother's wafer-computer and snapped a few quick vids. It was a gesture, a small something, a piece of Ethan to carry back home.

But when she looked at the pictures she'd captured, she felt a swell of disappointment. The great mountain's height flattened out from on high. Jessamyn knew she didn't have time to land her craft—she was borrowing time from the people of Mars even now. She hesitated but then decided to descend a couple thousand meters for a better picture.

Kilimanjaro rewarded her—from this altitude, it dominated everything. And even the ground astonished her, mottled with distinct greens and yellows so different from Mars's rusty-browns. She used her brother's wafer to snatch image after image as she made a lazy circle around the mountain. She still thought the pictures didn't do justice to Kilimanjaro's sprawling bulk. As Jess dropped a last thousand meters, the mountain became suddenly a large and majestic being that dwarfed her, and her craft, and even the needs of her far-away planet for food. She felt thinned out, ghost-like, as if Kilimanjaro were the living creature and she a mere breath, dissipating in a blink of the great mount's ancient existence.

And then something caught her eye. An undulant river, brown, sinuous, flecked with white. She marveled at how swiftly it flowed, saw with wonder how it pressed against its banks, spilling along the sides and then returning.

But as she watched, she realized it wasn't a river at all. The vast and swiftly- snaking flow was a procession of animals, all charging together, making adjustments for one another's movements that pressed them right or left.

"Ohhh," Jessamyn sighed and the flat-smashed heart inside her expanded.

She strained her eyes to find the beginning of the herd, but it moved far onward, beyond what she could see. Jessamyn felt her heart beating faster and a part of her yearned to dive and join the herd on its pell-mell journey. Who could resist such a call? She adjusted her craft when it began to drift away from the herd's migratory path. And still, she was nowhere near the front of the line. The creatures must be fast, but not in comparison to her vehicle, which meant she'd flown past thousands, maybe hundreds of thousands, already.

She circled back to take it in again, knowing she was using precious time. Back home, Jessamyn had considered the planetary dog as something to amuse children. But these wild creatures? Driving forward like a mighty river swelling its banks, they made Jess want to laugh and dance and cry all at the same time.

How she wanted this great swell of wild creatures for her own grandchildren's children! And for her brother—yes, she desperately wished it might have been for him—but this feeling went beyond her own personhood, her own losses. And suddenly it mattered to her—mattered terribly—that she return homeward. So that the next generation on Mars would survive and someday make *her* world into a place where wild things ran free. So that humans on Mars could have the breath knocked clean out of them by this kind of beauty, so full of dread and wonder that you wanted to laugh and dance and cry.

Jess swept one last time alongside the great herd. Then she set a course west that would swing her along the equator and out to the Atlantic Ocean. Slipping the wafer back into her sling-pack, Jessamyn saw an incoming message flash upon the screen before her.

"Deviation from flight plan detected. Please correct your course immediately to ensure your safety and the safety of others."

Jess turned the screen off, grimacing at the irony. By changing her course to return to the Red Galleon, she was ensuring the safety of others. Abruptly, she heard an audio signal. Not from her earpiece, which lay smashed upon the floor, but from the ship itself.

"This is Central African Air Control requesting to speak with the pilot of Skylight Orbiter Alpha-Zero-Niner," said a crackly voice.

Jessamyn was not in the mood for speaking with anyone right now. She had a several hours flight ahead of her. Ignoring the message, she aimed her vessel north-west to Scotland. The audio messages continued, annoying and frequent, and Jess wished she could find an "off" switch for audio relay in the unfamiliar craft. But after hearing the same messages for a steady quarter hour, they became for her a kind of white noise.

The messages ceased, finally, and for a full five blissful minutes, Jessamyn enjoyed peace as she flew onward. But then she saw a small approaching craft on her starboard side. Moments later, its twin appeared on her port side. Both sported flashy Central African Air Control logos. The pilot in the craft to her left tapped a headset as he contacted her by audio, ordering her to return to her logged route or face immediate penalties.

She took a few sharp turns, curious how determined her escorts were to stick with her.

Maddeningly determined, she observed, scowling.

Her refusal to cooperate earned her an additional escort as well—a third craft dropped into position just ahead of her.

"*Holy Ares*," she swore, throwing the ship into a steep climb designed to make accompanying her craft less convenient. She managed to shake off her starboard and port escorts, but the one that had dropped down in front of her looped over backward and tailed her with a disturbing resolve. She received several additional messages, which became increasingly threatening and promised *aerial intervention*, whatever that might mean.

And then the craft that had dogged her for an annoyingly intense three minutes was simply gone. Gone, too, were the threatening messages. Jess turned her craft back toward Skye. Relieved, she spent the next several minutes trying to figure out if she could use anything aboard her ship as a means of communicating with Wallace and Crusty, so as to let them know the Galleon had better be ready to lift off.

Unfortunately, Jess had never paid much attention to her brother's attempts to teach her more than rudimentary communications skills aboard ships back home. The Terran ship's communications system baffled her, absorbing more of her attention than turned out to be good under the circumstances: Jess had company again.

When the four ships representing "aerial intervention" showed as blips on Jessamyn's radar, she felt resolve like a cool band encircling her core.

"Intervene *this*," she murmured, hurtling her ship through a series of drops and turns that her nav-screen warned her were *inadvisable at current speed.* The stiff language of the message brought a grin to Jessamyn's mouth.

"Inadvisable?" she said aloud. "Really? You want to see inadvisable?" She examined her nav-com and punched out a string of commands. Ethan's lesson on disabling safety protocols had been something Jess *had* paid careful attention to. Grinning at her success, Jess pulled the ship into another steep climb, then looped over into a winding corkscrew. The extra g's felt *good*, she thought to herself as she checked onscreen to see who was still with her. It took a moment to locate her own screen-blip, blinking bright blue like the blips of her pursuers. She thought of how her brother would have designed a more practical screen display with differently colored blips.

But as she watched three of them flying rings around one another, she felt a surge of hope. They appeared confused as well. Maybe she could lose them while they played a game of *Who's Who.*

Her hope proved short-lived. The four ships quickly regrouped and once more gained in their pursuit. Her ship had to be emitting a signature of some kind. Jessamyn wished she'd paid more attention to what her brother had tried to teach her about vessel tracking.

A new message crackled over the ship's audio. "Alpha-zero-niner, you are under detainment protocol. You will be fired upon if you continue to resist contact and communication."

A quick glance at her dashboard told Jess she had no weapons of her own to return fire. She felt her skin flush warm with indignation.

"I did *not*," she growled, "Come all this way—" here she broke off to dive into a narrow valley—"Just to get shot out of the sky!"

She attempted a move she used all the time back on Mars, weaving back and forth within the confines of the channel. Only here, nothing about flying felt quite like what she expected. "*Holy Ares!*" she shouted, pulling left from a too-near canyon wall. Earth-air was so *thick*, and her craft didn't respond as she expected.

The ship tailing her was far less fortunate than she.

A fluttering on the nav-screen caught Jessamyn's eye: one of the blue blips disappeared, and from a rear view screen, she saw the disintegrating craft paving a trail like a comet. She gasped. *Now you're in trouble*, she thought. She scrutinized the valley walls—could she use them as weapons to destroy the other three ships? A missile exploding against a wall just to starboard cut short her analysis.

Jess threw hurried glances across screens and windows. Her ship appeared unharmed but there was a red blip now tailing her ship. *Another missile*, observed a cool part of her mind. Automatically, she banked left and up, then dove down again, narrowly missing a sudden rise in the floor of the valley.

"*Hermes*!" she shouted, correcting for the rising ground as the missile exploded on impact beside her. Jessamyn felt a flapping kind of panic building inside her belly: she didn't know how to fly on Earth. The strange atmosphere, so much thicker than that of Mars, made it impossible for her to pilot with precision.

The narrow valley spilled into a vast plain and Jessamyn felt exposed. Chill fingers played through her abdomen and up her spine. *How am I supposed to fly on this planet?* she asked herself. And then she found her ship climbing, climbing, climbing, as a part of her that didn't rely on thought took over.

"*Of course*," she whispered, "*Of course*."

She needed *less air*. If she stopped hugging the planet's surface, she could find that part of the sky where she could manage her craft with ease. She soared into the thinner air of the upper atmosphere.

"Just like back home," she said softly. "Now we'll see who knows how to fly." A smile crept across her face. It had been no accident she'd chosen a craft with orbiting capability. Running a hand over her gut, she murmured, "You knew."

Her unexpected climb had bought her a few precious moments and she used these to scan her dashboard, looking for a way to render inoperative the signal her ship transmitted to the pursuing vessels. Finding something called an *emergency beacon locator*, she attempted to disable it, holding her breath to see if they'd lost her signal. But three trailing blips on her screen told her they still knew *exactly* where she was.

She fired a forward thruster, squinting as the g-force slammed her against her restraint harness. A missile flared past her, curving in a slow arc as it adjusted for her sudden change in direction. Using a combination of her jet engines and rocket thrust, she rolled into an elongated corkscrew. *Hades*, but it felt good to be free of those extra millibars of atmospheric pressure.

One of her pursuers snuck in close and tight, nearly matching her maneuvers. She fired a port thruster and dove in time to see a flash of bright light—the craft that had followed her exploded as the missile struck it instead of her.

"Wings and rudders don't work quite the same in thin atmo, do they?" Jess murmured. She'd yet to see anyone fly in a way that suggested they knew how to use rocket-thrust to advantage up here. Did their ships even have it? She needed to find out. Using bursts from her forward thrusters to slow herself, she allowed the nearest ship to close on her. Then she looped back in a tight circle to position herself behind the other ship.

"Harder to fire on me if I'm hunter instead of prey, huh?" She examined her enemy's ship. And then she grinned: it was clear their vessels ran on jet engines only. She had an incalculable advantage.

"And I know how to use it!" she shouted firing both rear thrusters.

Just then the second pursuer passed across the back of her ship. She sucked in a quick breath—his mistake was more than she could have hoped for. The pursuer was caught unawares in her jet wash, spinning flat, in a jerking motion that smoothed out until it reminded Jessamyn of a child's toy, spinning across the floor. She felt a moment's pity—it wasn't a spin she'd want to try to recover from. The pilot would likely pass out long before impact. A sudden rush of hope replaced pity: only one pursuer remained. She liked those odds.

The real question now was whether or not she could lure her pursuer to follow her into a *higher* orbit. She suspected the answer would be *yes* as she aimed her craft toward the heavens. A bright necklace of satellites glinted and sparked above her. She fired her rear thrust rocket and watched as the satellites seemed to pull her forward.

Onscreen, she saw the remaining ship veer drunkenly toward her. "Jet engines don't like it up here, do they?" she muttered. An alarm flashed across her nav-screen. *Warning: insufficient oxygen. Jet-engine failure in twelve-point-five seconds on these coordinates. Warning: correct course immediately. Warning*—Jess slapped the cautionary screen to black and smiled as she hurtled into the deep.

The other ship fired at her again and Jess had to use her rockets to veer off her intended course. The missile sailed past her, unable to correct itself effectively in the thinning air. She waited for her jets to notice they had no oxygen.

"Come on, come on, come on," she said, urging her engines to cut. But what if Terrans had different technology? What if jet engines didn't die here, even without oxygen? The enemy ship was gaining on her once more. Would it fire? Would it break off pursuit?

The ship sent another missile hurtling toward her vessel and she burned her starboard rocket, hating how it aimed her ship back toward Earth and oxygen. But it happened anyway: her first engine flamed out and then her second followed suit. Jess held her breath watching the pursuing ship. And there it was: she saw a last gasping flare as her enemy's engines darkened. The pursuing ship glided out and away from Earth on a trajectory into the stars. Her gamble had worked. That ship was not changing course.

Unless the pilot started firing missiles, thought Jess, looking at his problem as if it were her own to solve. She felt a part of her brain whispering: *Fire them, idiot! Fire them!* She didn't actually want the drifting ship back on her trail, but she hated knowing the vessel would've made it back to Earth if she'd been piloting it. She murmured a prayer for the doomed pilot, and then, sighing, Jessamyn fired her thrusters in a series of burns that directed her Earthward. Maybe seeing what she'd done with her thrust rockets would give the other pilot the idea to try the missiles. But she wasn't sticking around to find out.

"I've got my own planet to save," she said aloud.

Slowing her re-entry into the lower atmo with repeated rocket burns, Jessamyn was nonetheless relieved when her engines restarted. Landing without them, with Earth's heavy gravity, wasn't something she wanted to experience. As she crossed the Terran north pole and aimed for the Isle of Skye, she realized she had a small decision to make. Should she bring her craft to a landing beside Wallace's cottage or beside the Galleon?

Cursing her inability to figure out how to contact either Wallace or Crusty, she decided to try the cottage first. Crusty might well have decided to hunker down and await her at the Red Galleon, but she had to speak with Brian Wallace. It was possible someone would trace the Marsian crew or their vehicle back to the Isle of Skye. She owed Brian Wallace a warning; it was what Harpreet would have done.

Her landing disturbed more ash than she'd expected, reminding her why Wallace had located his dwelling those few kilometers away from the storage barn. Holding her shirt over her mouth and nose, she approached the front door, an apology for the ash—now floating like snow—on her lips. As she knocked, she remembered Wallace's preference for shoes-off and was attempting to slip out of her footgear when the door flew open.

"Ye're back, then!" said Brian Wallace. He frowned, looking past Jessamyn for the others.

"It's only me," she said. She explained the events of the last two days with detachment—things that might have happened to someone else. Concluding, she asked where Crusty was.

"Aboard the Red Galleon," replied Wallace, "Fretting that he'll have to fly back alone. I told him ye'd make it back. But ye say that ye fought off a detainment squadron to get here?"

Jess nodded.

"Ye'll have disabled the beacon for the craft before landing her here, then?" said Wallace, looking nervously to the sky.

Jessamyn inhaled in alarm. *She'd forgotten about the tracking device*!

Wallace groaned. "Damned good thing I transferred the tellurium off-island yesterday," he muttered, shaking his head. Then, placing his hands on his hips, he took a deep breath. "We'll be having company shortly, lass. There's not a moment to waste. Quick now, get aboard that Mars vessel and get yerself off-planet!"

Jess nodded and turned for the stolen ship she'd abandoned moments ago.

"No," called Wallace. "Leave that beaconed ship for me, if ye please. Here." He grabbed a hovercart from beside the cottage. "These are swift." Wallace hollered after her, "Ye've given me a right fast escape ship, for which I thank ye!"

Jess hopped aboard the hovercart, swerving alongside her Terran friend. "But, what about the beacon?"

Wallace grinned. "I know how to disable a beacon, lass. Now get out of here! I'll contact Crusty to begin pre-launch!"

Jess pointed the hovercart in the direction of the Red Galleon. Only the topmost section was visible, but the sight made her sit a little taller, throw her shoulders back. The Galleon was a beautiful ship and it would be a honor to fly her again.

She pushed Wallace's tiny cart as fast as it would go. The ride was exhilarating, if jolting, and it made her think of piggy-back rides on her father's back. She let slip a brief giggle as the cart jounced along the curve of a low hill. But what she saw over the rise extinguished all laughter.

A small puff of ash drifted in the air from a recently landed craft. Three figures dressed in vivid red armor jumped from the vessel and aimed weapons at her. She swerved, nearly flinging herself to the ground. Grasping the sides of her small carrier, she hurtled forward. She could see the Galleon, gleaming, beckoning. She heard the slightest of rumbling shudders—Crusty had gotten Wallace's message and was commencing the pre-launch sequence. She would make it—she had to!

And then suddenly she heard a loud shot ringing out beside her. The Galleon disappeared from view and Jess found herself staring up at a whirling sky as she was violently dislodged from the hovercart. She tried to focus on a single cloud, tried to stop the world from spinning, tried to stand and flee. Strong arms restrained her.

She heard herself screaming, told herself, *You must break free—you must!* But her torso was held fast in a manacled grip. She wasn't strong enough. Things were too *heavy* here. She felt her legs collapse as someone tugged her, dragging her backwards. She stared in wonder at a bright bloom spreading along her left arm, a match to the crimson-clad guards who pulled her in the wrong direction, away from the Galleon. There was a sharp ache in the arm, but she had no time for pain.

"No!" she shouted. "No!" A third *no* trailed out into an anguished cry as she struggled to free herself, to race back to the Galleon and hope and the salvation of her world.

She heard shouted commands, but the world's edges seemed to be growing fuzzy. A part of her recognized she'd been shot, which explained how she'd become dislodged from the cart. As spots danced across her vision, she stopped struggling physically and instead struggled to maintain consciousness. She focused on her feet as the secures dragged her backward along a path to the front door of Wallace's cottage. Her feet bounced along the uneven surface and one shoe slipped free.

"Throw the prisoner over your shoulder," said a deep voice. "She's in no condition to fight."

Jess watched the world tip so that grass and ash became *up*, sky *down*. She shook her head. *You will not pass out*, she ordered herself. The ash and grass dimmed and then darkened.

And then the world up-ended itself again as Jess felt herself being hurled onto something hard. A chair. Her vision spun, steadied, and righted itself. Her hands had been bound and a bandage slapped over her arm wound. It disturbed her that she couldn't remember either of these things happening. In fact, she'd missed re-entering Wallace's cottage altogether. But she felt awake now, and the pain in her left arm helped keep her alert.

Across from her, Wallace sat at his computer, gagged and handcuffed, rather sloppily, to the desk. He was shouting at the Red Forces officials, who looked puzzled to see him. One stepped closer and removed Wallace's gag.

Brian Wallace twisted wild eyes at Jessamyn, shouting meanwhile at the secures. "That's her, I tell you! She's parked a nuclear weapon in my sheep pasture!"

A secure addressed Wallace. "She tied you up?"

"Aye," said Wallace, wagging his head up and down, "Only minutes ago, when she found me, hiding here. I've been sending messages to the constabulary on the mainland for two days now about her missile, but no one would listen. You've seen it, haven't you? That great bloody inciter missile?"

The two officers conferred. While their heads were turned away from Wallace, he aimed a long slow wink at Jessamyn. Her eyebrows flew up. He nodded briefly and in that gesture she saw reassurance. Whatever he was up to, it didn't involve giving away her planet's secrets.

Jess could play along, she decided; she bowed her own head slightly, mouthing an "okay" to him as well.

"Inform the prisoner of the charges against her," barked the superior officer to the one who had carried her before turning himself to interrogate Brian Wallace.

"Citizen," droned the guard beside Jessamyn, "You stand convicted of attempting to launch a nuclear weapon of mass destruction to destinations unascertainable which is an act of terrorism against the people of Earth and treason against her government."

Jessamyn's mind spun. She knew what came next—the part where they shot her and she collapsed unconscious.

"You are required to perform acts of manual labor to benefit the citizens you have attempted to harm. You will receive reorientation training during the balance of your years of life. Your current body will be entered into general reclamation and you will be assigned a geriatric body in which to carry out your sentence."

Jessamyn's breath caught, stretching the moment to an infinity, but no one raised a weapon at her.

"You're not going to shoot me?" she asked. Hope rushed in. She was bound and she was under armed-guard, but she was conscious. The Galleon lay just outside. And Wallace was now unbound. *They believed him.*

Emboldened, she spoke. "You have to take me to the . . . to my weapon. I'm the only one who can disarm it." The guard watched over her, expressionless.

She clawed through the back rooms of her brain, looking for anything that would end with her aboard the Galleon. "You must release me. The fate of the planet is in your hands!"

"The Chancellor is *en route*," reported the commanding officer, ignoring Jessamyn.

"Release me or everyone dies," she cried. "Desolation! Destruction."

"Seal the prisoner's mouth," barked the officer in charge.

As a piece of skin-heal was slapped roughly over her mouth, Jess sank farther back into the unyielding chair. She considered screaming continuously, but if the officers hadn't been convinced by her words, stifled groans probably wouldn't go far. In fact, based on how annoyed the secure looked at the moment, he might decide to render her unconscious. She held silent.

Through one of the windows, Jess could see the top of the Red Galleon. Everything in her strained toward the ship. Could Crusty make it alone? Her gut whispered, *No*. She had to escape. What resources did she have? She was no Harpreet with negotiation skills, obviously. *What do you have, Jess? Think!*

She was conscious. Miraculously, she retained the use of her legs, unsecured—she could run if the opportunity presented itself. Jess glanced at the weapon trained on her. Outside, she heard an animal noise. A dog's *woof-woof-woof*. She remembered their hope-filled arrival: Wallace's dog bounding beside them, barking. And something in that memory undid her. Despair settled upon Jessamyn like a mantle ice cold and brittle. But even as she bowed under the imagined weight, she commanded herself, *You will not give up!*

Another noise shook the windows: the rattle of a large hover-transport as it descended. The dog barked at an even more excited pitch. The security officers stood at attention and one opened the front door.

"Welcome, Madam Chancellor," said the commanding officer, in tones of deep respect.

Half a dozen angry drops of rain blew in through the open door.

Craning her head, Jessamyn saw a woman who was tall by Terran standards. A middle-aged threebody. Thin enough to pass for Marsian. Her wide-set eyes looked cold—exactly as they had when Jessamyn had seen them first, in this very room, upon Brian Wallace's video screen.

Lucca Brezhnaya.

Wallace's eyes flew wide.

As Pavel's aunt stepped inside the house, Jessamyn saw the Chancellor wasn't alone. Someone wearing physician's garb stood behind her in the narrow entrance.

"This is the girl?" asked Lucca, directing the question to the doctor accompanying her.

He stepped from behind her so that Jessamyn was able to see his face.

Pavel.

30

A STORM

Avoiding eye contact with Jessamyn, Pavel murmured, "It's her."

What have you done, Pavel? Had he told his aunt everything? And if he had, would that save her planet or damn it?

Lucca Brezhnaya spoke to Jessamyn. "Do you know who I am?"

Jess, seeing no benefit in pretending otherwise, nodded.

"Is that a bandage covering her mouth?" asked Lucca, incredulous. "Oh, for the love of . . ." She broke off and turned to her nephew. "Remove that."

While Lucca berated the security officer standing beside her for overzealousness, Pavel crossed to Jess.

"I need a hot, moist cloth," Pavel said to the other secure.

"Go on," said Lucca to the officer. "You heard my nephew."

The man strode briskly to Wallace's kitchen.

"Who are you?" Lucca asked Brian Wallace who had been nodding and bowing at her since she crossed the threshold.

"Such an honor," said Wallace, smiling at the Chancellor. "Welcome to me humble dwelling. I'm afraid the weather's none too pleasant for the honor of yer visit." Thunder rumbled far off, punctuating the oily greeting.

Jess hadn't known he could sound so . . . unctuous.

"Now, then," said Pavel, "Let's see how that seal's been applied." After saying this, he leaned in close and whispered, so softly Jess almost missed it, "*I've got Ethan. Lucca thinks you're an inciter. Don't tell her about Mars.*"

The secure, returning with a cloth, handed it to Pavel. Wallace continued his tale (of nukes in his garden and no one paying any heed) to an increasingly irritated Lucca Brezhnaya.

"This is filthy," said Pavel, refusing to take the damp towel. He dug through his med kit, found a clean cloth, and handed it to the security officer. "Run this one under hot water and bring it back to me at once."

Pavel sounded like Lucca, thought Jessamyn. The thought wasn't a pleasant one. But he was keeping the truth from his aunt, exactly as Jess had asked. Pavel caught her eye briefly and she saw the boy she trusted.

Outside, rain began to spatter the windows.

Before the security officer returned with the cloth, Pavel leaned in closely as though examining Jessamyn's eyes with a small bright light. "*I'll help however I can. Stall. And don't try anything while security's here.*" Then, taking the steaming cloth from the secure, Pavel gently dabbed at the piece of skin-seal and pulled it away. "You can question her now," said Pavel to his aunt.

Lucca ordered the junior officer to stand guard outside.

As soon as the secure had stepped out of the cottage, Pavel's aunt took two slow steps toward Jessamyn. Jess drew herself tall, noting she had a few centimeters on the Chancellor.

"I know all about your pathetic attempt to destroy New Kelen Hospital," said Lucca as she stared at Jessamyn. "I know you bargained with my nephew, exchanging your release for a promise *not* to destroy the hospital. Which means I know two important things about you. First, I know you stick to your bargains." Lucca stepped so close that Jess could see a small stain of lipstick on one of her lower teeth. "And second, I know you're not the type to throw your life away for the so-called *greater good.*"

"Or maybe I wasn't in the mood to die yesterday," replied Jessamyn.

"Oh, I'm certain I could put you in the mood to beg for death," said Lucca, red lips pulling back from white teeth in a false smile.

"Perhaps," agreed Jessamyn. *Keep stalling,* she told herself. "This woman is your aunt?" asked Jess, addressing Pavel.

"Yes." Pavel replied warily, his eyes narrowing.

Jessamyn spoke to Lucca. "You should be proud of him. He is incorruptible."

"He let you go," said Lucca.

Jessamyn shrugged. "He made a deal for the benefit of others rather than for his own benefit. Did he tell you what he turned down?"

Lucca laughed harshly. "Let me guess: you?"

"Aunt Lucca, please," muttered Pavel.

"As a matter of fact, yes," said Jessamyn. "But that's not all."

"Pray, continue," said Lucca, seeming amused by Pavel's discomfort.

"Your nephew turned down *butter* as well," Jess said, landing on the first thing she could think of.

"Butter?" repeated the Chancellor, turning to the security officer. "What do we know about *butter*?"

He shrugged as he dug through Jessamyn's bag. "Might be the street name of those potent narcotics coming out of Greenland."

"You offered narcotics to a physician?" Lucca asked Jess. "You're bluffing." Her clear eyes piercing Jessamyn's. "And you're wasting my time."

"He also turned down a double kilo bar of pressed tellurium," said Jessamyn.

"Don't be ridiculous," snapped Lucca. "Where would *you* get tellurium?"

"Excuse me, Madam Chancellor," interrupted one of the security officers. In one hand he held Jessamyn's sling pack. In his other, the thin bar of pressed tellurium from her emergency supplies.

Lucca's mouth fell slightly open. Then she spoke in clear tones to the security officer. "You never saw this." She seized the tellurium from him. "Do I make myself clear?"

"Absolutely, Madam Chancellor," replied the officer.

"Where did you get this much tellurium?" Lucca asked Jessamyn.

Jess shrugged. "There's more where that came from."

"Hmm," said Lucca. "Somehow I doubt that. Also, unfortunately for you, incorruptibility runs in the family." Saying this, she tucked the bar into a case she carried and barked an order to the remaining officer. "Search her transport for tellurium. And *butter* or any other valuables."

"With all due respect, Madam Chancellor," replied the officer, "Perhaps you might not wish to remain alone with the prisoner?" He glanced at a window as lightning sparked outside.

"You will *not* question my orders if you value your . . . position," said Lucca, her voice a soft purr.

Noting the officer glancing at the window again and seeming to hesitate, Lucca raised her voice. "I want you outside! Your armor's not going to rust, imbecile."

As the remaining security officer exited, Jessamyn's heart beat faster.

"Everyone has a price, Madam Chancellor," she said, trying to match Brian Wallace's *oily* tone. "What would yours be, measured in tellurium? Perhaps we can come to an agreement."

Jess saw Lucca's pupils dilate, watched her nostrils flare. The Chancellor wanted tellurium.

Lucca walked to Jessamyn's side. Placed her mouth beside Jess's ear. "Whatever my price might be, you couldn't have enough," whispered the Chancellor. "You couldn't possibly." Lucca walked back to the other side of the room, crossed her arms, and gazed out the window at the darkening sky. "Now, let's discuss your disarmament of the weapon sitting out there."

"Oh, aye," said Wallace. "Please can we discuss that."

Without even turning to him, the Chancellor uttered an order. “Silence this man.”

With no one there to act upon her order, Wallace continued speaking. “I’m sure I’m honored to have ye at me own humble dwelling, Ma’am,” he said. “Can I offer ye something? Goat cheese griddle cakes, perhaps? Or a lovely bit of goat steak?”

Jessamyn’s heart did a sort of hop as Wallace slipped free of the “restraint” that had attached him to the desk.

“This is your dwelling?” asked Lucca.

“Aye,” said Wallace, grinning proudly. “Me own castle in miniature.”

“I’ll take a coffee. Black. Make it strong.” The Chancellor turned her back to Wallace, dismissing him.

Jessamyn, finding herself with two allies and only one enemy, grasped her head and groaned, as if in pain.

“Aunt Lucca?” called Pavel. “The prisoner seems to be in pain.”

Jessamyn moaned again, swaying her head and collapsing to her knees. “My head,” she cried.

“Go on,” said Pavel’s aunt. “Examine her. Who knows what those idiots in armor did to her before we got here.” She lowered her voice. “I want that body *kept whole*.”

From across the room, Pavel spoke to his aunt. “This cast was inexpertly applied,” he said. “She has untreated burns and a wound to her left arm as well.”

"Fix her," said Lucca. "I need her alert for questioning."

Wallace shuffled back from the kitchen, coffee in hand, murmuring about there being a proper storm brewing.

"*My hands,*" whispered Jessamyn to Pavel.

Pavel cut them free with a small scalpel.

"*Let me take you hostage,*" she said.

And then things began to happen very quickly. Wallace presented the Chancellor with a mug of coffee. As soon as Lucca's hands were occupied and her eyes turned from her nephew, Pavel passed something small into Jessamyn's hand, tipping his head toward his aunt. Only after this did he give Jess the requested scalpel. She placed the bright instrument at his throat, using the opposite forearm to lock Pavel's head into her shoulder, which left a hand free to grip the unknown item he'd passed to her. In the moment before Lucca looked up, Jess glanced at the object: a med-patch. What did she need a med-patch for, she wondered? She kept it hidden in her hand.

"Order your guards to set their weapons aside and to lie face-down with their hands clasped over their heads," Jessamyn said. Thunder rattled the windows.

Lucca, her eyes now upon Jess and Pavel, uttered two short words: "Or *what?*"

Jessamyn blinked in confusion. Could Lucca really be that stupid? "Or I slit your nephew's throat, obviously."

"Oh, that," said Lucca, waving a hand to indicate disregard. She took a slow sip of coffee. "Yes, well, by all means . . ."

Jess stood, dumbfounded. "I'll do it," she said.

"Will you *really*?" asked Lucca, lazily, taking a moment to stare as the rain pelted the windows, a sudden tattoo.

"Call off your guards," said Jess. "*Now!*"

Wallace made a whimpering kind of sound.

"And you, goat-herder," said Jess to Wallace, "Stay out of this unless you want the boy's death on your head."

Brian Wallace covered his eyes with both hands as if terrified. Another flash of lightning, the snap of thunder close behind.

The Chancellor took a couple of slow steps toward Jessamyn.

"I mean it," said Jess. She felt Pavel's breath, warm and rapid upon the hand gripping the blade.

"Do what the terrorist asks," Pavel said to his aunt.

"No, my dear boy, I don't think I will," said Lucca, advancing slowly upon the two. "You see, if she intended to kill you, *I* think she would have done it already."

Jessamyn swelled with anger at this woman— at Lucca's seeming disregard for her nephew's life, at the skill with which Lucca read the situation, at how Lucca stood between life and slow starvation for her world. Something in Jess pulled taut and she said, her tone venomous, "Or *maybe* I'm just waiting for you to come close so I can kill you instead!"

"Give me the knife," said Lucca Brezhnaya. Her voice, cutting like the wind of a Marsian winter, sent a chill along Jessamyn's spine.

Jess shook her head. "Come closer," she whispered. "I dare you."

The Chancellor did. "The knife," said Lucca, holding her hand out.

Straining against a fury boiling inside, Jess held her position, the knife at Pavel's throat becoming the center of her world, the core about which the universe revolved.

"You're a *child*," whispered the Chancellor. Lightning revealed for a brief moment her face, white with anger.

Jess saw again the smear of red lipstick upon white tooth. She felt the knife dropping away from Pavel's throat as if by the sheer force of Lucca's desire. And then the rage inside Jessamyn exploded outward and she struck at the Chancellor's outstretched palm with the bright blade.

The windows shook in their casements, and Lucca howled in fury, and Jessamyn, suddenly understanding the power Pavel had placed within her hand, slapped the med-patch hard against the Chancellor's throat. Gasping in surprise, the Chancellor's eyes flew wide and then, just as quickly, fluttered closed as Lucca Brezhnaya slumped unconscious to the floor. Jessamyn dropped the bloodied scalpel from her hand.

"It's a very short acting sedative," said Pavel as Jess released him.

Wallace shouted, "Go!" to Jessamyn as he aimed a small gun at Pavel.

"Don't shoot him!" Jess cried. "He's with me."

"Right," said Wallace, lowering the weapon. "Lucky I held off firing then, isn't it? I contacted Crusty while I was making that creature's coffee. The ship launches in four minutes and thirty seconds. I suggest ye move quickly." A coolly efficient Wallace had replaced the whimpering, blustering one. "Can ye bluff past those two outside?" he asked Pavel. "Because this gun will be worthless against their armor."

"I'll say my aunt wants Jess aboard the shuttle," he replied, "And you can carry her, like she's unconscious."

Wallace nodded. "That lad's a good one to have on yer side. Four minutes, ten seconds."

Wallace scooped Jess up as if she weighed nothing and the three moved outside and into the storm.

31

FOLLOWING ORDERS

"Where are you going with the prisoner?" asked the soldier guarding the door.

The other secure looked up from his inspection of Jessamyn's stolen vehicle.

"My aunt has ordered me to transport her to the nearest hospital," said Pavel.

"I'm going to have to confirm that before I let you escort the prisoner any farther," said the soldier.

"Suit yourself," said Pavel. "But I should probably warn you, Aunt Lucca's orders are that no one goes inside until she opens the door. She's on a private call with the viceroy."

The secure hesitated. His commander shrugged.

"The Chancellor's a real pain when her orders are disobeyed," said Pavel, blinking at the rain striking his face. He smiled sympathetically at both officers. "But you interrupt her call. I'll wait."

"Don't look at me," said the man guarding the door. "It's more than my life is worth, disobeying the Chancellor's orders."

The commanding officer apparently agreed, motioning Pavel and Wallace forward to Lucca's ship.

"*Three minutes, forty-five seconds*," Wallace mumbled.

Pavel released the hatch on the near side of the vehicle and Wallace carried Jessamyn inside. As soon as he closed the door, she dashed for the controls, firing the engines.

"*Shizer, shizer, shizer*!" groaned Pavel.

"Let's move it!" Brian Wallace shouted to Jess.

"Where's my brother?" Jess called as she swung the transport up, aiming it toward the Galleon. She threw a glance back at Pavel, who was staring at what looked like a hard-sided travel case, opened and empty. They cleared a slight rise and Jess could see the Galleon, bits of cloaking camouflage on one side, its hover boosters ready to fire.

"Jess," said Pavel, his voice hollow. "Ethan's gone."

"What do you mean 'gone'?" Jess felt her heart contract. "You said you had him."

"I hid your brother in this travel case and he's *gone.*"

The transport landed in a muck of grass, mud, and ash beside the Red Galleon.

"He must have made a run for your spacecraft," suggested Wallace. "Smart move, really."

"He's got no chance of making it. Jess—aw, *shizer*!" Pavel's voice had a defeated accent that made Jess's skin clammy.

"What?" she demanded as she opened the transport's door.

"Your brother's in an amputee's body now. Getting out of that suitcase and off my aunt's hover-ship? I don't know how he managed that, but there's no way he dragged himself five kilometers to this ship. One of his arms is useless, Jess."

Two minutes forty-five seconds.

Jessamyn's stomach wrenched and she felt as if her own legs had turned to jelly. "An amputee?" she wheezed. A gust of wind shuddered the Chancellor's craft.

"His new body has no legs," said Pavel. "Jess, two minutes to go. What are we doing? My aunt will be awakening any second."

"You can't ask me that," she said, her voice a whisper. "I have to . . . I've got to . . ." She looked at Pavel, every muscle in her face straining against the horror of the choice before her.

"Tell me what we're doing," said Wallace, a hard edge to his voice.

Jessamyn stumbled out of the shuttle. She reached for the Galleon's hatch, but the door flew wide before she reached it.

"Jess?" It was Crusty. "*Ares,* you're a welcome sight. I hear it's just you, then. Ship's set to lift off in two minutes. Gonna need a pilot for that."

"Let me go in your place," said Pavel. "I can fly an old *M-class* like this . . ." His voice trailed off as he ran his eyes along the ship's curving surface, evaluating it.

For the space of ten agonizing seconds Jessamyn considered her friend's offer. *You could stay and find Ethan. Your brother needs you.* And then she remembered her words to Mei Lo—*I won't fail you.* Remembered the golden light sweeping across the gentle rise of Mount Cha Su Bao. Remembered the people who would perish and see that light no more if she failed them. And she spoke the hardest words she'd ever uttered.

"I made a promise." Turning to Pavel, she murmured quietly, so quietly, a simple request. "Will you find Ethan?"

"Yes," he said. "I swear it."

"Get him a dog. He loves dogs." Her feet refused to move.

"We'll get him to safety, lass," said Wallace. "Yer planet's counting on ye. Go."

"Tell him I love him," she murmured, wind whipping her bright locks into a reddened fury. "Tell him I'll be back and I'll find him."

"Not if ye don't get yerself on that great ship *now*!" warned Wallace.

Shoulders pulled back, head tilted Mars-ward, her eyes streaming, Jessamyn lifted one foot and then the other from off the water planet.

"Let's go," she whispered to Crusty.

32

AWAKENINGS, RUDE AND PLEASANT

Lucca Brezhnaya, awakening in a manner utterly unlike the one she favored, noted the rain had stopped. She noted as well the unpleasant stink of *dog* as she lifted her head from a worn patch of rug.

"Pavel?"

Hearing no answer, she ran through a series of silent curses. *I need that boy*, she thought. Rising, she glanced out the window. One of the guards—she neither knew nor cared which—remained at his post outside the door. Had the girl snuck out a back way? Were plans afoot to ransom Pavel?

Rage welled up inside her. Lucca needed to kill something. The dog? She looked about her, but the smelly creature was evidently not in residence at the moment. No matter—there were other things soft and worthless nearby. She strode to the front door, head pounding from the sedation—*damn the girl!*—and stormed outside.

"Idiot! Do you realize what you've done?" shouted Lucca.

The secure hesitated, evidently weighing the wisdom of responding. "Just following orders, Madam Chancellor," he said at last, reasoning that the Chancellor liked having her orders followed.

"Give me your weapon," said Lucca, her voice calmer.

His final act was to follow the Chancellor's order.

As the soldier fell dead, Lucca smiled at the weapon. She really needed one of these for herself. Feeling rather better, Lucca continued to the small craft Jessamyn had stolen from New Kelen's hoverport.

The remaining officer was just peering around as Lucca strode into view.

"Madam Chancellor, I thought I heard weapon-fire," he said.

"Nothing wrong with your hearing, then," said Lucca, baring her teeth in an artificial smile. "Or, wait, perhaps there's something wrong with it after all. I don't suppose you noticed the sound of *my* hover-transport as it flew away?"

"Yes, Madam Chancellor. That would be two minutes ago."

"I'm surrounded by idiots," Lucca said softly. She discharged the weapon a second time. She felt much better now. Much better indeed. In the distance, she heard the rumble of thunder. Although she'd mocked the officer lying at her feet for his hesitation to go into the rain, she had no desire to experience it herself. Sighing she turned back to Wallace's cottage to await transportation.

Then, feeling a shudder that vibrated the very bones of her body, she realized it hadn't been thunder at all. The inciter's missile arced across the blue and white sky. Or perhaps it wasn't a missile at all. "Of course," she murmured. "A transport. How foolish of me."

Saying this, she emptied several rounds of ammunition into the sky. The bullets fell far short of their target and she did not feel better.

~ ~ ~

The storm which raged over Skye was passing on to the mainland now, having shifted great swathes of ash in its wake. Clusters of Brian Wallace's goats searched for the newly revealed patches of green, paying little heed to either the Galleon or to the Chancellor's craft as both flew past.

Brian Wallace laughed softly.

"What is it?" asked Pavel.

"There's no tracking beacon of any sort on this ship." His fingers flew across a small screen. "It's meant to fly without leaving a trace."

Pavel grunted. "Sounds like my aunt."

"We'll bring her down right there," called Wallace. "On the north side of that wee stone croft."

Pavel observed a small building constructed of rock that had been white-washed many years ago, but now stood neglected, blending with the island's ashen-greys.

"You think her brother came all the way here?" asked Pavel, puzzled.

"Nay, but we've a need to keep this vehicle out of sight. This is as close as we dare approach me cottage, lad. And Elsa likes to slumber here, the great slacker."

"Elsa?" asked Pavel.

"Aye, me dog. Elsa. She'll find the lad faster than ye or I can ever do."

Saying this, Brian Wallace punched open the door hatch and leapt out of the craft, Pavel on his heels. Wallace withdrew a silver cylinder upon a chain from his shirt. It was no bigger than his little finger. He blew into it, but nothing happened.

"Will your dog—will *Elsa* hear that thing?"

"Aye," said Wallace. "More importantly, those men in red armor *won't* hear it any more than ye could have just now."

"I hear barking," said Pavel.

"This way," said Wallace, grabbing a hovercart that leaned against the stone hut.

The two leapt upon the cart, Wallace urging it as fast as it could go, toward the sound of Elsa's bark.

"She's nae coming to me," muttered Wallace, after blowing into the dog whistle a second time.

"Try again!"

"She's a stubborn lass, Elsa. As like to run if it suits her."

Pavel's lips pinched thin as he calculated how likely it was his aunt had awakened already.

Wallace brought the silver whistle to his lips once more. Elsa barked in response and the cart sped toward the sound. She barked again and again.

"Perhaps she's found him already, then," murmured Wallace. "She took to the lad uncommon fast, the other day." He blew into the whistle once more.

Elsa barked in reply, sounding nearer than last time. The hovercart glided over a low hillock to reveal a deep, grassy hollow just below them. The wind shifted.

Pavel saw him first. In the quivering grass lay a man, old, bereft of legs, and about his head curled a black and white dog. The man's one good arm lay buried in the dog's soft coat.

Wallace slowed and Pavel leapt from the cart, sweeping Ethan into his arms. "I'm sorry. I know you don't like to be touched. Your sister told me."

Ethan looked in confusion at Pavel, but seeing Wallace jump from the cart, he calmed.

Pavel lifted Ethan onto the small transport. Another cart, spilled at an odd angle beside where Ethan had lain, told his story—he had fallen off and been unable to hoist himself back on. The dog whined anxiously, darting between legs, herding the three until all were settled upon the cart.

"Jessamyn," Ethan said in a whispered hush. He raised a palsied hand, pointing to the sky. "Jessamyn," he said again. His rheumy eyes met Wallace's. "Did she make it?"

"She's on her way to Mars," said Pavel. "You're a very lucky man, having a sister like that."

Ethan closed his eyes, a sad smile upon his lips.

Wallace pulled to a halt beside the Chancellor's ship and the cart jolted. Both men reached for Ethan, grabbing him to prevent his falling off. Pavel murmured another apology, hurriedly carrying Ethan inside his aunt's craft.

Ethan laughed softly. "It would appear that this body, despite its several faults, is not strongly affected by touch. What a pleasant thing to awaken to." As the ship departed for the safety of the skies, Ethan laughed to himself again and sank a gnarled hand into Elsa's thick fur.

Epilogue

Dear Pavel,

You may wonder why I am writing to you.

No, I guess not.

You won't wonder because I have no way to send this message. But as I watch Earth shrink farther and farther behind us each day, it seems sometimes like none of it was real. Not pizza or that silly orange dress or even you. So I'm writing because I need to remind myself it was real. You are real.

The wisest person I know once told me that I need to accustom myself to the harmonies of minds unlike my own. (Her words, not mine.) I can think of a few who qualify in that regard. Kipper. The dean at my flight school. Your aunt. But I think I need to start with someone I don't feel active hostility toward.

So I thought of you. Well, to be honest, I was already thinking of you. It's something I do often. I imagine you finding and rescuing my brother. I see you standing up to your aunt. I picture you becoming a great leader some day.

I'll be home soon, and I'll try to see my world with your eyes. I think that's part of what Harpreet meant with all that harmony language. I hope, as I look at Mars through your eyes, that you will love my planet.

Please tell my brother that I miss him. No. Tell him that I wish he'd invent a switch I could flip so that I would not think of him because it hurts so badly when I do. That might make him laugh. Then you can tell him never mind, because by the time I see him again I won't need the stupid switch anymore.

I will return for him, Pavel. Tell him that. I will return with my memory full of how Mars appeared through your eyes: what you thought of the shadows of the Valles Marineris at sunset; how you smiled to see Zhinü and Niulong set in a veil of stars a thousand times more numerous than what you can see from Budapest; how sweet a morning wet ration can taste when drunk with those who love you.

Farewell for now.

Your friend,

Jessamyn

End of Book One

Author's Note

I am no astrophysicist. I'm just a writer who talks with her imaginary friends all day. I've done my best to keep the (meager) science in *SAVING MARS* at least somewhat accurate, but there are many points where I felt free to get quite speculative, and I'm sure there are numerous out-and-out errors as well. These errors are wholly my own.

If you are curious whether humans could live on Mars someday, or whether "terraforming" is real, I suggest Robert Zubrin's fascinating book *The Case for Mars.* (He has another title, fictional and hilarious, called *How to Live On Mars,* which I highly recommend as well.)

Would you like to see humans on Mars? Or journey there yourself? You many find the following organizations helpful as you explore the possibilities!

www.planetary.org
www.nss.org
www.spacefrontier.org
www.marssociety.org

Acknowledgements

Very special thanks to Toby and Isabel, who have been listening to this book morph for over two years, passing from one voice to another, one tense to another, and reinventing itself way too many times. For help with key plot problems, thanks to Chris, Jacob, and Toby. Also, for when the physics started making my brain hurt, an extra helping of *merci* to Chris. Jacob and Nathan convinced me that the ending had taken a wrong turn at a critical moment. Thumbs up, guys!

And to you, dear reader, I am grateful beyond what words can convey. To be able to sit and imagine my days away beats anything I know, including pizza of pepperoni.

THANKS for giving *SAVING MARS* a read; I hope you enjoyed it! Please consider leaving a review on Amazon--even a line or two helps other people decide if the book is for them or not.

LET ME KNOW about the review via email, and I'll send you (or a friend) an e-copy of *Rippler*, Book One in the Ripple Trilogy. I love email from readers!

SIGN UP for my New Release Email List. You'll get two or three emails per year (tops) letting you know when the next book in the **Saving Mars Series** comes out.

VISIT ME online—I'm highly distractible!
cidneyswanson.com

Made in the USA
San Bernardino, CA
01 March 2013